DEMONS OF STONY RIVER

A true to life adventure about North America's meanest animal, Alaska's Wolverine, alias devil bear, demon bear, and devil beast.

Tom Willard

P.O. Box 221974, Anchorage, Alaska 99522-1974

ISBN 1-888125-03-9

Library of Congress Catalog Card Number: 96-67379

Manufactured in the United States of America.

Table of Contents

There have been countless narratives written and reported about the wolverine, its voracity, cunning, and resourcefulness. Almost all of them seem to be based upon tales passed from one person to another, most of which would shock any wolverine.

Demons of Stony River, is a wonderful life history of a truly remarkable animal. It is written in a style that will not only enlighten the readers, but will add to their knowledge of the natural history of a remote corner of the Earth. Indeed, every plant, bird, or mammal included in this book is depicted in the same way one sees them when visiting the far reaches of the Kuskokwim River of Alaska. Having studied the flora and fauna of those areas in years gone by, I am taken back to times of adventure in a vast boreal wilderness, and can vouch for their authenticity.

Tom Willard, artist and naturalist in his own right, has spent many years studying, painting, and drawing this northland and its wildlife which he so obviously loves. That knowledge and ability makes his endeavors come to life in writing, and fine works of art. He gives his characters names instead of numbers a research party would, thus bringing readers much closer to each animal in a way that makes one smile when things go right and feel sad when they don't. Who would have thought they would ever feel that kind of emotion for the "Demon Wolverine?" Only in the works of Ernest Thompson Seton does one feel that particular emotion to a wild predatory animal. Unlike Seton's writings, Tom makes us look at everything within the Wolverine's territory, and puts all living things, including plants, within that environment at a high enough status that we are enlightened and in awe of the beauty and complexity of nature. When he interrupts the narrative to add additional information on a subject, it is always based upon his personal observation and the latest known data available. Activities of foxes, wolves, bears, and native birds, which play an important part in the lives of wolverines, are depicted just as they are seen by a biologist or adventurer who studies wilderness.

The lonely call of a raven is often the only sound heard on cold, quiet winter days—sometimes not even that. There are tracks and signs of a great deal of activity which is rarely seen by the "once in a while" visitor. There are however, a surprising number of year 'round resident bird and mammal species. They seem to appear suddenly, often in large numbers, only to vanish again. There is a feeling of the vastness of the country and the desire is always present to cross the next hill to see what lies beyond.

Tom Willard has crossed and recrossed many of those hills, stalking, trailing, and hunting. Usually traveling alone, one with the wilderness, and armed with a vast knowledge of northern wild places, he is able to read sign and observe nature in places where many would fail to see a thing. Being a pilot with his own airplane, he learned the terrain he studies from the viewpoint of the gyrfalcon to the underbrush and forests of those creatures limited to living on the ground.

When a writer and artist naturalist, like Tom Willard, travels through a wild place, little is missed—every nuance of light and shadow, every sound, and every movement has much more meaning than it would to someone who merely hunts or fishes. Tom never misses a single plant species, bird, or mammal, and has the healthy attitude that, he has so much more to learn. The wild places will always call out to that kind of person, they call out to Tom Willard.

Prof. Boyd J. Shaffer
University of Alaska

Demons of Stony River would never have been written without the encouragement of Boyd Shafer, friend and mentor. Thank you, Boyd. This book is dedicated to you.

Demons of Stony River has been written with the intention of both instructing and entertaining the reader. There is probably no animal in North America with so many myths perpetuated about it than the wolverine. It is in the order: *Carnivora*, family: *Mustelidæ*, subfamily: *Mustelinæ*, and is the sole species of the genus. *Gulo gulo* is known by several names, each prominent in different areas where it is located. French trappers of North America used the names *Loup Garou* and *Carajou*. Glutton, skunk bear, devil bear, and devil beast have all been used at various times and places.

There are two listed subspecies, the European wolverine, *Gulo gulo gulo*, and the North American wolverine, *Gulo gulo luscus*. Most will agree there are, at best, only minute differences between the two, and many would be hard pressed to tell them apart with any degree of accuracy. Coloration can run from pale to dark phases, dependent upon the gene pool of the area. However, these differences can also show up within a single litter.

Stories about its fantastic strength and tenacity, and its intelligence, are frequently blown out of all proportion for an animal that rarely reaches fifty pounds. The wolverine in Alaska has a body length of thirty to thirty-two inches with an additional nine inches of tail. The males average thirty-five pounds, the female twenty-five. Only an exceptionally large male will top fifty pounds. The muscles in their legs are larger than normal for other animals the same size, giving them a strength that is in comparison with the tremendously powerful bears. Indeed, the wolverine does resemble bears, both having heavily muscled legs. Semi-retractable claws are light colored, sharp, and over one and one-half inches long. Not only are they suitable for digging, they do well in climbing, and are used to capture and kill prey.

Many tales are heard of wolverines driving large bears off their kills, demolishing remote cabins, and wreaking havoc on trap lines. For their size, they are strong and can, on rare occasion, do a great deal of damage to a cabin, much as a bear can. However, I wonder just how many torn up cabins were actually vandalized by bears, and the wolverine left his sign when he happened upon the scene at a later date. Possibly a wolverine could drive a small, timid black bear off its kill, but a mature bear could easily kill a wolverine and have him for dinner.

They can do a lot of predation on trap lines, eating caught animals anytime they are found in that helpless condition. Once they learn a meal can be found at those locations, they will revisit until the trapper sets a heavy trap or snare. At those times, the wolverine is quite vulnerable. The trapper winds up with another valuable fur to replace those that were eaten. The idea that a wolverine is too smart to get into a trap, and too powerful to be kept there, should be regarded as nothing but a tall tale. They have little fear and consequently are quite easily caught in snares. Still, only heavy duty traps and snares can be used on them as they are much too powerful for those used on small mammals.

Wolverine fur is much prized by natives of the north. It is said to have a special property in that frost will not adhere to it as it does to other furs. This makes it desirable for the trimming of collars and hoods on parkas and several hundred are taken for their fur each year in Alaska.

Not a plentiful animal, its numbers are stable, and it is not considered endangered anywhere in its range. It is solitary in habit and does not like to stay in areas where there is much human activity. Few Alaskans are ever privileged to catch a glimpse of this creature because of this trait. Even those who do see one, get only a quick look as *Gulo gulo* always seems to be on his way somewhere else. His loping gait is broken only when he stops to examine a new smell.

He is relentless in search of food, and even if not hungry, he stores in caches anything he finds or kills to be consumed later. A highly developed sense of smell helps him to relocate the cache, frequently weeks or even months later. The cold ground helps to preserve whatever is buried, but then, some ageing probably only adds to the flavor.

A considerable portion of his diet is carrion. Caribou, and moose found dead or ill are readily consumed. Voles, lemmings, and ground squirrels are eaten in great numbers. Ptarmigan, grouse, and any other bird, as well as their eggs and chicks, are eaten in substantial numbers.

The wolverine is not a fast runner, a well-conditioned human can run him down on open ground. However, this is not to be recommended. Just what would you do when you caught up with him? A wolverine could kill a man easily and cornering one would be the height of folly. His temperament is much like a pit bull dog, the more he is hurt, the harder he will fight. A single, full-grown wolf two or three times his size would never attack a wolverine, and would have little chance should he try. He is quick and with stealth and persistence, guided by a fantastic nose, easily captures the fastest of prey species. The wolverine is usually a well-fed animal.

The setting for this story is the Stony River of Alaska. This is a small tributary of the Kuskokwim River which flows into the Bering Sea. It drains an area of the Alaska Range, and is some one hundred fifty miles due west of Anchorage. There are no roads west of the Alaska Range connected to the Alaska road system; therefore, the area can be reached only by airplanes equipped with floats. Water travel would be possible, but very difficult and would take a long time. The small city of Bethel, near the coast, is over three hundred water miles from this locale. *Gulo's* area is isolated, remote, and visited only by hunters, trappers, and other outdoor persons.

Although this is a fictional story, there are many scientific names and terms used. Therefore, I have done something unusual for a work of fiction, I have included a glossary, an index, and a section of descriptions and drawings of some of the flora and fauna residing in Gulo's world. Many terms will be familiar to most of you; however, in nature some words are used to mean things different from the common definition.

I have tried to make this narrative as true an account as is possible of the wolverine's life and habits in an actual setting. Hopefully, after reading *Demons of Stony River*, you will have a better understanding of the mammals, birds, and flora that make up *Gulo's* world.

 It was dark. A soft breeze was winding its way among the spruce trees. Soft noise of branches was the only sound heard in the deep cold laying over the valley. In the east, the moon was rising slowly above the horizon, but the land was already alight with reflected brightness of unending snow. Even trees were laden, their branches moving sluggishly in response to puffs of air. Inches of settled snow covered the ground and in places there were drifts several feet deep.

Not far from Alaska's Stony River was such a drift, but this one was unusual; it was occupied. Dug into it for a distance of nearly thirty feet was a snow tunnel. At its end was an oblong cavity. There lay the mammal who had worked nearly nonstop until completion of the den.

Not understanding why, she nervously dug the tunnel and excavated the nesting area at its end. Then she gathered leaves and grasses, carrying them into the room. She scratched them together, turned her body round and round until she was satisfied with the nest she had created. Several times she laid in it to rest, but her extreme nervousness prevented anything more than a few moments respite until she felt the urge to move again. She made frequent trips to the outside where she loped first one direction and then another, sniffing the air frequently before returning to the tunnel.

Daily, the agitation built until this night when she lay in the nest in near total darkness. The coming day would bring light through the snow ceiling, however for some time it would be of little use to its occupants.

Gulo, a two year old wolverine, began feeling labor pains in early evening, and nervousness she felt in the preceding days now became intense. Pains became more frequent and sharper until she was forced to strain against them. At their peak, straining produced some relief and a small, wet bundle was deposited in the soft grasses of the nest. Gulo instinctively severed the umbilical cord with her teeth and immediately began to clean the kit, licking till it was nearly dry. This was no sooner accomplished

9

when contractions returned, signaling that the night's events were not yet over.

The first born was a female, only five inches long, and covered by fine, white fur. Carajou's fuzzy tail was one fourth of her body length, just a little more than an inch long. Weighing only a few ounces at birth, she and her siblings would show a phenomenal rate of growth, reaching the size of their parents before their first birthday. Carajou made tiny, squeaking cries and did not appear to be too glad to be outside the warm womb. Cool air of the den was considerably lower than inside her mother's belly and she protested as loudly as she could. But her mewing was ignored by her mother, who was too busy with her own pains to be concerned.

Contractions once more intensified and Carajou was soon joined by two males. Each, in turn, licked clean and dry by Gulo, who then cleaned up the placenta by consuming it. In this manner, most of the birthing odors in the nest area were removed, making it more difficult to be located by an enemy. Instinctively the kits nuzzled in their mother's fur, soon locating her teats, and without guidance clamped onto a nipple and began nursing. Gulo's previous agitation was now gone, her breathing returned to normal and she relaxed, enjoying the gentle pulls of her new born. The den became quiet except for the contented sounds of the kit's first meal.

A hazy light came through the snow ceiling the next day; however, Gulo remained in the den with her kits until full light, her maternal instincts subconsciously telling her they were extremely vulnerable at this time. Emerging from the den, she moved to a nearby rock, lightly leaping to its top. She sniffed the air and turned about, looking with intensity in all directions. The sun had risen over the mountains turning the sky a soft gold that faded gently into the blue of a cloudless morning. No wind stirred the white spruce trees and a layer of new snow, dropped the night before, still hung on their bending branches. Far away she heard the grating call of a raven, and nearby, the soft chatter of a gray jay busy looking for its morning meal.

The beauty of the crisp, clear morning was wasted on the wolverine. She was intent only in the den's safety and paid no attention to the aspects of her surroundings. It was several minutes before she was satisfied all was well, neither seeing nor smelling anything out of place. Jumping from the rock, she made a quick, irregular circle of the area, further satisfying herself there was no danger. She returned to the tunnel, moved down it to the nest, and was greeted by three balls of fuzz who quickly located a teat and began pulling on it.

The next few days were repetitions of the first, with Gulo spending more time each day outside the den. Her trips were to nearby caches where, in previous months, she had stored ptarmigan, ground squirrels, and other foods not needed at the time. The caching instinct of the wolverine is strong. Now it was helpful to Gulo, who had little time to hunt for food. She could leave, find food for herself, and return to the den without having to be gone for more than a few minutes. Each day the kits became stronger, and after a few days were moving about the den, wobbling from side to side and stumbling over anything and nothing. Their eyes did not open until their tenth day. It was then, for the first time, they could see shadowy figures moving about the den.

The snow ceiling allowed only a faint light, and then only during a few hours of the day when the sun was directly overhead. This was March, and at this time of year in Gulo's territory, the sun climbs higher each day and spends several minutes more above the horizon. But deep in the den, it was dark much of the time, even at midday when the sun was at its peak. Outside there were still periods of driving snow and howling winds with temperatures sometimes dropping to zero and below. However, inside the snow den, their bodies kept the temperature well within the comfort range of Gulo and her babies. Whistling winds outside had no effect on the snugness of their home. Inside, the climate was constant, regardless of the gales blowing out of the north bringing more snow with them, or sometimes simply swirling around snow already laying on the ground. The wolverine family was well protected from the elements, insulated with snow under which the babies cuddled together, warming one another during short periods when Gulo was gone from the den.

Each day the kits grew in size and their aggression grew along with their size. Glutt, the second born, and his younger brother, Garou, spent the days jostling one another, including their sister, Carajou. They were constantly fighting to find a teat that had a little bit more milk, although the supply from each was much the same. The pushing and shoving did serve a purpose however, giving them much needed exercise, which strengthened their muscles. Gulo's milk was unfailing, and the three of them become more active and stronger each day.

March in the Stony River area is still a harsh time of year. Although the sun shines several minutes more each day, the time since its change from loss to gain has been short. The day of least sunlight occurred just three months earlier on December twenty-first, the winter solstice. At this latitude, the sun had been above the horizon slightly more than five and one half hours. Now the sun was up nearly eight minutes more each day and the difference was noticeable.

This fast change goes the opposite way during days near autumnal equinox, about the twenty-second of September. From that point on, the daily rate slows until it is down to only seconds per day during the few days near the twenty-first or twenty-second of December. Then, daylight begins to lengthen again. On June twenty-first or twenty-second, the summer solstice, the time of longest sunlight has arrived, and the sun is above the horizon for over nineteen hours. Then, night is mostly a twilight, and there is real darkness for only a couple hours. This is in Gulo's area. The further north one travels, the more the change, until the arctic coast is reached. There winter has no sun for many days and summer has no nights for many days.

The amount of light triggers many activities of animals and birds: molting, migrations, and sexual activity being the most prominent. Man understands little just how this happens and much has yet to be learned. Nature still holds many secrets from us.

By March, Mother Nature's light messages had been sent out, and the wolverine kits were soon to be joined by uncountable numbers of mammals, birds, and plants, all starting their new cycles of life. The catkins of spring were popping out on the willows, their gray fuzz nearly blending into the white background of snow. The snowy owl, who has been hunting the area for the past three months, will soon return to its northern summer range. A great gray owl will move into the area, along with his mate, returning to their breeding ground from their winter home further south. Their chicks will be the earliest birds to hatch, arriving while there is snow and frigid winds yet roaring from the north. Their hatching matches the arrival of their prey species, the new born hordes of rodents: voles, lemmings, and larger meals, the ground squirrels. Mother Nature's timing rarely is in error, new born of the predators arrive when their prey species is just becoming abundant. If the prey does not do well, neither does the predator.

The microtines (voles and lemmings) make up a significant part of the diet of the wolverine, as well as that of most other predators of the North. Although small, about one-half an ounce in weight, their tremendous numbers furnish a steady diet for many mammals and birds. These small mammals run in cycles, with population numbers peaking about every three to four years. The population of the predator species follow them in a delayed cycle, crashing when the food supply does and not rebuilding until plentiful food is again available. All of this follows a law set down by Mother Nature; nothing can live beyond the capacity of the land to sustain it.

Gulo was now able to leave the kits for more than a few minutes at a time.

Their eyes were open; they were well fed and healthy, but still too small to leave the security of the den. On their fifteenth day, Gulo roused herself well before dawn. Leaving the kits cuddled together in the nest, she quietly entered the tunnel. They took no notice of her leaving; their full stomachs from a recent nursing kept them sound asleep.

Passing through the tunnel, she reached the open air. The night was nearly gone and the sky was just turning light from a sun still below the mountains towering in the east. Pointing her nose into this light, she made her way through scattered spruces, casting about for any scents on the air. It was half an hour before her nose told her there was food ahead. Slowing her gait, she began a semi-stalk, knowing the prey was yet some distance away. As the smell grew stronger, her movements became slower until she pinpointed its location. Then she froze, moving only her head, watching intently for movement, and breathing in the aroma of a fresh meal. She saw the snow appear to move and directly ahead, in an open area dotted with scattered clumps of willows, she focused on a ptarmigan. Within moments she caught sight of several white birds. The brightening sky had awakened them, and they had begun to feed on willow buds swelling with new growth, making ready to put forth leaves for coming summer.

Gulo froze in a crouched position, watching them for several minutes. The ptarmigans' white feathers blended so well with the snow, that when they were still, they were nearly invisible. In the dim light Gulo would lose sight of them only to have them magically reappear the moment they moved. The birds were heading toward Gulo's right, making for a clump of spruce, picking buds from the willows as they moved along. Backing away, she got behind another group of low growing spruce and quickly moved to get into a position of ambush. Spotting the spruces the birds were feeding toward, she circled ahead and found a snow covered hummock built up of moss and grass. Gulo crouched down beside it, her dark fur melting into the shadows. She had now lost the scent of the birds as the breeze was no longer coming from them to her nose. Still, she knew where they were from the soft rustle in her ears as the ptarmigan brushed against willow stems.

Several minutes dragged by—her impatience grew until finally she had to raise her head and peek over the hummock. Nothing could be seen, but again she heard a rustling sound and let her head slowly sink back to the ground. The sky was getting lighter, and the coming dawn urged one of the ptarmigan to send out a few soft clucks. Now Gulo knew exactly were they were. From the continued sounds, they would come within striking distance.

13

A sudden roaring of wings caused Gulo to leap up and find the birds were off the ground, already too high to catch. They were just over her head and she rose on her hind legs, desperately trying to get nearer, but she was not able to leap so high. Back on all four feet she let out a growl of disappointment then suddenly caught movement out of the corner of her eye and understood the reason she had lost her meal. On the other side of the small clearing stood a red fox with a ptarmigan pinned beneath her front paws. Its head was in the fox's mouth, but the fox had almost forgotten the bird, the horrifying appearance of the wolverine so close had nearly startled her into dropping it. A flood of fear caught the vixen. Still holding the bird by the head, she turned and ran, snow flying into the air from her frantic efforts.

Hampered by the bird bouncing against her fore feet, she went no more than fifty feet before she had to stop to get a better grip. During this stop Gulo quickly made up some distance between them until no more than ten feet separated the two. Looking back, the fox saw the danger she was in and took off with a burst of energy. Burdened with the bird, her progress was just good enough to slightly open the distance until she reached an open, flat area. There her speed increased, and soon she had a comfortable lead on Gulo. Finally, realizing she was not going to catch the fox, the wolverine slowed and came to a stop. Totally frustrated with the morning hunt, she snapped at a willow stem, biting it in two, venting her anger.

A half-mile away, the vixen slowed to a trot and soon after, stopped to catch her breath and survey the back trail. Assuring herself the dangerous enemy had given up, she picked up the bird and trotted for another mile before feeling comfortable about stopping to eat. In a few weeks, she would be giving birth, and her body needed all the nourishment possible. This would be her second litter, having given birth to four kits the first time this past spring. This year, six would arrive and the drain on her system in providing for such a large family would cause her to lose two to three of the twelve pounds she now weighed.

The male who had bred her a month earlier was still at the location of their den. He had stayed when the vixen left to hunt, as he was not yet satisfied with the den's condition. He would soon be kept busy hunting, as the vixen would leave the den area only occasionally after the birth of their kits until the time they were weaned. Once weaned, they would both be working hard to provide for the young. At first they would regurgitate food, then progress to bringing home whole or portions of raw meat from mammals and birds. This would continue until the kits were able to follow them on the hunt.

Gulo's temper was not good as she went back to hunting. The frustrating morning, combined with the need to get back to her young, was telling on her patience. She straddled a hummock and without thinking about it, marked the spot with her ventral gland. Its musky odor would let any other wolverine know this area was taken. The ventral gland, on the lower abdomen, is used to mark territory, as are anal glands and urine. When she marks with the ventral gland, Gulo straddles a hummock, or other high spot, and rubs her belly on it, thereby leaving her own individual scent. This scent not only identifies her as a wolverine, but also a specific wolverine because each has its own distinctive smell.

Again, working into the wind, she again picked up the smell of prey. This time the air had a hint of blood in it, giving her an urgent incentive to investigate. Moving to the right, the scent disappeared, and she turned back the other direction. Quickly the smell was found again. Now knowing the direction, she cautiously started her stalk. Her movements were quick until her nose told her she was getting close, then she slowed to a quiet walk. She moved slower as she drew close. Finally, spotting movement, she came to a halt. In a small hollow, a young caribou cow stood. The movement that had caught Gulo's eyes had been the cow licking a newborn calf.

Gulo watched, savoring the unusual odors coming to her. The calf had been born only minutes before and was still lying helpless on the snow. The cow continued to clean her young, oblivious of the danger looking at them. As she licked the calf, more pains coursed through her body and then one final contraction came upon her. Spreading her hind legs, she passed the afterbirth and another wave of scent flowed to Gulo. Still, she did not move. The cow went back to licking the calf whose head was wobbling back and forth, not yet able to hold it steady. Steam rose from its warm, moist body. Large dark eyes glistened in the light of the morning sun, seeing the world for the first time.

Down wind, Gulo watched the cow complete her clean up of the calf and consume the placenta. Odors of birth quickly dissipated— still a slight odor of blood remained. The next movements of the caribou brought to Gulo the realization that it was injured, the left hind leg did not work normally. When the cow turned, dried and fresh blood could be seen around several cuts on her left flank and hind leg. The leg was stiff and the cow's movements were slow and deliberate. New blood was oozing from the cuts, opened by her efforts in giving birth to the calf.

The previous night her herd had been attacked by a pair of coyotes that had a den a few miles to the west. Only by her determination, using vicious swipes of her antlers and forefeet, was she able to discourage them. However, she had received severe cuts. Her leg was now stiff from the deep gashes left by the coyotes' teeth.

Not only had the coyotes injured her, the stress from their attack had brought on the early birth of the calf. The small herd with whom she had been migrating north were on their way to their regular calving area, at least another week's travel. When the first contractions came upon her, she left them to find this small hollow where she felt somewhat secure. But without the company of her herd, she was nervous and had good cause to be. She was alone, injured, and with a newborn calf, a combination likely to have serious consequences.

Three ravens flying overhead spotted the animals below, and suddenly made a tight turn to alight in nearby spruce trees. The scene caught their attention, and sitting in their trees, their croaks sounded for all the world like humans talking over the situation. As interested as they were in those below, the ravens were ignored by the participants on the ground. Nothing was about to distract Gulo from her quarry. The caribou, used to raven sounds, did not even realize they were there.

Moving behind a screen of spruces, Gulo stayed down wind and slowly crept forward, freezing when the caribou lifted her head. It took her several minutes to cover ten yards, lifting her feet one at a time in extreme slow motion, then setting them down soundlessly. The cow was nuzzling her calf, trying to get it up on its feet so it could nurse. Still weak, its attempts were feeble, but with each try, it got stronger until all at once everything worked together and the calf was on its feet. Swaying precariously, it stood, legs wide apart. The cow and calf touched noses, taking in each others breath. Sight and smell were now imprinted on each other, making it possible for either to identify the other, even in a herd with hundreds of other caribou.

Imprinting happens at the time of birth, not only for caribou, but for many animals. It is a necessary function, so, if they are momentarily separated, they will know one another and be able to get back together. A few mothers will accept the young of another in some species; however, most will not. The caribou is one of those that will not. A nursing caribou calf that gets separated from its mother is doomed to starvation or predation, as no other cow will give it protection or allow it to nurse. Wolves follow caribou herds, and it would be a rare lost calf to last long enough to starve.

Only in recent years has it been learned that a brown bear mother will take over the raising of another's cubs. In fact, cubs have been noted moving from one sow to another and then back again. However, bears are normally a solitary animal. It is usually around salmon fishing areas, where large number of bears congregate, this switching of cubs happens. This goes to prove we have much yet to learn about animal behavior.

Birds also imprint at the time of hatching; however, each bird and mammal, has their own peculiarities as to how far this is carried. While a mammal may become separated from their young and reunite later after finding them in a new setting, it is not so with some birds. Young birds, falling from a nest, will be cared for by a few parents on the ground, but some will no longer recognize their own chicks once they are away from the nest. Others carry this even farther in that if their nest is moved by a human or the area around the nest is changed, the parents do not recognize the nest or young as theirs and will abandon it.

The caribou calf was now on its feet, although perched most precariously on them. The cow moved between it and the wolverine, blocking Gulo's full view. She crouched lower so only her eyes and ears were above the grasses where she lay. The cow continued to clean the calf, her rasp-like tongue nearly pushing the unsteady youngster off its feet. Soon the soft hair covering it was clean of birthing smells and only damp enough to hold the hair in curls clinging tightly to its body.

Finished with necessary chores, the cow moved to the side of the clearing, limping badly on the injured leg. Clumsily the calf tried to follow, falling when uncoordinated legs did not work in proper sequence. Again there was a struggle to rise. This time it was accomplished easier. The next steps were taken on wide spread legs, but now they stayed under it and the distance to the cow was slowly closed.

The movement of the calf caused Gulo's muscles to twitch—before the calf reached the cow, she released them in a sudden charge. The caribou cow, hearing the noise, was able to turn toward her nemesis, but was too late to get between the calf and the oncoming demon. The unsteady calf detected only movement before being knocked off its feet and feeling the sharp pain of teeth in the back of its neck. The wolverine moved her jaws from neck to the head, and with all her power, clamped down. There was a crunching sound—the calf was dead.

Gulo released her hold on the calf, whose legs were still twitching, and turned to face its mother. The terrified cow backed off several paces, too startled to fully understand what had happened. She made a halfhearted lunge at the wolverine, which brought a throaty growl from Gulo, who was now prepared to defend her kill. The caribou backed off realizing she was also in mortal danger. Gulo took two steps toward the cow, growling menacingly. Again the cow retreated. Two more steps from Gulo and the cow's courage left entirely. She turned and fled the scene.

The small herd with which the cow had been traveling had long since left the area and she was alone. Frightened, she had the urge to leave, but her maternal instincts would not let her. They told her, she must stay near the calf. Her movements in getting away from Gulo had reopened the cuts, and once more they were bleeding freely. One long gash in the abdominal area had partially closed and already infection was starting to set in. In a few days the infection would spread to her leg and inside her abdomen. She would travel only a few miles from this spot during the weeks left to her.

After the caribou's retreat, Gulo returned to her kill. Smelling blood about the crushed head, and seeing no movement, she knew it was dead and no longer capable of getting away from her. She licked off the blood that had oozed from the head, then moved to the abdominal area and started tearing into the paunch. The newborn's thin, tender skin was not much of an obstacle, and soon she was feeding in earnest, slicing off large chunks of still warm viscera. Blood and body juices covered her muzzle, but she did not stop her feasting. It had been some time prior to the birth of her kits when she had last had a large, satisfying meal, but today she would feed until her stomach was round and tight.

The ravens watched for a while, then lost interest and left. A gray jay arrived and perched on a nearby willow limb, waiting for a chance at a few morsels, but would be disappointed as Gulo would leave nothing for it to eat. Only blood would stain the snow and mark the spot of the kill.

By the time Gulo was full, there was still much of the calf left. She picked up the remains and carried it off with her. She held her head high as she moved from the scene, the calf's legs making parallel drag marks on each side of her own tracks. Ploughing through the willows, she left tiny tufts of soft caribou hair on the twigs, but her strength was such that the hard going was not difficult. Well away from the site of the kill, she found a snow bank to her liking and dug a hole through the snow into frozen moss. She deposited the remains of the calf and covered it, concealing the location as best she could. After checking the area about the cache, she turned toward the den, answering the call to return to her young.

Crawling through the snow tunnel, she found the kits still asleep, but they awoke when she got inside the den. They greeted her with excited cries until each found a teat and clamped firmly onto it, sucking as though they were starved. Soon the den was quiet, all were content, and they slept with round, tight bellies.

CHAPTER TWO

Tired of constant squabbling of who got which teat, Gulo left the den. It was midday and the sun was as high above the nearby mountains as it was going to get. The air was sharp and clean, but the bite of it was more subdued than in preceding days. There was a warmth that hadn't been felt since fall, and the afternoon promised to be warm enough to start melting the snow pack. Already the snow's depth was less, due to settling. New snow yet to come would not be able to keep up with melting.

Soon there would be dark ground showing. It would absorb more heat from the sun and further hasten melting of snow, and ice in the ground. With warming, the roots of perennials would begin to show signs of life, using the stored energy from fall to send out new roots and start new growth above ground. Seeds from last year will begin to swell from warmth and moisture, germinating into the plant its DNA programmed for it, a near duplicate of last year's species.

Gulo's territory covers an area about twenty-five miles long by fifteen miles wide. It backs up into the low range of mountains to the east and extends west to encircle a prime hunting area along a stream. Her neighbor to the north, a female, was her own litter mate, both having been born in this same area two years previously. Their mother allowed them to set up their territories next to her, and even extending well into the range she claimed for her own.

These neighboring areas were left vacant when the occupant succumbed to injuries received when caught in the open by three wolves. She fought a vicious battle with them, by backing up against a large boulder, and had been able to save her own life for the short term. The wolves left her alone after sustaining several severe injuries themselves, deciding there was food to be had without getting bitten in return. But the wolverine's cuts became infected and she died after several long, agonizing weeks.

The other wolverine had the misfortune to locate the bones of a moose killed by a hunter while the hunter was still in the area. Spotting her on the carrion, he stalked to within shooting range and took her as a trophy. Her fur was of poor quality, not yet prime, as September is much too early for fur animals to have grown the dense underfur and long guard hairs needed for winter. It is these that make the most beautiful fur. In spite of this, she now adorned the basement trophy room of the hunter in the form of a full body mount. The poor quality of the fur was not noticeable in this way, nor was her small size. The rarity of the trophy excluded all such thoughts. Many hunters have spent years in the Alaska bush without being privileged with the sight of a wolverine, much less collecting one.

Leaving the quarreling kits secure in the den, Gulo headed into more mountainous terrain. Her travel was erratic, generally in an easterly direction, but with short side trips. Each new odor had to be investigated and nothing was passed without her having noted and accepted it as being in its proper place. Some distance from the den, she intentionally turned off course. Stopping at a willow protruding from the snow, she urinated on it. The scent was left to mark the area as her territory.

During the day's travel, she stopped frequently at willows and other sticks and clumps to repeat the marking. Twice during the afternoon, she halted at hummocks where the snow was raised above ground level due to a mound of grass and moss below. Gulo rubbed her anal glands on these mounds using a side to side motion. Depositing her scent in this manner also told others that this area was her home.

Gulo would allow her own family into the area without a fight; however, unknown females would be met and driven away. Seldom would actual fights result with these intruders, but they would not be accepted, and there would be much growling and posturing any time they came together. The newcomer usually backs down and leaves without a fight, continuing her search for an unoccupied home.

Gulo's father lived about forty miles away, his own territory overlapping that of her mother and adjoining that of the male in whose territory Gulo and her sister lived. The local male was the one who fathered the litter she was now raising.

The territory of males is much larger than a female's, and there will be several females having territories within it. But, the male will not allow another male in the area. His own male offspring will be forced to leave when they mature. Females are more tolerant as they will allow their female young to stay after maturity; however, they generally leave

21

after a couple years and find homes of their own. Females can, but frequently do not, breed before their second year. If food is plentiful, they breed every year, but if times get lean, they do as many other mammals, either have no young or have fewer young in their litters.

She crossed a small stream and continued into rising terrain. The sun was well up by now, at least as far as it was going to rise on this beautiful spring day. As she crossed a ridge, an odor was picked up and Gulo immediately stopped. A few more sniffs gave her a direction, but she stayed for several more minutes, testing the air until she was sure no scent of danger was mixed with the smell that caught her interest. She cautiously headed down the other side of the hill, adjusting her direction to follow the tantalizing odor. Gulo had been slowly climbing in her hunt and was now at treeline. There were only a few scraggly clumps of stunted spruce in the area. Weaving her way among them, her pace became slower as the scent became stronger. She made wide swings to each side of the scent trail checking for danger, but found none.

Cautiously she peered from behind a gnarled spruce and found the remains of a caribou poking through the snow. Sticking high above the mound was a gigantic antler showing the animal had been a mature bull. The old bull had not been able to survive the winter due to his physical condition becoming run down after expending an excessive amount of energy during rut the previous fall.

He had bred several cows, and in doing so had pushed himself to the limit driving younger bulls away. The shoving matches occasionally were long, and at the end of them, he would be panting and spent.

Seldom were there severe injuries sustained by the participants, but at times, one was blinded or received puncture wounds that later became infected. On more rare occasions, antlers locked together and fighters died a slow death of exhaustion and dehydration when they could not get free. Although uninjured, the bull was more interested in the rut than in feeding and his physical condition rapidly declined. Between fighting and eating little food, winter caught him without enough fat to sustain him through cold and lean dark days. But, the last of his genes were now carried by cows he had bred and will be carried on through coming generations. His remains would sustain those that would feed upon it, from large mammals down to microorganisms.

Gulo advanced to the dead caribou. After again checking for danger signs, she started digging packed snow from it. Uncovering part of the stomach,

Gulo tore into it with her sharp teeth until she had a hole large enough to begin gnawing on the frozen entrails. The past month had been a time during which she had eaten less than was normal. The past two weeks had been especially lean. She left her kits for only short periods during which she had cleaned up most of the caches near the den. Pregnancy, and now the milk needed for her kits, placed a heavy burden on her body. She was somewhat run down and in need of many large meals. The only reasonable meal over the past two weeks had been a ptarmigan she had stalked and killed yesterday. The bird hadn't been much more than a snack, but now she had food to keep her stomach filled for many days.

It was well past sundown when she left the carcass. Only starlight reflected from the snow lit up the area. The sky was cloudless. The temperature had again returned to freezing. Without cloud cover, night would be a cold one. After the hard work of gnawing a large meal off the frozen carcass, Gulo's instincts and swollen teats were telling her it was time to feed her family. The den was nearly three miles away, and she headed there, traveling in nearly a straight line. Twice on the way home she stopped to mark, but made no side trips other than a few feet. Darkness was no problem, she knew her territory well and was used to traveling and hunting in less light than she had tonight. A steady gait brought her quickly to the entrance of the den. A few quick sniffs told her that all was the same as when she had left.

Garou, the youngest male, met her inside the tunnel, several feet from the den cavity itself. Already he was showing traits that would follow him the rest of his short life: a lot of curiosity and an eagerness for activity. Carajou and Glutt were waiting in the den anticipating a meal that had been a long time coming. The kits were squealing and pushing as Gulo entered. They were fighting for a teat before she could lay down. In their hunger, they bit and pulled hard on their mother. Had she been able to think, she would have felt glad the kits did not yet have their teeth. After several minutes, they slowed, but continued to suckle until their bellies were as round and tight as their mother's. Peace finally came and all slept soundly.

Outside, clear skies brought colder temperatures while the moon rose and cast a shadow on the snow of one of night's silent creatures, a snowy owl. Nearly white, what few brown markings it had allowed it to blend perfectly with the night's snowy shadows. Sitting on a hummock near the caribou carcass it watched and listened.

The owl's eyesight is exceptional in the dark, and contrary to what is generally believed, has as good eyesight in day time. Normally a nocturnal bird, owls can, and do hunt in daytime. Owls of far northern latitudes have to do much of their hunting in daylight as there is little or no dark in summertime. Another little known fact is owls have the largest ears of all birds. Their hearing is enhanced by one ear being lower than the other, giving them the ability to pinpoint their prey just as eyes, being separated, can tell just how far away an object is. Owls can locate and kill prey in near total darkness by their hearing alone, using their eyes only secondarily.

The night was bright and windless, making things easy for the owl. It had been sitting on the hummock for only a short time before a northern red-backed vole came into sight. The vole ventured out of its snow tunnel for an unknown reason—out into the dangerous open. Nearly soundless, still the vole was heard by the owl and movement of the animal had brought the owl's large eyes instantly to it. It had moved only a few feet across the snow when a sharp talon pierced its skull, dripping a small spot of blood on the white snow. The owl's wings had made no sounds as it left its perch, nor in the short flight to the vole. Without even knowing danger was near the vole had died. The only trace left was the small spot of blood and marks in the snow where the owl's wing tips had brushed it.

Back on the hummock, the owl swallowed the vole without tearing it apart. It would furnish a fragment of energy for the trip that it was going to start in a few hours, migrating north, back to the area it had left in early winter.

At the other side of Gulo's home area, two coyotes were hunting along the stream. Both were hungry and eagerly gave chase when the young female jumped a snowshoe hare. The chase was short as the fleet coyotes were able to run down the hare and quickly kill it. Had the hare not jumped from its hiding place, the coyotes may have missed it, as the white of its fur blended perfectly with the surroundings. Even the few brown splotches already showing in its coat helped hide him in branches and shadows of spruce. Had he survived the night, his fur would have progressively turned brown to match the earth that was just beginning to show in spots through melting snow.

The coyotes quickly consumed the hare and resumed their hunt. More food would be needed. The female had been bred in early March by her mate and in a short time would give birth to a litter of five pups.

The coyotes (*Canis latrans*) are new to this far north locale and are still not plentiful. However, each year sees a few more of these carnivores in the area. They are one of the most adaptable of animals living today. Although they are not yet found in arctic regions, time will surely see some of them adapting to the harsh life there. And, baring some unusual climatic change, possibly they will develop a paw much larger than the narrow one they now have. Perhaps they will even begin to change to white fur in winter. But all of this takes thousands of years. For now, the coyote must cope with his surroundings with what he has.

His ability to change diet and lifestyle to fit new conditions is one of his strongest points. Already in the Lower-48, he has adapted to urban life, living within the limits of large cities, surviving on garbage, and killing and eating domestic cats and dogs. Not being hunted by man in those areas, the coyote population is growing steadily and is becoming more of a problem each year.

The coyotes had departed the area long before Gulo left early the next morning, after Carajou, Garou, and Glutt had their breakfasts. The day was again clear and cool. Stars were fading in the light of the sun that was still below the mountains. Her stomach was not as full as when Gulo had entered the den the previous night. After a mile of travel, she found a place to her liking, stopped and relieved her bowels. This was not to mark territory, marking is done with urine and with ventral and anal glands. Still it would further show her ownership, although that was not her purpose.

Today she knew where she was going and her progress was more in a straight line than the day before. Only a few side trips were made for marking purposes and to check for danger. Scents she picked up were quickly identified and she hurried on her way. One short stop was made when she detected an odor and only a few feet away found a spot of blood on the snow. The faint smell of vole still lingered and the scent of blood told her the story of the night before. Often in her short life, she had come upon the site of another carnivore's kill, at times finding something left she could eat, but that was when it was much larger prey than just a vole. Knowing that none of this was dangerous to her and there was no food left, she continued to the site of the caribou, eager to refill her now empty stomach.

As she approached her new food source, she became cautious, instinctively knowing that its smell could bring visitors who might be a danger to her. Bears were still in their winter dens and were no threat, but being unable to reason this, her instincts kept her alert. At this time of year, her only real danger was from wolves. Sensing nothing, she began feeding. The frozen meat was hard, but not a match for her powerful jaws and sharp teeth. Had it not been frozen, she would have been tearing off chunks to be carried away and buried in caches. Now, she could only fill her stomach, which she did with all possible speed.

Gulo did not like feeding in the open. The carcass was frozen down; she was unable to move it. There were no trees or dense brush next to it. Being so exposed made her nervous, especially during daylight hours. Several times, it seemed, she heard or smelled something, making her leave abruptly, but she never went far before returning. It was not until she was about to leave that she was discovered, but this was only by a raven who happened to pass overhead. It made several croaks and dove on Gulo twice, but since no other raven was there to help it harass the wolverine, the raven made a few scolding remarks and left. Gulo paid the bird little attention, giving it only a casual glance, and continued feeding until again her stomach was extended and she could hold no more.

On the return to the den, her nose picked up the scent of a snowshoe hare causing her to come to an abrupt halt until she detected the location of the animal. It was nearly invisible against the snow, but the wolverine's nose led her closer until she caught the glint of sunlight on the hare's eye. Gulo completed the short stalk, and with a quick pounce killed the hare. The wolverine was unable to eat any of it as there simply was no room in her bulging stomach. Gulo carried it to a nearby snowbank where she dug a hole in the snow, then down a few inches into the frozen moss below. There, she placed the hare, covering it with the moss and snow. Hopefully she would be the one to locate it in the future. Many of her caches were appropriated by others; foxes are especially adept at this kind of thievery.

Again she turned toward the den. When Gulo arrived, she was met by Garou, this time further out in the tunnel than he had come the night before. Carajou followed Garou into the tunnel; however, not having his bravery, she waited for her mother without getting far from the nest cavity. Glutt, not to be outdone, was just behind her. The kits were now a month old and had tripled their birth weight. Sharp points of teeth had penetrated the gums, and it would not be long before their mother would begin to wean them.

White fuzz with which the kits had been born was also starting to change. It was turning darker; a faint outline could already be seen where the classic pale tan stripes would be, above the eyes and from the shoulders down each side, then over the rump and on top of the bushy tail. Fuzz was turning into a fur that would eventually be dense and a rich brown color.

Day by day they became more active and were spending a good part of the time in not so gentle play. As before, a ferocious feeding followed Gulo's return. Again, all in the den went to sleep with full stomachs.

The next week was spent much the same, with Gulo feeding at the caribou carcass and staying away for longer periods each time she left the den. She was feeding mostly at night, early morning, and late evenings. Daylight made her uncomfortable, especially with the carcass in such an open area. Several ravens located it and were busy picking at the remains during daylight. Four foxes were helping Gulo devour it in the evenings in spite of her running them off on several occasions. The bones were being well cleaned and Gulo had used her powerful jaws to crush several of them to get at the marrow. Many smaller, softer bones had been eaten entirely for their calcium, helping to replenish that which she had lost during the formation of her babies.

The kits began coming to the opening of the snow tunnel, but their bravery left before they got entirely outside. Their teeth were now grown to needle sharp points and starting to cause discomfort to their mother. While nursing this morning, Carajou had clamped down on one teat, nearly bringing blood, and was immediately nipped by Gulo. She let out a yelp, but went back to her meal immediately, not understanding what the rebuff was all about. This was to be repeated more often in the coming days.

The kits were six weeks old when Gulo made her last trip to the caribou. Nothing was left except smell, and that was becoming faint. What few tiny bits of protein remained was hidden in moss and would be decomposed by bacteria. Within a month nothing would be visible other than a few tufts of hair. This would be gone long before fall, settling down into the grass and mosses, or picked up by birds or voles for nesting material. Its disappearance would leave nothing to show where the bull had died. Even the huge antlers would be gnawed away by the microtines and porcupines who needed the calcium for their own bodies.

After assuring herself there was nothing left to eat, Gulo angled along a bench, staying at the edge of the timber. Her wandering soon brought her back to lower ground and into an area growing only a few small spruces. Sniffing constantly, she followed the edge of a muskeg, checking everything that caught her attention. Twice her nose picked up the odor of voles; a quick pounce and dig each time resulted in a kill. The small animals were bolted down; the slicing action of the wolverine's teeth easily cutting them into swallowing size bites.

The sun was well up by the time the voles were eaten. She crossed an area of muskeg and climbed to the top of a small ridge. Pushed up by a glacier thousands of years before, the ridge was composed of gravel and rock with only sparse vegetation. Here, her nose picked up the scent of food and she soon located the source. A male spruce grouse (*Dendragapus canadensis*) had already filled his crop and had come to the ridge to get small pieces of gravel. The gravel would be used in place of teeth, grinding the food in its gizzard. During winter months, the grouse feeds heavily on spruce needles and buds, but soon his diet would turn to better foods. However this early in spring, he was still feeding almost exclusively on needles. Later green plants would be abundant, and he would switch to them. When berries appeared, they would round out his diet.

The grouse stood still, cocking his head and watching the wolverine approach. Gulo was moving slow, trying not to alarm the bird. When within a few feet, she made a sudden lunge, the grouse taking to wing at the same instant. This time the grouse was lucky; Gulo was just able to touch his tail feathers at the top of her leap. She started her charge just a couple inches too far away. The grouse flew to the top of a nearby spruce and looked down at her. Gulo gave a low snarl, looked back up at her lost meal and left. Climbing after the bird would have been easy; however, experience told her the bird would fly long before she could reach him.

Gulo turned toward the den. It was light and the kits would be hungry, but as she was not satisfied with the skimpy meal of two voles, she hunted on the way home. Later, when it appeared she would go hungry, she blundered into a snowshoe hare. Her quick reaction enabled her to catch it. Instead of eating it there, she picked it up and carried it with her to the den.

The kits were at the entrance as usual, and instead of immediately demanding to suckle, their attention was drawn to the hare. The odor of blood was stronger than they had smelled before. Previously blood odor had come from traces left on their mother's fur, but this was strong and exciting! All three kits hesitated, but soon were examining the hare's fur, for the moment having forgotten about nursing.

Gulo watched for a while, then went to the hare and tore part of the skin from it. She pulled out the entrails; as soon as the abdomen was opened, a new, powerful odor poured out. Carajou and Garou touched their noses to the intestines while Gulo ripped them apart. Glutt held back, too many new things were happening and he was unsure of himself. While Gulo was eating part of the entrails, Carajou and Garou touched the raw flesh with their tongues and instinctively started to lick it. The new odor was transformed into a delightful taste and both began to gnaw. Although the kit's teeth were not out enough to do much good, they chewed on the soft food, enjoying its flavor for the first time.

The bewildered Glutt still held back, not at all sure that this was something he wanted. He moved beside Gulo and the closeness reminded him of her milk and he began to nurse, forgetting about the strange smells. Carajou and Garou were able to chew off some of the more tender portions, and swallowing them, their weaning began.

Gulo let the kits chew until their jaws were tired. When they came to her to nurse, she finished the hare, then turned to enter the den, dragging the reluctant Glutt who refused to let go of her teat. She was followed by Garou and Carajou, who were whining and trying to keep up with her. As soon as she lay down, they were on her, each grabbing a teat and twisting their bodies into comfortable positions. The taste of hare had whetted their appetites and they pulled and bit harder than ever, each getting a nip from Gulo for their roughness. Peace reigned for a while, but for a good part of the day, the kits played and fought one another.

Gulo was up early the next day. It was still dark when she left the den. Clouds shut out the stars. The temperature was just below freezing and there was a hint of snow in the air. This morning, she left in a westerly direction and her hunt took her into the area of a small stream.

Reaching it, she turned to cover the south side of the water way, leaving behind a large area of muskeg. In this manner, she could stay where spruce trees were plentiful, as well as prey that would fill her empty stomach.

> White spruce (*Picea glauca*) are the most common trees in Central Alaska, but although they are plentiful, they are not large. The growing season is so short it takes many years for them to mature. It can take up to two-hundred years for one of them to reach twelve inches in diameter. Scattered among, and towering over the spruce, are cotton-wood trees (*Populus balsamifera*). These are much faster growing and do well along the moist banks of streams.

Numerous openings among the trees were overgrown with willows. In places they were thick enough to slow a human. However, Gulo had no difficulty in navigating among them. Her slender body glided through the thick shrubs with no more trouble than a whiff of air.

> Muskeg is mostly water with sedges and rushes, seldom do any true grasses grow there. White spruce cannot grow in these conditions; it is simply too wet for them. Clumps of spruce in these areas are black spruce (*Picea mariana*), a species that can exist with their feet continually wet. In this type of habitat, black spruce is a scraggly, stunted tree, dark and homely in appearance. When it is found in

drier places, it can be as pretty and as well formed as white spruce.

Muskeg is usually edged with willows, blueberries, and dwarf birch, along with many other plants that can handle both dry and wet conditions. Some muskegs can be dangerous. Plants can appear to be growing on solid ground when in fact, they are growing in mats floating on water. Stepping from clump to clump can get a hiker in trouble, when suddenly a seemingly solid clump sinks under him, and he is in several feet of water.

Getting wet in Alaska, even in the summer, is a serious matter unless one can get dry and warm quickly. Ground water here is always cold, and many lakes seldom get above fifty degrees during the short summer. Hypothermia sets in within thirty minutes if immersed in such water, and death comes soon after.

Gulo had put the muskeg well behind her when a fox barked, but knowing she had no chance to catch the speedy animal, she ignored him. A grouse in the top of a small spruce watched them both, but made no move. Gulo passed the tree oblivious of the bird and continued to hunt. The spruce grouse has survived and thrived in this country by the simple trait of being still. It is frequently called the "Fool Hen" by humans because it will allow them to approach closely and are easy marks for a gun. Man is new to the scene and the grouse has not yet adopted tactics to counter him. In the past, their principal enemies have been predator birds who cannot spot the grouse when it sits quietly, and some will not fly among the trees to kill it. Only since the arrival of man has their actions been a detriment to survival.

Further down stream, Gulo picked up the scent of a hare, started her stalk, and captured the prey with little difficulty. It was eaten underneath cottonwoods near the water. Finishing the hare, she turned back to the east, and in a circular path made her way in the general direction of home. Stopping frequently to mark her territory, she continued to hunt, finding several voles that were promptly put into caches.

Nearing the den, she made a side trip to a spot where she usually had success in finding voles. There she located two more, killing them, but leaving them uneaten. By this time the sun was well up in the sky and she felt the need get back to the den. She was now well fed and it was time to feed her young. Carrying the two voles, she made her way home.

The kits met her outside the tunnel, jumping up on her and biting her feet. Their playfulness fit in with Gulo's contented mood and she began to hop and jump about, acting like a kit herself. The play continued for several minutes until the excitement died down. By this time, the kits had noticed the two voles and were starting to investigate this new smell. Putting a paw on one, Gulo pulled it open and promptly all three kits started to chew on it.

Glutt had now learned there was something other than milk that tasted good, and was soon growling and fighting with the others, trying to get more than his share. Gulo tore open the other vole and then lay down and watched them worry the carcasses. She had little to clean up this time. It took the kits a while, but eventually the voles were gone, except the tougher parts. These she ate herself, then lay down outside the den and allowed them to nurse. After a few moments she got up, pulling her teats away from them, and entered the tunnel. The darkness was restful and reassuring to her. Making her way to the nest area, she again lay down, and again the kits found a teat and nursed until they were plump and round and could eat no more. Milk had been forgotten for a while, but was still needed to completely satisfy them.

During the following days Gulo continued to hunt, killing enough to satisfy herself and bringing more food home to her young. She started moving away when they became insistent to suck, allowing them to do so for shorter periods each day. Their teeth were out, sharp, and Gulo's nipples were beginning show signs of their abuse.

The sun was shining longer each day and Gulo and the kits spent more time outside the den. The play became more rowdy as they grew, and snarls and growls became a big part of it. This play took on aspects of the hunt and was good training for them in addition to the exercise that was needed for their muscles. They stalked each other, pouncing and biting in the places where they would later bite to kill their prey. Frequently too hard a bite brought a squeal of pain, followed by a growl and a retaliatory bite for the offender.

By eight weeks the kits were weaned and Gulo was hard put to find enough food to bring back to the den. She hunted day and night, spending long hours, with little time at the den except to rest up for the next hunt. The kits were growing at a fast pace and were already several times their birth weight. The plentiful supply of food from Gulo was giving them a healthy start in life.

At the beginning of their ninth week, the weather again turned cold and patches of bare ground that had shown up were again covered with snow. Winds came from the north and temperature dropped to low levels. It did not last long however; within a day the new snow was gone, and by the end of the week it had warmed again. Gulo again left the den before daybreak and was four miles away when the sun rose above the mountains. It cast a soft yellow glow on the ridges. Clouds holding over the mountain tops were rimmed with gold. The bright warmth was inviting to the kits and they came out of the tunnel. A nip by Glutt started them chasing each other; soon they were playfully fighting and rolling about in the softening snow some distance from the entrance to the den.

Unknown to the kits, a mile away, a mature female goshawk was perched in the top of a tall spruce tree. In spite of the distance, her eyes immediately picked up the kit's movements and she focused her attention on them. It took her only moments to determine they were unprotected and vulnerable.

Swiftly she dove from the tree leveling off just above the ground. Pumping her wings, she wove between the trees, gathering full speed within a few beats. Glutt saw only a flashing shadow before the goshawk hit him, her sharp talons piercing his skin and penetrating his chest. He screamed in pain, but by then the goshawk was again airborne and heading toward a tall, white-branched cottonwood tree. Glutt was dead by the time she selected a limb on which to light.

The goshawk waited for a time, making sure her kill was dead, then headed for her nest where her own young waited for a meal. Arriving there, she perched on the side of the nest and tore open the soft underskin. Pulling bits of flesh and entrails from his body, she stuffed them into the gaping mouths of her chicks. Noisily they gulped them down, eating until they could hold no more. Then the mother ate a large portion, leaving what was left on the side of the nest. The remains would be consumed later.

Inside the snow tunnel were two cowering kits, both well back from the entrance. The sudden appearance of the vicious bird, and the dying cry of their litter mate, had struck a terror in them they would remember each time a shadow passed over them. After a time, their fright eased; however, a feeling things were not right persisted and they did not go back outside. Retreating to the den nest, they curled up and waited for Gulo's return.

While all of this was happening, Gulo was on her way home. Had her eyesight been better, she would have seen the flight of the goshawk as it carried off her second born. She reached the den about half an hour later and for once found the tunnel vacant. Dropping the hare she had brought, and sensing something was not right, she tested the air, but found nothing unusual. Gulo checked the ground for several yards each way from the entrance, detecting only the smells of her family, then entered the tunnel and made her way to the nest. There she found two kits who were eager to see her. She looked over both and again picked up no unusual smells. Still she was uneasy, and again went down the tunnel and outside, checking everywhere. Something was missing, but not being able to count or to reason, she was not capable of understanding it was one of her own babies. Returning to the remaining kits, she lay down. Carajou and Garou suckled their fill, cuddled against Gulo, and were soon asleep.

Gulo did not sleep. Twice more she left the den before settling down. The balance of the day and all of the following night she stayed at the den, leaving only for frequent trips outside, checking the area repeatedly.

Garou and Carajou came out of the den with Gulo in early morning. Finding the hare still lying beside the entrance, they worked on it for a while unsuccessfully until Gulo tore it open for them. After filling themselves, they lay down outside, staying only until Gulo ate what was left.

They returned to the den when Gulo finally decided to hunt for more food. She was still uneasy. Her hunt did not take her far before she was fortunate to locate, kill, and eat a ptarmigan. She then found and killed another hare, which was brought home whole. Carajou and Garou were again at the entrance to the tunnel—this time they had not ventured outside.

The family had been uneasy the entire day, not comprehending what had occurred the day before. Things were somehow different. Although they were missing one of the family members, they could not think or reason like a human and say to themselves, "Glutt is missing! He was taken by the bird!" This is what sets man apart from all animals; he can reason and feel emotions of love and hate. The wolverines could feel none of this, but with one of them missing, their lives were different. This they could sense as not being normal and their activities changed as a result.

Gulo ripped part of the skin from the hare and left it lying near the entrance. While she rested nearby, Carajou and Garou gnawed and worried the carcass, eating as much as they could. Their teeth were well erupted by now and they did a good job on the meal, eating a good part of the hare. Gulo cleaned it up after the kits were full and had entered the den to sleep—their recent loss was no longer a concern to them.

It was as if Glutt had never lived. His death had become a part of the survival of the family of goshawks. Normally a predator animal, Glutt became the prey and his flesh was now sustaining others as others had sustained him. Nature is so devised that everything must feed upon something else, be it flesh or vegetable.

Something must die that others may live. This is a lesson that many humans never learn and they place human feelings and emotions on animals they simply do not have. Animals do not reason. They do not act because of any thought process. They simply react to stimuli, whether it is external, such as running from an attack of a predator, or internal, such as mating or eating. They do not teach their young how to mate, eat, or hunt. This is ingrained somehow in their genes. Even a newborn human baby knows how to suckle. They do not have to be taught this basic action of survival.

Animals learn by observation and repetition, but only in the most basic manner. Only humans communicate to the point they can convey a thought to another human. Some animals give warning calls to others, but this is the crudest form of communication, barely above "body language" in which an animal's posture may convey aggression or submission. These calls and actions are a result of traits handed down through generations; they are not learned and certainly not taught. They are done without thought—simply reactions.

Mankind would be more helpful to its wild brethren if they would stop humanizing them. Fantasy movies have spawned a generation of humans who believe animals think, feel emotions, and actually communicate intentionally with each other. The more extreme believe they should be equated on a par with humans. Yet, these same people think nothing of squashing a spider or killing a snake, dangerous or not. Do not these have as much going for them as other animals? For that matter what about cutting a flower? Why shouldn't plants have the right to be unmolested? "They can't feel anything!" you say. But wait, how do we know they cannot feel pain just because they cannot visibly or audibly react? The chance that a plant can feel pain is so remote that it needs to be discounted out of hand, just as the fallacies about animals having human emotions needs to be discounted.

Some animals are more intelligent than others. Through repetition, some can be taught simple things, some can be taught little or nothing. Is this a basis to decide which has special "rights?" Some humans think so, then some think all are equal, but somehow draw the line when it comes to snakes or mosquitoes. We have all heard the remark from an animal right's activist equating a boy and a pig, making them of the same "value." I doubt a human would give a pig the same treatment they would their own child. Can you imagine funeral arrangements and emotional loss of a child as being no different from the loss of a pet pig? Of course that is ludicrous, just as that person who made the analogy originally must know.

Values cannot be placed on things in nature unless it is value for purpose. A dog has no more value than an earthworm, unless you define it. The worm has great value in building soil; for this the dog is practically valueless. The dog has value as a pet (unless it is your neighbor's dog that barks all night); as a pet the earthworm leaves much to be desired.

The point of all of this is, each thing has its own intrinsic value and it is impossible to equate one to another. Each has its own place in nature, just as man has his own place in nature. Man is a predator, no different from a bear, weasel, or goshawk. But, man has a more profound effect on the world because he can reason, plan and create. He can build cities and roads, harvest forests, and clear land and plant crops. And he can multiply...then clear more land and build more cities and roads so he can multiply again, and again.

Although there is no statistics to prove the point, I doubt any biologist would argue that an average farmer takes more wildlife out of nature each year through his farming than any sport fisherman, hunter, or trapper does in a lifetime. The mere fact of the land no longer being available for natural use precludes its use by millions of insects, thousands of rodents and birds, and hundreds of small and larger mammals. Therefore these lives are denied, year upon year, simply for the sake of the intelligent human.

The city dweller is no different from the farmer. He buys the farmer's grain and livestock or the farmer would not be farming. The cities need building supplies and most of all, more land for buildings, and more roads to transport grains and other foodstuffs the urbanite buys. Many urbanites believe it is cruel for a fisherman to hook a fish, hunter to shoot a deer, or trapper to snare a mink, then thinking nothing of eating a hamburger or steak. They have given no thought that in actuality, they have hired the farmer to keep the steer or hog in virtual slavery, penned for its entire life, selectively bred, and specially fed, for the purpose of feeding the urbanite. Not only is he paying the farmer to do this for him, but he is paying the slaughter house to kill the animal and process it for him. Since he does not see this, he places himself above others; however, he is a predator, no less than the hunter who shoots and processes his own meat.

The vegetarian frequently places himself above the meat eater, but he himself uses land that could be used by wild animals, land on which the grains, fruits, and vegetables he eats are grown. Roads, homes, and even businesses that produce the goods he buys, totally unrelated to food, all take up space, denying it to wildlife. Many vegetarians will eat fish, caught by others in nets where they usually are asphyxiated (gill nets interfere with the gills and they can no longer get oxygen from the water). All are dumped into holds where the rest are asphyxiated, later to be sucked out by vacuum hoses for processing and shipped to the consumer. Poultry, frequently on the menu of vegetarians, is handled the same as a cow or hog, imprisoned for life, specially fed and slaughtered, little different from a pig. So the vegetarian is a predator too.

All humans are predators whether they like it or not. Man, with his intelligence, is at the top of the food chain, but that is simply his niche. Each animal, insect, plant, fungi, bacteria, etc., has its own niche, none is better than another, and since man is changing the world so much, all must be kept in balance.

With man being such an efficient predator, he must care for and manage wildlife, not on an emotional basis, but on biological facts, or at least the best information available. Acting on emotion without using knowledge does animals far more harm than good. Protecting something past the point it needs protection is like using radiation to kill a cancer; beyond a certain point you begin to kill what you are trying to protect.

But now Glutt was gone, the predator that had taken his life had done so for survival of its own species. Its young were being sustained by Glutt's flesh and with that of other creatures that would be killed in the future. And so it has been since time began, all living things feed upon something else. Glutt was gone—the wolverines quickly adjusted to the change.

CHAPTER THREE

May arrived; along with it came improving weather conditions. Snow turned to rain showers and snow pack on the ground melted, pouring water into the small gullies feeding larger streams until finding a river going to the ocean. Muskeg and marsh held as much water as possible this spring— winter snows had been often and deep. The many different kinds of willows, birches, and cottonwoods were leafing out, each leaf an individual, green, and absorbing sunlight, feeding its parent and restoring it to last summer's glory. Even spruce, green all year, was sending out new growth on tips of their boughs, the new needles, a yellow-green color in contrast to the dark blue-green of the older needles. New plants were springing up. The white scene of winter, then brown with old vegetation, now turned to green of a thousand shades.

Those plants propagating from seed must sprout, flower, and mature quickly to reseed for the following year. Others regenerate from rhizomes and roots that are dormant during the winter, reviving when spring comes. All have to adapt in some way to the short summer, even trees and shrubs must store food for the long winter. If they cannot do this in the time allotted, they will not survive. Many plants, transplanted to Alaska from warmer climates, do well here in summer, but without being able to mature their seed or store enough food in the short growing season, are unable to return the following spring.

May is the time for the first blooms, more will come in June, be profuse in July, and start to wane by August. Late September will find flowers gone as frost again returns. Willows and cottonwoods are among the earliest to bloom, but color of their catkins are somewhat drab, running from off-white to yellowish-green. There are many species of willow in Gulo's home area, only a few easily distinguishable because the family, *Salicacæ* crossbreeds readily and many species blend together. Only a few do not cross and therefore retain their identifying features.

Cottonwood and aspen are also in the family *Salicacæ,* but while the balsam cottonwood is plentiful along streams, more rare in this area is the quaking aspen which grows on drier hillsides. Cottonwood grows tall, its bark whitish in the upper branches, with dark, rough bark on its lower trunk and heavy, low branches. The aspen is smaller and has a smooth, greenish colored bark with dark, warty patches. When rubbing against an aspen, a white powder is left on clothing and is visible on dark, smooth material. Aspen leaves are on flat stems and twist and turn easily with the slightest breezes. At times the trees appear to be shaking and trembling as leaves rustle noisily against one another, hence the common name, quaking aspen. In spring new buds of the cottonwood is resinous, fragrant, with a reminder of turpentine. The aspen does not have this resinous odor.

Birches (*Betulaceæ*) have several members of its family growing locally, and again there is much crossbreeding with species blending into one another. One tree in this family, the alder, consisting of mountain alder (*Alnus crispa*), Sitka alder (*Alnus crispa sinuata*) and *Alnus incana* (no common name) are found in patches, sometimes in pure forms but often in cross strains. Even pure forms are difficult to distinguish from one another; mountain alder has oval leaves with a finely serrated edge while Sitka's leaves are wider, larger, and almost lobed with coarser serrations along edges. *Alnus incana* has narrow leaves with edges more smooth; also, its bark is reddish where others are gray.

Thickets of alder are nearly impassable to man. Other than Devil's club, alder is probably the most cursed plant of the North. It comes from the ground in many branches, forming a bowl-like plant. These trees grow close together with limbs crossing those of its neighbors. Frequently the lower limbs are only a foot or so off the ground, growing outward and intermingling with other alders before turning skyward. Heavy winter snow mashing them down when they are young are blamed for them growing nearly parallel to the ground before they get strong enough to grow upright. In this manner a nearly impenetrable barrier is formed.

Man, with his upright posture, is at a distinct disadvantage, and if he is encumbered with a backpack or rifle, his progress can be measured in feet per hour. Though limbs are often three inches in diameter, large bears can, by using their great strength, force their way through them. The wolverine, with his smaller size, can run between branches nearly as fast as on open ground. Hunters following a wounded bear into alders do so with great peril, for they are at the mercy of ambush and frequently unable to get off a killing shot before it is chewing on them.

Gulo was having an easier time now spring had truly arrived. New growth of plants was being matched by mating and nesting of birds and animals that she needed to feed her family. Her nightly forays furnished more food than before and with more variety. Now becoming available were whole new families of lemmings, adults having been dormant during winter, and ground squirrels that had actually been in deep hibernation.

Arctic ground squirrel (*Spermophilus parryii*) furnishes a sizeable meal, with adults growing to two pounds and occasionally a little more. This rodent burrows into the ground and lives principally on vegetation with only an occasional meal of a smaller rodent, bird's eggs, or chicks. Their young begin arriving in June, continuing through July, with as many as eight in the litter. Being prolific, they are an important prey species for predators of the North. For some reason, bears are especially fond of them and will spend an enormous amount of energy digging them out. Sometimes they expend more energy than they receive in nourishment from a kill. *Gulo* also digs them out, but usually her stealth and quickness enable her to catch them before they can get back into their dens. Frequently the den has only one entrance, making digging for them practical, as they cannot get away.

Only a few days after the death of Glutt, Gulo took Carajou and Garou with her, at first enticing them to follow her, finally picking them up and carrying them when they stopped. Each in turn was taken in her mouth and gently held there, her powerful jaws and teeth closing only tightly enough about their chest and shoulders to hold them. Their snow den finally melted to the point it was becoming unusable. Since the natal den is only used for a length of time by wolverines, they now would be more nomadic.

Gulo had traveled no more than a mile before she found a hole between two boulders. After giving it and surroundings a cursory examination, she shoved the kits into it. This was to be their home for the next few days. Gulo had been uneasy since the loss of Glutt. Although she did not connect his demise with danger about the den, her instincts told her it was time to leave. They would move about frequently from now on, staying only a day or so at each location.

With the kits safe in their new temporary home, Gulo left to hunt along the stream to the west, a place that was one of her more productive hunting areas. Voles and lemmings made up most of her catch for the night, enough to satisfy herself, and some to bring back to her young.

Returning to the kits, she found them exactly where they had been left, sleeping peacefully. The new surroundings were strange to them and they had moved from the hole only three times to sniff around and relieve themselves. Gulo again helped them to eat by tearing open the lemmings, but this was becoming unnecessary as their teeth and jaws had developed enough for them to do it on their own. Before the sun was high, they were curled up together, well fed, contented, and asleep. Now out in the open, Gulo was more alert. She lifted her head often and tested the air for any odors.

Morning dawned gray. As the day progressed it became grayer still. Clouds that had been covering the nearby mountain tops early in the morning later crept down until it became a fog, blurring everything that wasn't within a few feet. Gulo paid no attention to this and even became less attentive, spending more time napping. Fog always seemed to give her a sense of security; she slept more deeply than she normally would have in such an exposed location.

Thick fog held throughout the day, swirling gently among the trees. At times, trees a few hundred feet away were visible but mostly only those nearby could be seen, and these were fuzzy and appeared to be in deep shadows. Just past, what would have been sunset, a light breeze brought an odor to her nose causing her to wake up. A moment later she identified the smell as one that could be a danger to her kits.

Arousing her young, she shoved them with her nose, forcing them back between the boulders as far as possible. Gulo turned into the wind with the smell still tickling her nose. She knew the enemy was some distance away, but the faint odor was growing stronger each moment.

Gulo instinctively moved away from the kits to meet the danger as far from them as possible and her anger mounted with every step she took. She headed directly toward the intruder until the scent became strong, then Gulo stopped. Her enemy was close. While trying to pinpoint its location, she heard an almost noiseless sound and then saw a shadow move. It was heading almost directly toward her.

Gulo crouched beside a small spruce and in the dark shadows she was nearly invisible. She now picked up two separate scents, one her enemy and the other the smell of a familiar food. As the shadow approached her muscles tensed until they were nearly quivering—suddenly the shadow disappeared. Gulo nearly rose to see better but her hunting instincts stopped her. Blocking her sight was a dense clump of willows. She concentrated on them waiting for movement. Suddenly the shadow reappeared no more than ten feet to her left. The movement triggered the release of the coiled springs that were her leg muscles. Within two bounds she hit her enemy. She struck him nearly head on and with a loud growl, clamped down on what she took to be its neck.

The coyote was knocked on his side and Gulo dug in with her claws. Biting as hard as she could she violently shook her head side to side. Suddenly a large chunk came loose, startling her, until she realized she had only a mouthful of snowshoe hare. Instead of getting her teeth into the coyote's neck, she had merely taken his night's catch from him. By this time the coyote had regained his feet, and with a frightened yelp was running as fast as he could. Gulo jumped in pursuit, but with several leaps head start, the scared coyote had the advantage and was making hard use of it. She realized it was useless and gave up the chase.

Returning to the site of her ambush, she growled several times, releasing her tension. She tested the air for other danger and found none, but not satisfied, she cast about, thoroughly checking the ground for any smells. Several times, she picked up the trail of the coyote and followed it back to the spot of the encounter. Finally her growls and agitation subsided to the point where she was able to return to her kits. Gulo picked up the hare taken from the coyote, and headed for the rock den. The frightened youngsters had not moved. Excited to see their mother, they jumped upon her, bit her ears, and licked her muzzle.

Gulo was still not ready to settle down. After seeing her kits were safe, she made short trips about the area, checking for scents and anything that should not have been there. Not until she was completely satisfied that all was well, did she lay down beside them. They had already started eating the hare, its skin having been torn open from being ripped from the coyote's jaws. Evening was early, Gulo had not hunted, and already they were being fed. She helped them finish the hare, and they were satisfied for the time being. Gulo was still highly alert. Although the kits tried to initiate some play with her, they were rebuffed and had to settle with playing with each other.

It was not till the sky started to grow light that Gulo got up. Before leaving the area entirely, she made a check to see if there were any coyote smells or other signs of danger. The morning hunt was kept short. The wolverine never went more than a mile from the kits. She located a family of voles, killed and ate them, then left the boggy place she was in and moved to an area of thick grasses.

Gulo had not hunted in this new area long before she scented a spruce grouse. Sneaking up on it, she jumped, and with a bite on its head, had more food to take back to her hungry young. The hen had been reluctant to fly as she was sitting on a clutch of eggs and her delay was fatal. Finding several eggs under the hen, Gulo broke them and greedily licked up their contents. This was not the first nest she had destroyed and most certainly would not be the last. The eggs were eaten with relish, and for the moment her hunger was satisfied.

Picking up the grouse, she returned to the kits who were hungry again. The bird was enough to satisfy them both and the kits finished their meal by rounding out their stomachs with Gulo's milk. Between naps, the day was spent in rough play, and Gulo was at times forced to join them when they climbed on her, biting her ears and tail.

Now past two months of age, Carajou and Garou were growing rapidly. Already their fur had taken on much of the wolverine's basic dark brown color and the creamy markings were becoming more pronounced. Their play brought on much growling and squealing. Gulo sometimes had to be rough in return to protect herself from them. Before they slept, a red squirrel scolded them from the top a nearby spruce, but he was smart enough to stay off the ground. When he did decide to leave the area, he did so by jumping from tree to tree. The squirrel was ignored, the wolverine family never looked up or even appeared to hear the chattering.

The coyote that had been unfortunate in getting too close to Gulo's kits had, for once, gone to his family without food. He was an exceptionally good provider and this had rarely happened before. But since his pups were still nursing, only he and his mate felt hunger pangs. Entering the den, which had been dug into the hillside beside a clump of willows, he lay down and licked the wounds he had received. He had been fortunate when Gulo had clamped down on the hare instead of his neck. His only cuts were from her sharp claws. These were minor and would cause only a slight discomfort. It could have been far worse. Except the hare, Gulo would have found the throat. It is doubtful he would have survived the assault. His few sore spots would not hinder him in hunting, and with his mate helping, their five pups would get plenty to eat. Not all of them would survive to become adults, but it would not be from lack of good care.

Within a few days, Gulo again moved the family to another location, this time well over a mile away. The kits were now able to keep up with her and she no longer had to carry them. From now on, Gulo would continue to move them every few days until they were able to follow her on the hunt. The new den was a hole found beneath a cottonwood growing on a mossy knoll. Only a small amount of digging had been needed to make it large enough for them, which was fortunate, as Gulo would never have dug a hole in the bank without the start of it already being there. She was not averse to digging, but it was just not in her nature to dig a den in dirt.

Snow tunnels were frequently dug in winter. Unless a den was needed in which to give birth and house newborn, they were short and used only for temporary shelter and to cache food. Their summer dens from now on would be safety spots—holes under rocks and trees, or simply just a dense growth of grass or shrubs that would keep them from being too visible.

May was gone, June arrived with its days of long, brilliant sunshine broken only by occasional showers. Summer rains are nearly always light, rarely would there be more than an inch of rain in twenty-four hours. In this area of Alaska, some of these rains develop into storms that have lightning and thunder; however, even here, a full-fledged thunderstorm is unusual. Further inland they would be more common as summer temperatures are hotter. Hot weather is needed for them to develop. Ocean waters keep temperatures lower along Alaska's coast and stops the formation of thunderstorms; thunder and lightning is rare. The south coastal area can be experiencing sixty-five or seventy degrees while the interior has temperatures in the nineties.

Everything grows profusely in June. Brown of winter has changed to greens of endless shades and catkins of cottonwood and most willows have matured with white "cotton" scattered by winds. Many wild flowers have already bloomed and many more have yet to do so. In wetter places coltsfoot (*Petasites*) had been one of the first to show up, with lavender tinted white blooms at the top of a stalk maturing into puffs of soft, white down. This plant blooms even before its leaves come out, the flower stalk oddly standing alone until maturity when it is then joined by the leaves coming directly from the ground. Soon after this, the dead appearing limbs of shrubby cinquefoil (*Potentilla fruticosa*) leaf out. Later this brushy plant would be adorned with five petaled yellow flowers all summer long. The area is covered with plants having beautiful and unique flowers, each blooming in its own time and in its own preferred habitat.

Blueberries are everywhere. Patches of them crowd the open areas and are at home in both wet and dry places. They need sunlight to bear fruit as heavily shaded plants have few berries. Several species are found in the area, *Vaccinium ovalifolium*, which prefers forest edges and drier locations and *V. uliginosum alpinum* (alpine blueberry), which inhabits the bogs.

Lingonberry (*Vaccinium vitis-idaœ*), known as Low Bush Cranberry, is also plentiful, using both sunny and semi-shady spots, but needing open sunny areas before they can do well in bearing their sour fruit.

While the ripe blueberry is sweet and delicious when picked and eaten directly from the plant, lingonberry is tart, tasting similar to the true cranberry. It needs to be cooked and sweetened for humans to enjoy it. The true cranberry (*Oxycoccus microcarpus*) is found here in wet places, but it is a tiny plant and seldom can enough berries be found to waste time picking them. Both lingonberry and cranberry are in the Heath (*Ericaceæ*) family but are separate species.

Not to be left out is the crowberry (*Empetrum nigrum*), the only local member of the crowberry (*Empetrum*) family. It is probably the most widespread of all local berries, living not only in bogs, but throughout the tundra and into the mountains. The fruit is blue-black and grows on a ground hugging plant looking for all the world like a tiny evergreen stem. Seedy and juicy, the berries form a large part of the diet of bears in the fall.

The berries furnish food, not only for birds, but also many mammals, and for bears, they are almost a necessity. The wolverine, fox, and coyote will eat berries, but the bear uses them extensively in the fall. Their high sugar content is needed to put on fat so that they can survive the long winter without food. Near human habitation, confrontations between them and bears during the berry season happen occasionally, usually with both parties leaving the area in a hurry. Seldom is anyone hurt at these times, but the encounter is well remembered. Pumping adrenaline embeds it deeply in one's mind.

Lesser known berries thrive locally, but in much fewer numbers. They are eaten only when encountered. Rarely are they found in large patches where they can be more than a passing snack. In this group are currants (*Ribes sp.*) which belong to the *Saxifrage* family (*Saxifragaceæ*) and raspberry, trailing raspberry, cloudberry, nagoonberry and salmonberry (*Rubus sp.*) all of which belong to the rose family (*Rosaceæ*). These berries are edible, some are tart, but in jellies and jams, they are delicious. Those in the rose family are sweet when picked and eaten raw, just as is the blueberry. They halt many hikers and hunters and make for pleasant rest stops.

CHAPTER FOUR

Gulo took Carajou and Garou with her when she left for the evening hunt. They were now nearly one-third her size; Garou slightly bigger than Carajou. He would continue to grow faster than she. When fully grown he would be over one-third larger. He was dominating their play; already his strength was more than hers. For the past week Gulo had been taking them with her for part of the hunt and leaving them in secluded places while she did the actual stalking of prey. Tonight would be different.

Their journey took them to the edge of a muskeg area, grassy with a few willows, and many blueberry bushes. Blueberries, now beginning to form, would later turn a dark blue, getting sweeter as they ripened. When frost comes in September, the spot will be visited by a small black bear. He will gorge on them using his lips and tongue to strip them off and eating any stems and leaves that get in the way. Sugar in the berries will quickly add fat to the bear, which is necessary, or the animal will not be able to lay dormant for nearly seven months without eating.

Grass and moss surrounding the muskeg was infested with voles. Their tunnels under the grass kept them hidden most of the time, but the sensitive nose of Gulo easily located them. A quick pounce pinned them down to be immediately killed. The kits watched with interest as she made her first two kills, but aggravated that Gulo refused to share. She bolted the small mammals down as soon as they were caught. Then a third vole was killed and Garou leaped to pull it from his mother's mouth. She quickly turned, avoiding him. With a toss of her head she swallowed it.

Garou's temper flared and he jumped on his sister in frustration. Biting and snarling, the two tore into each other, and for once, an actual fight happened between them. Garou pulled fur from his sister's neck and she promptly retaliated, biting him severely on the lip. For the first time he was really hurt and blood came from the cut he received. Startled, he backed off, shaking his head, then immediately resumed the battle by jumping on her back and sinking his teeth into the nape of her neck. But the fight came to a quick conclusion as Gulo came from behind, clamped down on his hind leg and pulled him off Carajou. Her snarls told them the fight was over. When she saw them back away, Gulo returned to hunting voles. Garou blamed Carajou for his trouble and gave her one last growl, but then turned aside, not wishing to bring his mother back into the conflict.

The disturbance had driven the nearby voles into hiding, so they had to move a short distance. Carajou and Garou began picking up smells of the voles in the grass, but were still expecting one to be given to them. It was not until the fourth vole was caught and eaten by Gulo that they started to leave her alone, finally realizing she was not going to feed them.

They now turned their interests to their own noses and in short order Garou located his own vole. Instinctively, he pounced, but being somewhat uncoordinated he came down on the wrong spot. Seeing the grass move, he put his paw on it and felt a softness underneath. A quick sniff told him the vole was there. With both paws digging and his teeth snapping, he came up with the small animal. By the time it was free of the grass it was dead, but Garou sniffed and worried it for some time to make sure. He then bit it in two, his new teeth now able to shear it easily. The pleasure of food hitting his stomach energized him and he began hunting with enthusiasm.

Carajou was several minutes in locating her first vole. Not as deft as her litter mate, it got away from her. A tunnel under willow roots blocked Carajou from further pursuit; however, it was not long before another vole was found. This time she was successful in killing it. The kits had now learned to hunt and over the rest of their lives they would eat thousands of voles and lemmings. Although they were awkward, it would not be long before they would be able to hunt efficiently and would seldom fail to kill one of the microtines when they went after it. The family continued hunting the edge of the muskeg until they were satisfied. Then finding a thick clump of dwarf birch, they curled up together, resting until nearly dawn.

Predawn found them traveling parallel to the stream as Gulo cast from one side to another while working into a slight breeze. The day promised to be clear. There were only a few fluffy clouds breaking up the brightening, blue sky. Under the trees it was still dark. Their progress was quiet with only moving shadows marking their way. The kits had no problem keeping up, and at times, even got ahead of Gulo. Inquisitive Garou was usually the one in front, but Carajou occasionally became bold enough to lead the way.

Suddenly a crashing sound brought them to a halt. Gulo froze, testing the air. The kits promptly imitated her by sniffing quietly until at last a faint odor came, one familiar to Gulo, but new to the young ones. Knowing her quarry, Gulo quietly made her way toward the sound that had alerted them. Keeping low and moving without sound, they got close enough to hear a scraping noise. A short distance ahead of them, a tree was seen moving across the ground. At its butt end was a large brown creature.

The crashing noise had been a birch tree falling, having been gnawed in a circle around the trunk until it gave way. Some limbs were to be used by the beaver to repair its dam. Some would be buried in the bottom of their pond. Those buried would be used for food during winter when they would live almost entirely inside their house, or under the thick ice that would form on the pond. Beaver live on leaves, grasses, and ferns during summer, but these foods would not be available in winter. Then their food would be the bark of birch, aspen, cottonwood, and willow that had been cut during summer and stored underneath the water. Forays on land to search for these foods would be limited to the milder periods of winter. Harsh times would find them feeding on what they had stored.

The large beaver (*Castor canadensis*) spotted by the wolverines had his own family nearby, a female and five kits that had been weaned only a short time ago. The kits were still inside the house protected by its sturdy construction and water surrounding it. Built of interwoven sticks, plastered with mud and lined with leaves and grasses, the beaver house is snug, warm, and nearly impenetrable.

Although the birch was nearly three inches in diameter, the beaver was having only a little trouble pulling it toward the water. He weighed over fifty pounds and his short, powerful legs were well designed to move this and even much larger loads. Beavers are the heaviest rodents native to North America and their incisor teeth, like other rodents, never stop growing. They have to gnaw constantly or the teeth will grow too long and eventually make it impossible for them to eat. Unknown to Gulo and her kits, the beaver's mate was just a short distance on the other side of the fallen tree. All of their attention was fastened on the only animal they could see, the large male.

Carajou and Garou instinctively knew to freeze and did not move a muscle as Gulo began her slow approach. The beaver's attention was solely on his job, moving the birch which had caught on some willows and was temporarily stuck. It took a few extra hard pulls to break it loose. The sudden release sent it down the bank in a quick slide. Seeing her quarry nearing the water, Gulo knew her charge had to be now or it would be too late. Although she was still further away than she wanted, she rushed anyway, ploughing through the thin brush between her and the beaver. The sound of her passage was drowned by the noise of the birch limbs scraping on the ground. Garou and Carajou remained frozen in position, intently watching the action before them.

Gulo was nearly upon the beaver before she was finally seen and he had time only to get partially turned to meet her charge. He was knocked sideways when she struck, and immediately felt the wolverine's jaws clamp down on his shoulder. His turn had been just enough to divert her attack from his neck to this less vulnerable area. Gulo's front claws dug in fiercely and tufts of beaver fur went flying into the air. The beaver was still on his stocky legs. Their compact strength was able to withstand the violence of the assault and the added weight suddenly on his back. Pivoting on his hind legs he was able to reach Gulo's left hip and his teeth ripped open the skin. The pain infuriated Gulo and she transferred her bite from the shoulder to the nape of his neck. Clamping down, she buried her teeth but the size of the beaver protected him and her teeth could not reach the vital spinal column.

By now, Gulo had been able to get onto the beaver's back and had the claws of all four paws dug in with many of them penetrating the animal's tough hide. But she was not able to stop his dash for the water. To him, water was safety, and all of his effort was now made toward reaching it. All this time, Gulo had no knowledge the female was even there, not having seen her because of the fallen tree. The attack on her mate did not elicit a response to protect him, but the kits in the nearby house did, and she moved to protect them. She reached Gulo and the male just as they got to the water, striking them both with her charge. The impact jarred Gulo; she was barely hanging on when the beaver dove into the water. Shock of the female's blow and icy water closing over her head was too much, and she let loose.

Gulo popped to the surface, and looking about for her quarry, saw only widening rings and a few bubbles where they disappeared. She swam about in circles, but shortly gave up, even the strong scent of the beavers was dissipating. Reaching the bank, she shook herself of water and nosed about, still looking for the beaver. But they had disappeared, and finding nothing more of interest, she turned to where Carajou and Garou waited. Garou extended his nose to touch with hers, but was met with a nip on his ear. Gulo was not in a good mood. Shaking herself again, showering the kits with water, she give a low growl and moved off.

They had not traveled far before Gulo finally took note of the burning sensation in her left hip. She stopped, turned to the source and found blood streaming down her leg. The beaver's huge incisors had torn loose a flap of skin half an inch wide and an inch long; however, fortunately it was not deep. The flap was dangling and the sharp, prickly pain caused her to lick it. She cleaned up the blood and soon the wound stopped flowing. Still the flap dangled. Ignoring the stinging pain, she returned to the hunt.

As the morning progressed, they located a hen grouse and her seven chicks feeding in an opening. The hen was alerted by their approach and was able to fly up into a spruce and escape. But the chicks were not yet able to fly well enough and all of them were caught, killed, and eaten. If Gulo had eaten the hen's eggs before hatching, she possibly might have re-nested and raised another brood. However, since this brood had hatched, she would not nest again until the following spring—if she lived that long. She was already two years old, and the life span of grouse is short. Many do not live as long as her present age. Only about fifteen out of a hundred survive their first year of life.

It was nearly midday when they found and killed a large snowshoe hare. The group tore it apart and gulped it down before giving up the hunt for the day. The meal had precipitated another fight between the two young ones as each was determined to get a full share. By this time, traveling had become too warm from the heat of the sun directly above them. Finding shade under a large spruce, they napped until well past sundown. The days are long in June and night is short, mostly a time of twilight. If the weather is clear, it gets really dark only in the deep shadows under trees. Gulo and family were now being forced to do much of their hunting in daylight.

During the night, Gulo was awakened by the dull pain in her hip. Licking the wound, she was bothered by the flap of skin hanging loose and chewed it off. Without knowing what she was doing she had just saved herself from infection. The dead skin would have rotted and formed a place for bacteria to grow. Infection of wounds in wild animals is one of the more common causes of death. Most of the time, if the wound is not extensive, and they can reach it with their tongue to keep it clean, infection is averted.

Over the next several days the kits continued to develop their hunting skills. They were missing less and less when they pounced on voles and lemmings. Their noses could tell them exactly where the microtine was, and with improving muscle coordination, they became more efficient each day. The prey were now having their young in large numbers and was easy to find. The kits became able to eat their fill in a short time and even started to cache many of those they couldn't eat. This is a natural instinct and was not learned by Gulo teaching them. Although they had watched her do this often, they would have done the caching on their own without ever having seen her do it.

Stalking and killing movements begin when the young are still at the natal den and these actions are visible in the kit's play. This is long before they have ever been away from the den to observe their mother's actions in an actual hunt. The kits caching food is also done without being shown or knowing its purpose. They have no idea why they are doing it. The same goes for marking their territory. Garou and Carajou began marking territory themselves when they first started leaving the natal den. They needed no one to show them how or why, they simply do these things by instinct. When the proper time comes, neither of the kits will be shown what to do to reproduce; the sexual act will also come naturally.

One day in early June, Gulo and the kits were traveling through the foothills at the eastern edge of her territory when the smell of rotting flesh came to them. Keeping down wind, she waited until she was confident there was no danger. The kits followed some distance behind as she slowly advanced and found the carcass of a cow caribou in a shallow swale. The animal had been dead only a couple days, but with summer heat, she was already bloated to twice her normal size. Flies were buzzing in a large swarm, and small, yellow-white eggs had already been laid by the thousands in her nostrils, mouth, and every other orifice. On her left side and hind leg were signs of the massive infection that had caused her death.

Gulo did not realize it, but this was the cow whose calf she had killed and eaten some weeks before. The wounds she had received from the coyotes had become infected. The deep ones in her leg had kept her from migrating away from the area. The infection had spread into her abdomen—her slow death had been agonizing. She had been unable to keep the flies from the open wounds and their eggs had hatched into maggots. These had eaten deeply into the dying flesh. She was an ugly sight. This had been an ugly death—but death like this is repeated countlessly in nature. There is no pity for the weak, ill, or injured. There is no one to comfort them, no one to ease their pain, and no one to mourn their death.

The stench was overpowering. Gulo circled the carcass from a distance to check the area thoroughly before they approached. Once assured that all was safe, she cautiously made her way to the caribou. The kits, unaccustomed to this new odor, held back, and followed only after Gulo, hopping about the carcass, had finally stopped and gotten a mouth full of skin. She bit into the stomach area and with a few tugs was able to tear it open. A loud hissing noise came from the hole and the kits jumped back. Gulo paid no attention to it and kept pulling and tearing until the pressure inside forced the entrails out. Their odor was heavy and rank, but only increased her appetite. The kits joined her and it was not long before they were gorged. The trio moved a few hundred yards down wind where they located a clump of spruce trees and cuddled together digesting their meal.

It was twilight when they roused themselves with stomachs again nearly empty and ready to be refilled. The family could pick up no scent of danger on the breeze and started moving toward the caribou. The approach was again cautious, but not nearly so much as before. The carcass had not been disturbed other than having been picked at by a couple of ravens and a whole flock of gray jays. The ravens had plucked out the eyeballs first, and then had eaten their fill of the rotting flesh. The jays had pecked and pulled at any exposed flesh and anytime they had been able to get more than a tidbit had flown off to hide it in cracks and crevices in trees some distance away. Already some of their caches had been found by chickadees and were promptly being eaten or carried off by them to be stored in their own caches.

Just past midday, a northern shrike, perching in the top of a partially dead spruce tree half a mile away, spotted the movement of the birds flying about the site. Winging closer, it lit in a nearby spruce and watched several gray jays busily filling their craws. One had eaten all it could and was pulling off bits and flying into the trees to cache them. On the second trip after the shrike had arrived, the jay was met in midair by the gray fury. The shrike's beak, similar to a hawk's, grasped its prey and both fell to the ground. The shrike ignored the morsel in the jay's beak, he was not there to rob him as the chickadees were. A few sharp bites to the back of the neck and the jay was dead, its vertebrae severed. Although almost the same size as the shrike, it was no match for its viciousness.

The prey was too large to be carried off by the shrike, so it began eating it where they had fallen. The shrike is actually a song bird, but is much like a miniature hawk in both appearance and actions. Its beak is curved as are the falcons, hawks, and eagles. Although small, it has sharp talons. The shrike uses these weapons much as hawks do. Being a small bird, they are limited as to what they can carry away from a kill site. Anything over an ounce becomes a heavy burden.

After eating until it could hold no more, the shrike flew to a nearby spruce top to rest. There he sat while digesting his meal and watching his kill. Soon it flew back and attempted to carry the remains of the jay in its beak, but the weight was too much. With its full craw, it could not fly carrying the rest of the jay. The shrike accepted his predicament. After giving a few more pecks on the remains he flew away.

The Northern shrike (*Lanius excubitor*) does not use his talons as extensively as do hawks. Hawks, and those predator birds having heavy talons, are powerful enough to kill their prey with them. But the small shrike (only two to two and one-half ounces!) does not have that kind of power. His kills are generally made by using his beak to sever the neck vertebrae of small birds that he uses for his main diet. Voles and lemmings are also killed in this manner. Insects are included, but make up a small part of his food consumption as there are not many large insects in much of the northern shrike's territory.

He carries food with his beak much of the time if it is small. Larger prey are held by the beak until it gets into flight, then the prey is dropped and caught in its talons for transportation in that manner. He can carry prey nearly one-half his own weight.

His cousin, the loggerhead shrike, who lives in the south, uses thorns of trees, such as locust and some cacti, and even points of barbed wire to impale their victims for a storage cache. Not having these handy spikes, northern shrikes have to make do with crotches and crooked limbs. These places are also used to help them eat by holding food while they tear it into bite sizes.

The wolverine's approach at dusk was not challenged. With minor squabbling over positions at the carcass, they again ate as much as possible. By now the animal was well opened. Gulo had stripped the tough hide from a large section. She tore off sizeable chunks and the kits did as well. These were carried off for several hundred yards and buried in caches. While doing this, they frequently stopped at various places and marked with urine and scent glands to signifying to others that this was their place and the caribou carcass was claimed. They worked until just before daybreak, when tired and full, they left the area to rest. Moving down wind, they found a thick willow patch and lay down to sleep through daylight hours.

During the morning, clouds that had been holding over mountain tops became thicker and darker and spread until finally they blocked out the sun. By early afternoon, a mist started and long before evening, it changed into a light rain. However, the fur on the wolverines kept them dry, and they did not get up until it was again twilight. Shaking off rain drops, they started toward their evening meal. The wind had switched, and they were unable to smell the putrid flesh. Gulo made a circling approach until its scent was picked up once more.

Gulo used less care than before. With her kits following closely behind, she was nearly to the caribou when there came an odor making hair on the back of her neck stand up. She froze, and immediately the kits followed her lead. Slowly she swiveled her head. The scent, now there, and then gone again. The rain was deadening the smells around her much as it had deadened the sounds of their movements. For long moments, they stood, immobilized, knowing danger was near, but not being able to tell just where it was. The moments turned into minutes. Still, they did not move. Then a sudden shift in the wind brought a strong, wet smell and Gulo knew where her danger lay. Fifty yards toward the mountains was a dense clump of spruce forming a ring, the center of it nearly open and covered with a thick mat of needles. The needles formed a soft bed and lying on this bed, not visible to the wolverines, was a young brown bear.

The bear was three years old, and already weighed about three hundred pounds. His fur was ragged. There were several places where he had previously rubbed himself on trees, scraping loose winter hair off, down to bare skin. New growth had covered the skin, but this and loose hair in other spots, gave him a rough, unkempt appearance. Within the next month all of his winter hair would be gone, his summer coat would be full, and again he would look slick and clean. His coloring was somewhat different than most bears of this area. His legs were a deep chocolate brown, as was his ears and muzzle. Otherwise, his pelt was creamy-yellow. The contrasting colors gave him an outstanding and distinctive look.

Brown bears (*Ursus arctos*) in the interior regions are called grizzlies, but the brown bear and the grizzly bear are the same animal. *Ursus arctos* lives in the northern less inhabited part of the world and is abundant in North America, Russia, and other parts of northern Europe. Despite their local name, they are all brown bears. The only differences is coloration and size, and size is principally a product of food availability. The Kodiak bear of Kodiak Island, the brown bear of nearby Kenai Peninsula are larger than the grizzly bear of the interior. They have access to more food, principally salmon, and do not spend so long in the winter den. More food, and a longer time to eat, means bigger bears. However, genetics also plays a roll in their size. Despite the differences in size, coloration, and local common name, these are the same bear, *Ursus arctos*.

The young grizzly was in a foul temper in spite of his full stomach. Over the previous few days, he had been driven off by his mother as she was coming into estrus and no longer had any maternal feelings toward him. The change in hormones gave her a new mood, and she began to snap at him when he got too close. She refused to let him share any foods near her. Especially discouraging was that she would not let him dig any ground squirrels when she found a den of them. Each day, she became more quarrelsome. Finally, she began chasing and nipping him when he came near.

The end came when a large male had shown up and chased him for several hundred yards. His mother paid no attention, ignoring them both, and continued feeding on the newly grown sedges she found. He had been too frightened to return to her, and watched them from a distance for some time before leaving to find something to eat. He was thoroughly confused; she had always protected him before. Now, she had ignored him when the dangerous large boar had chased him. Later he returned to the area, but found the scent of the big boar too strong for his courage—he did not attempt to follow their trail.

Once more, he left the area. It was that day he located what was left of the caribou cow. Smell of wolverine was strong, but hunger pangs in his stomach gave him all the added courage he needed to stalk the carcass. Finding it unprotected, he ate his fill, then wandered off a short distance, finding a comfortable bed within a ring of small white spruces.

Gulo and her kits were uncertain what action to take. Reluctant to leave their food, they were also hesitant to try and take it back. Edging closer to the caribou, they found it was covered with litter. Leaves, sticks, moss, and dirt had been scratched over it by the grizzly. In doing this, the ground had been torn up for ten feet around. When their approach did not bring any response from the bear, they went closer. Nosing under the trash, they found little was left. Little though there was, she still felt possessive; also, she was hungry. The young brownie was still asleep and had no knowledge the wolverines had reclaimed the carcass until Gulo brushed aside some of the covering, and in doing so made a slight noise.

The bear's exceptional hearing picked up the noise, slight as it was, and he rose to all four feet, then reared onto his hind legs. Trying the breeze, which had changed slightly since he had laid down, he encountered nothing. Swinging his head, he looked at his cache, and at first saw nothing. Then a slight movement brought everything into focus, and he spotted those trying to take over what was now his. A loud explosion of air escaped his lips, and the alerted wolverines turned to face him.

Being young and on his own for the first time, the bear was not sure enough of himself to charge, and he hesitated. Gulo did not want to leave although the instinct to protect the kits was giving her strong messages to do so. The bear stood and watched, popping his teeth, working his saliva into a froth. The lack of action by the wolverines gave him courage. He dropped to all fours and started toward them. Laying back his ears, he was in full charge within a couple steps. Gulo turned, snapped at the kits and they took off, away from the charging bear. After a few yards, she turned again, facing the grizzly, but was slowly backing up at the same time. Seeing the wolverine stop, the bear slowed his charge, and, at the edge of the torn up ground, came to an abrupt halt.

The two stood facing each other for a short time, only yards apart, with the bear popping his teeth, and the wolverine snarling as if she were as big as the bear. Gulo took two steps backward and the bear came forward one. Again two steps back and the bear one forward. The slow retreat took only a couple minutes, but finally the bear reached the caribou and turned to sniff at it. With his attention diverted from her, Gulo turned and loped to catch up with her kits. The bear, seeing her leave, paid little further attention, let out a low rumble, and turned to see if his food was disturbed. Still full from the early feeding, he walked about it, scratched more trash over it, then lay down on top. Not much was left, but it was his and he was not going to give it up.

Gulo caught up with the kits, who had not gone far as they were reluctant to be separated from her. They had been frightened, but faith in their mother's protection quickly calmed them, and they followed as she passed them by. Gulo was still growling with low sounds deep in her chest just as if she were muttering under her breath, angry at losing an easy meal.

The night was otherwise uneventful. The wolverines found several voles and lemmings and rounded out the menu with two young snowshoe hares. The spring crop of hares had been a good one. The young, inexperienced leverets (baby hares) were easy prey for these efficient predators. Sunup found them several miles from the bear, who now had been completely forgotten. Stopping in a small depression on a side hill, they lay down, spent a short time licking themselves clean, and went to sleep.

The sun broke the skyline of the mountains and turned their snowy tops into crests of glistening yellow and orange. Colors extended up into the heavens where it blended into the cerulean blue of a clear, crisp sky. The spectacular sight was unseen by the wolverine family who were dozing contentedly while piled one on another.

Food was plentiful at this time of year as hares were reaching the peak of their population cycle. There were leverets in abundance. Within three years, their numbers would plummet and hares would become scarce. However, now they more than kept Gulo and the kits well fed. Their hunts were short, usually only a couple of hours a night were needed to kill all they needed for food. Lemmings and voles supplemented the hare diet, along with grouse, and ptarmigan. The naive young of these were especially easy to catch.

By late June, Carajou and Garou had both became skillful hunters and seldom missed when hunting voles and lemmings, but not doing so well on birds and hares. However, they were improving with every attempt. They had even surprised a red squirrel on the ground, catching it before it was able to get to the safety of a tree. Carajou received a sharp bite through her lip from it before crushing it in her jaws. The bite had enraged her and it was several minutes before she quit mauling the small form and ate it. It tasted especially good.

July found Carajou and Garou nearly half the size of Gulo; their fur was marked almost identically to hers. Their legs were a deep chocolate, nearly black on the feet, which were large for the animal's size. Their size would be a help to them in winter, making it possible for them to walk on top of snow that some of their quarry would sink down in. This way they would be able to catch and kill many of those that normally could get away from them. These large paws also held claws that resemble those of the cat family, being semi-retractable and sharp.

> Unlike wolves, coyotes, and foxes (*Canidæ* family), wolverines are capable of inflicting considerable damage with their claws, much like cats (*Felidæ* family). Also, like cats, they can use their claws to climb. However, being large, they are not agile in trees and are much more efficient hunters on the ground and seldom climb trees. Their cousins, the fisher (*Martes pennanti*) and the American marten (*Martes americana*), are much smaller and extremely fast in trees and can easily catch speedy red squirrels among the branches. The fisher does not live in this area, but marten is a common occupant of the thickly wooded lowlands of Gulo's territory.
>
> The kits' muzzles and ears are a lighter shade of brown than the legs. Above each eye, nearly joining in the middle of their foreheads, is a creamy-tan marking that looks like high eyebrows. On the underside of Carajou's neck are several bright spots of light tan. These are not so pronounced on Garou, and nearly invisible on Gulo. Starting on the back of the neck, they have the same dark brown hairs of the belly. These are tipped with tan, much like the hairs on a silver-tip grizzly. These grizzled hairs extend to about one-third of the way from

the head to the shoulders, then divide, going down each side, meeting again on the rump at the base of and on the top of the tail. This leaves a dark brown area free of the tan-tipped hairs on top of the back. The entire appearance somewhat resembles a distant relative, the skunk of the southern areas of North America, although the skunk's stripes are white. The wolverine has musk glands similar to the skunk, but it does not spray. The odor is light and not offensive. Contrary to old tales, wolverines are clean and have less odor about it than many animals.

The first of July brings a time when most of the plants are in full bloom. A surprise to many are orchids. Many orchids grow and do well in Alaska; however, these do not have the showy flowers of cultivated orchids. Growing in bogs are ladies' tresses (*Spiranthes romanzoffiana*), having tiny, creamy-white flowers that bloom in a spiral about the stem. *Corallorrhiza trifida*, known commonly as coral root orchid, has small greenish-white flowers with purplish spots and bloom at the top of a leafless stem. Its name is derived because its roots resemble an ocean coral. This orchid is unusual in that it has no leaves at all.

In the less wet, but still damp areas *Plantanthera obtusata* grows, topped with flowers of green tinted white. It is different in that it rarely has more than one leaf. In the same conditions are found rattlesnake plantain (*Goodyera repens ophioides*), an orchid distinctive in that the veins in its leaves lack chlorophyll and are white, forming patterns that resemble a green colored snake's skin. The flowers on all the orchids are tiny, delicate, and beautiful, in spite of their lack of brilliant colors.

A few of the lakes have yellow pond lilies (*Nuphar polysepalum*) and at the edges occasionally are seen the unusual wild calla (*Calla palustris*) with shiny heart shaped leaves. Its flower is not a true flower, but a spathe, which looks like a leaf standing upright. The back side of this leaflike spathe is green and the front white. This forms a white background for the light red fruit that stands upright in front of it. The wild calla is scarce in Gulo's home area but more plentiful further north. It is similar to a better known relative, yellow skunk cabbage (*Lysichiton americanum*), but is decidedly unlike it, in that it is poisonous if eaten raw.

In wet bogs surrounding these lakes and in adjoining meadows are lily flowered marsh violets (*Viola epipsila repens*) and water smartweed (*Polygonum amphibium lævimarginatum*) which is a favored food of waterfowl in the fall. It is prolific in its production of tiny seeds extensively used by waterfowl of many species.

The drier areas have another orchid, the pink, purple spotted, lady's slipper (*Cypripedium guttatum guttatum*) which is well known and without question the prettiest of Alaska's orchids. Pink blooming bistort (*Polgonum bistorta plumosum*) with a flower head resembling clover is also found here.

Beside streams, in their wooded areas, are lungwort (*Mertensia paniculata paniculata*) of the *boraginaceæ* family, commonly called bluebells or chiming bells. Their blue-violet flowers hang in showy panicles in profusion in this type of habitat. However, it is not a bluebell, nor even closely related. True bluebells are in the bluebell family (*Campanulaceæ*).

The flowing waters have the marsh marigold (*Caltha palustris arctica*) with brilliant yellow blossoms and along the gravel bars are yellow dryas (*Dryas Drummondii*) also with bright yellow petals.

Yellow blooms of *Geum Rossii* and poppies (*Papaver alaskanum*) are in sandy areas and, on mountainous, rocky slopes are spider plant (*Saxifraga flagellaris setigera*) which sends out stolons with buds on the end that root and form new plants. Also found in this habitat is roseroot (*Sedum rosea integrifolium*) with purple blooms and thick, fleshy leaves.

Everywhere is there are various kinds of Arnica with yellow blooms, *Senecios* with blooms from yellow through orange to purple, and possibly the most wide ranging plant of all, fireweeds (*Epilobium* angustifolium). Different fireweeds have adapted to fit almost every type of habitat, and are known and enjoyed throughout the world; however, the local name of fireweed is used for different plants in other places.

Lupine (*Lupinus arcticus*) in the interior are dark blue, much deeper than the light blue and lavender of the south coastal regions. Dry areas are covered with bearberry (*Arctostaphylos alpina* and *A. rubra*) that hug the ground. Their green leaves turn brilliant red in fall, making hillsides appear to be on fire. Taller, but still a low growing plant is another bearberry (*Arctostaphylos uva-ursi*), known as kinnikinnick or mealberry. It has been used as a tobacco by those desperate enough to smoke it.

July's profusion of flowers dwindle as the days go by and few are left by its end. All seeds this far north must mature rapidly to become viable before the killing frosts arrive. Blooming until frost are lupine, fireweed, and a plant known around the world, the hated weed of immaculate lawns, the dandelion (*Taraxacum*). But the earlier blooms of these have already matured and will furnish the seed for next summer's display.

CHAPTER FIVE

L ife was easy in July; lemmings and voles were plentiful as were hares. Nesting birds were no longer found, but the young, not yet mature, were easy marks, and Carajou and Garou were able to hunt well enough to kill all they needed. Many caches were made with the excess, some of which were promptly found by others, usually a fox. But then, Gulo and the kits also found some of the fox's caches, partly evening out the score. Bears and coyotes also took their share, digging them up whenever they located one. Of the predators, only the lynx could walk next to a cache without detecting it. This animal is a sight hunter. Its nose is not developed to the extent of the others.

In mid-month a small group of caribou migrated into the area from the north. It was shortly after sundown when the wolverines came upon their trail at the northern edge of their territory. Following the trail of the herd they came upon them in rolling hills. Willows and alders were scattered about in thickets. Here and there were dark clumps of stunted spruce. The sun dips only a short distance below the horizon in July. The night would be nothing more than an extended twilight. The only dark possible would be brightened by a moon. The wolverines would have no difficulty keeping their quarry in sight as well as by scent.

Gulo led her kits directly toward the herd in a steady, loping gait, paying little regard as to concealment. They were seen by the caribou while still two hundred yards away, but not alarmed, they stood and watched. Some even dropped their heads to continue feeding although they looked up frequently. One large cow trotted toward Gulo, and was then followed by another smaller cow accompanied by a young bull. When the distance between them came to less than a hundred yards, the caribou turned and pranced back to the herd. Quickly the wolverines closed the distance and then the entire herd started moving away.

In the group were several cows with calves born this spring and some yearlings from the previous spring. Three young and two older, large bulls had joined the cows only a few days before. The bull's antlers had now completed their growth, but were still covered with velvet. One old, barren cow had antlers from the year before, her hormones were no longer in balance, and she had failed to shed them. They were brown, hard, and clean in contrast to the cows who had had spring calves. These cows had shed their antlers and were now completing the growth of new ones.

Caribou are the only deer whose females grow antlers, in all other members of the deer family antlers are restricted to males. When a caribou cow gives birth to a calf they drop their antlers and regrow them like bulls do each spring. If they are no longer capable of having young, their hormones fail to tell them to shed and antlers are kept.

Gulo and family followed the caribou with a steady gait, but gave up after a mile or so as all in the herd were able to keep up and none showed any sign of disability. Had an ill or injured one been detected, the chase would not have been abandoned. Also, when deep snows of winter cover the ground, the situation will be different. Then, the wolverines will be able to use their large feet to stay on top of the snow while the caribou hooves sink in. At those times, even a healthy caribou would be at risk.

Shortly after giving up on the caribou, they came upon a colony of arctic ground squirrels. Two were caught away from their burrows and quickly consumed. Then brisk digging yielded several adults and numerous young that were only a few weeks old. Although the young were small, the one to two pound adults made a sizeable meal.

Ground squirrel dens frequently have only one exit. A digging wolverine has little trouble in getting to them unless blocked by large rocks. For some reason, a large number of ground squirrels will panic after several minutes under siege, and come out of the den on their own and are easily caught. One bite from powerful jaws dispatches them in quick fashion.

By the time they had completed their meal of ground squirrels, the sun had risen and the heat was becoming uncomfortable. The open area where they were provided no protection from the sun so they moved back north, down the side of the mountain. Entering a small copse of spruce and willow, they found a cool spot next to a small stream and lay down. The heat of the day would be blunted here. They would not leave until evening when the sun was low.

By mid-afternoon the temperature had risen to nearly ninety degrees; even birds were quiet. Alaska's interior has an amazing spread of temperatures; nineties in summer and fifty below in winter. Only the hardiest survive here year 'round. The south coastal area is much more moderate, in both winter and summer. There, the extremes are blunted by the Japanese current, a moving stream in the ocean having near constant temperatures.

During the last week of July the kits began to detect an unusual odor from their dam. Gulo was starting to come into estrus. Carajou and Garou paid little attention to this new odor other than simply being curious. They were too immature to be aroused by it. Only one new male had been seen in their area over the past month. He was young and immature. He had been passing through while looking for a range of his own. The resident male detected him nearly as soon as he arrived in Gulo's territory and chased him for over a mile. Learning that this was not the place for him, the young male kept moving. The local male, although he had not been seen for some time, wasn't too far away and would soon pick up signals from Gulo's body.

The large male came upon Gulo's scent when it became stronger. He was over a mile away when the scent reached him, at first only a tantalizing indication, but quickly a full breath of air confirmed it. His nose rose in the air taking in the faint aroma and a slight curl came on his lips. Rolling his head and turning it from side to side, he was able to get more scent in his nostrils. A tightening came upon his stomach muscles. He started in Gulo's direction, following the scent and making frequent stops to check the air. With each halt he became more aroused.

Coming to the stream, he stopped for only a moment, then plunged in. The shock of the cold water went unnoticed although it was no more than ten degrees above freezing. The far bank was less than twenty feet away and shallow enough that only the first few feet of water had to be swum. He paddled those few feet in short order, and when his feet hit the rocky bottom, made lunges until he reached the other side. Climbing out, he raised his nose, and finding the scent stronger and more exciting, pushed through a dense willow thicket. He worked his way from the thick underbrush growing next to the water and climbed a slight knoll. There the smell was strong and he stood up on his hind legs to savor it.

This male was the father of Carajou and Garou, having bred Gulo the preceding summer. He lived in this territory since taking it over three years ago, finding it vacant at the time. Now, at eight years of age, he was large, weighing nearly forty-five pounds. His color was slightly darker than Gulo's. He had the yellow-orange spots on the side of his jowls and neck he had passed on to Garou and Carajou. These spots were missing on Gulo. Although animals may appear identical, each are different in subtle ways. To the trained observer, individuals can be easily identified. Number, size, and pattern of spots were different on each family member.

The male stood on his hind legs for several minutes while the scent was arriving in waves carried on the wind, now strong, then faint, but always detectable. His excitement grew by the moment as his nose pointed high toward the female. His lips curled into a grinning response to the sexual stimulus. Still unable to see her, the male dropped to all fours and went down the other side of the knoll. Here, he nearly lost the scent, but keeping on course, he topped another small rise and there it was overpowering. The waiting female was near!

For several minutes, he watched the area in front of him until a movement caught his eye. Not fifty yards away was the object of his quest. Gulo, busily hunting lemmings in the grass, was unaware of his presence. At the time her kits were off on their own hunt, more than a mile away. As the male came closer, Gulo picked up on the movement and stood on her hind legs to peer over some blueberry bushes. She quickly identified the newcomer and ran a few paces to greet him. Touching noses and smelling each other, she knew him as the male who had been with her the summer before. His presence brought up urges that had been building over the past few days and she became excited he was there.

Rubbing their shoulders together, they became reacquainted. She danced about, pleased to see him. The greeting took several minutes, during which the male kept trying to smell her vulva. Gulo kept twisting away from him, refusing to allow his nose to get close as she was not yet ready. When the initial excitement abated, she lay down. The male kept trying to determine the state of her readiness. Although laying down, Gulo turned to keep him from behind her. After a time, he gave up and lay down beside her, his initial excitement blunted by her rejection.

The next few hours passed with the male getting up every few moments, meeting with rejection, then laying down again nearby. Later they were joined by Carajou and Garou who came back from their hunt and were startled by the presence of the visitor. Frightened by this new turn of events, they did not approach closely, but kept together many yards away. The two youngsters did not know what to make of the situation. Although they had seen the male before, they had never been this close to him. They were decidedly uneasy, wanting to go to their mother, but were afraid to do so. Gulo paid no attention to their distress and finally the kits lay down well away from the mating pair and just watched. Having been successful in their hunt their bellies were full and it was not long before, combined with the warmth of the day, put them to sleep. However, it was not a deep sleep as every movement of the male or Gulo brought them alert, and they did not lay their heads back down as long as there was any movement.

Throughout the day the group was restless, the male more so than the rest. He kept trying to sniff Gulo and she kept rebuffing him. Toward evening, she arose and moved off to look for food with the male following. But he was not thinking of eating, even if she was.

The kits watched them move away but did not attempt to follow. Gulo moved swiftly and with purpose, heading down hill toward a grassy area near a small stream. Arriving at her destination, she began hunting, knowing the spot housed a large group of lemmings. Gulo was efficient and quickly was able to locate, kill, and eat several of the small mammals. The male spent most of his time just watching her; however, he did locate several lemmings himself, gulping them down. But his feeding was mostly only reaction, as his mind was not on food.

The rest of the night was spent in this manner, Gulo intently hunting, and at the same time, moving away from the male when he became too inquisitive. The male followed as closely as Gulo would allow, but he was paying little attention to the hunt.

Sunrise found them still near the stream where there was an abundance of cover and shade to protect them from the sun. Under a large spruce, they lay on a soft carpet of moss, tired both from the hunt and the stress of the situation. They napped for a couple hours, waking up when they were joined by the kits who had trailed them. Again the kits stayed some distance from the couple, sensing their presence would not be accepted. Gulo and her mate acknowledged their arrival with only a glance and promptly went back to sleep. All were oblivious of the clouds that rolled in over the mountain tops in early afternoon and of the light rain and cooler temperatures they brought. The evening promised to be much more comfortable as the heat of the past few days had been wearing on them.

The male was the first on his feet and immediately went to Gulo, sniffing and poking her with his nose. She turned and nipped at him, but not with the intensity of the night before. Getting up, she touched noses with him, then danced away. He followed, and she started running but the male easily kept pace with her. Gulo stopped, turned and nipped again, but this time it was all play as she had lost any desire to keep him away from her.

The two courted for some time, rubbing against each other and bumping

63

shoulders. The male kept trying to get behind her, but she always spun about to face his advances, constantly teasing him. Gulo kept swishing her tail from side to side, then raising it so that it stuck high in the air. Her female scent was strong. There were traces of blood on her vulva.

In frustration, the male finally took her neck in his jaws and threw his forepaw across her body. At last Gulo did not fight back but submitted to him. Twisting her tail up and off to the side she allowed him to mount her. The coupling was frenzied for several minutes, finally slowing to a steady rhythm. They stayed joined for over an hour, his penis kept stiff by the baculum bone. The long period joined together helped to stimulate the female to ovulate, enhancing the probability of her becoming impregnated.

Upon separating, the two lay next to each other, nuzzling one another and rolling in the cool moss. When at last they were relaxed they slept, nose to nose. The kits had observed the evening's activity with innocence, totally unaware of its significance. When their parents lay down and slept, they did the same. Later, during the night, they were awakened when Gulo and her mate were again copulating as they would repeatedly do over the next few days. She and the male would eat little during this time. Carajou and Garou were not inclined to go without food and they left to hunt.

Heading down stream they progressed for over a mile before picking up the sounds of splashing water. Listening for a few moments, they decided to see what was causing the commotion. Slowly moving into position on the bank, they could see across the water where a small, slender animal was dragging a larger animal out onto a gravel bar.

The creature was a dark chocolate brown with a white chin. Twenty-eight inches long, including his slender eight inch tail, he weighed less than three pounds. The long slim body was beneficial, making it easy for it to enter dens and burrows to kill animals larger than himself. This mink had done just that. Entering the den of the muskrat, he had found it at home and dispatched it with a bite to the throat.

The mink (*Mustela vison*) is related to the wolverine and has many of its characteristics; a fearless nature and fighting ability to attack and kill animals much larger than himself. More adapted to water than most mustelids, other than the otter, he spends most of his time in or near it, and feeding on prey found there. As with others in this group, the caching instinct is highly developed. Anything he does not need for immediate consumption is stored for later use. Fish, muskrats, and waterfowl are staples in the mink's diet, along with any other small creatures found in its vicinity.

The muskrat (*Ondata zibethicus*) is a rodent with a stocky body about fifteen inches long and a tail another eight or ten inches. The tail, which is flattened, is used as a rudder when swimming. This one was big, over three pounds, and with the large, strong incisor teeth common to rodents. They can inflict severe damage when they get to use them; however, speed and aggressiveness of the mink was too much, and he had been unable to bring them into play. He died quickly, and was pulled from his underwater burrow and towed to the gravel bar when the wolverines spotted the action.

Garou stood on his hind legs to get a better view and was immediately seen by the mink. Giving a low growl, the mink redoubled his efforts to move the muskrat up the bank and out of sight. But before he was able to do this, Garou and Carajou were in the water and swimming toward him. The mink pulled on his prey until the wolverines got to the gravel bar. As they emerged from the water they were met, head on, by a brown blur of action. Startled by the sudden onslaught and hampered by the water they backed up, but not before Garou had received a cut on his lip and Carajou a bite on her nose. The assault had been totally unexpected. Never before had food attacked them.

By the time they had collected themselves, the mink had returned to the muskrat and was again trying to pull it into the grass. The slender killer had no intention of handing over his kill to them without a fight. Squealing and growling, he reached the slick moss and grasses of the stream side and began to make good progress over it. However the two young wolverines, who were several times the size of the mink, also had no thoughts of letting this easy meal get away from them.

By now they were out of the water, and with their courage regained, went straight for the mink. Seeing their determination, the mink began to back away, voicing his displeasure with snarls and bared teeth. Confronted by two predators larger than himself, he realized the futility of the situation, but still he could not turn and run.

The wolverines reached the abandoned muskrat and stopped to smell it, the fresh blood exciting them. By now the mink was nearly ten feet away and they paid little attention to him. Garou grabbed the bloody head, and just as quickly, Carajou bit into the stomach of the rodent. A tug-of-war resulted, which tore open the abdomen, and between the two, the animal was quickly consumed. Before it was eaten, the mink left the area when it realized his dinner was gone and he could be next item on the menu for the pair of thieves.

Their stomachs filled for the time being, the kits rested by the stream until nearly morning when they got up and began hunting again. Finding a concentration of lemmings, they refilled themselves. By the time the sun was up they were again lying down, at first with the warm sun on them, later moving to shade when the heat got to be too much.

Late in the night, Gulo and the male went hunting on their own, eating voles and lemmings, but only enough of them for a snack. Their hearts were not in the hunt. It was cut short by a return to mating activities. At this time, it was the dominate factor in their lives; everything else was pushed into the background. Procreation is second only to survival in the instincts of animals, but then procreation is also a form of survival…survival of the species.

As Gulo went out of estrus, she began to reject the overtures of the male. The coupling slowed until finally she refused him altogether, snarling menacingly and actually biting when he got too close. The male became less aroused as her mating odors lessened. By the time he was getting painfully rebuffed, he was losing interest himself. He stayed with her for another day then left to hunt and did not return. Gulo had been impregnated again, but like other mustelids, the fertilized eggs were not implanted in her womb at this time. They would stay in a state of suspension and not grow until implanted during winter. In this way, birth of young would take place in spring, just as their food sources become plentiful.

The kits and Gulo found each other the day after the male left the area. Once more they became a family unit. Garou and Carajou were now well able to fend for themselves, but still they felt the need of their mother's presence.

Days passed. August arrived with the family still intact; however, in Garou there was a stirring, a need for something, but just for what he had not an inkling. The kits still hunted together when Gulo was off on her own, but now, Garou was taking the lead, going where he wished, and usually being followed by Carajou.

On those times, when Carajou followed her mother and Garou was left on his own, he felt more at ease and his hunts were more satisfying. Without knowing it, he was starting to establish the solitary trait that would be with him for the rest of his life. The male wolverine is a lone animal, not tolerating another male near him nor even in the territory he claims for his home. Females are another matter. They were allowed to freely roam in his area. But seldom did he spend much time with them unless they were in season, ready for his sexual advances.

CHAPTER SIX

September arrived. Along with it, a chill in the air as the night temperatures drew close to freezing, then surrendered to a hard frost. It came on the heels of a sudden storm, not yet severe, but one foretelling of cold times to come. The sun became cooler, rising less above the horizon, and for a shorter time each day. Midnight was once again dark, and the wolverines felt more secure in their nightly hunts.

Aspen, birch, and cottonwood leaves began turning to their varying shades of yellow with the loss of light. By the time frost arrived, leaves were beginning to drop. Blueberries, crowberries, and all other berries had matured by August. The frost changed them to a sweetness, luring bears to them. While the crowberry plant itself stayed green, blueberry leaves turned a rusty-red color with a hint of lavender. Willows joined the transformation, as did grasses, and other ground covering plants. But the most beautiful of all was the ground hugging bearberry plant (*Arctostaphylos alpina and A. rubra*). Its leaves turned a deep scarlet, making whole hillsides aflame with its brilliance. This color would last until snow covered it for winter.

Some distance down the valley, where the coyotes had whelped in the spring, the female had long since weaned their young. Large numbers of snowshoe hare, being on an up-cycle, provided plenty of food for the pups, and gave them a good start toward hunting on their own. The bitch had given birth to five pups, but the last one born was small, and not able to push others away from the teats, it had slowly weakened and died. It was unceremoniously carried from the den by the mother to a point some seventy-five yards away. There she scratched some leaves, mosses, and sticks over it, just barely covering it from sight. Turning, she went back to the den. Before arriving, all thoughts of the lost pup were gone. Inside the den, she was pummeled by the remaining four as life went on without so much as a skipped heartbeat.

The pups were cared for much as the wolverine kits had been, with the major exception of the father coyote. Unlike the wolverine male, who bred Gulo and left, the male coyote stayed with his mate and hunted for all of them the first week. Later, he helped tend the pups while the female went off to hunt. The parental chores are shared in the dog family. Parents may even raise several litters together, although they do not necessarily do so.

The pups were weaned by eight weeks, then started on a diet of food regurgitated by their parents. This slowly graduated to small mammals, both dead and alive, brought to the den. The young had the opportunity to play with, and learn to kill their own food. They soon were able to follow the adults on short hunts, and their education mimicked that of the wolverine and most predators. They learn by seeing and doing, but even then, most of their abilities come naturally. The main thing they have to learn is coordination. That comes only from hours of practice. The siblings "hunt and kill" each other in countless mock attacks in their play—training for the life they will lead.

The coyote pups were feeling extra energy the coolness of fall brought on, just as Garou and Carajou had. Crisp air gave them an excitement that was hard to hold down; also, like the wolverine kits, they were now going off on hunts with one or two siblings in the company of each other. Every hunt seemed to teach them something new: the best way to find and kill a vole, the futility in trying to climb to reach a red squirrel, the super-stealth needed to get close enough before making the final charge, and above all, when to back off and leave the area. This final lesson was painfully taught one afternoon.

It had been one of those especially invigorating days with a temperature in the low forties, a light wind, and a sun that frequently peeked out from between fluffy clouds. The day started on a high note with a wild rough-and-tumble fight among the pups, and the parents quietly left to hunt by themselves. The sun was well above the mountain peaks by the time they learned they were on their own. The opportunity was not to be wasted. With a few more playful nips, they left the area to explore and hunt. The largest male took the lead, followed by the other male, and the rear was brought up by the females. Though they were nearly the same size, the males were ever-so-slightly larger and were dominate in activity about the den.

Following an old moose trail, they headed toward the stream, one behind the other. They had not been particularly quiet. A muskrat feeding on the bank heard them coming. The pups were rewarded only by the scent left and rings on the water where he had dove in. Somewhere down in their minds, this was filed away and they would be more circumspect in the future.

Moving more quietly, they traveled down stream until they came upon an area of voles. They separated, each hunting on his own. They fed quietly, eventually filling themselves. Rejoining, they climbed a tall ridge and found a spot where the breeze kept mosquitos and biting flies away. Here they lay down and rested. The small mammals they had eaten were digested quickly, and by the time the sun was low on the horizon, they were feeling pangs of hunger. With a few yawns and playful growls, they arose nearly as one, and started down the crest of the ridge.

The ridge elevation was near the point of treeline, and there was much open ground. What few trees grew there were gnarled and short. The view on either side of the ridge was spectacular. Distant mountain peaks in the east, still snow covered, were glowing brilliant yellow from the setting sun. In the west, gold was outlining a bank of purple clouds, and the hills were rimmed in red. Pinks, golds, and lavenders accented the darkening trees in the valleys.

To the south, hills rose steadily into a low range of mountains that were barren, except for some stunted willows growing in the gullies carved in their sides. In one of the lower valleys, there could be seen a large white spot, now wavering, now still. It brought only a cursory glance from the coyote pups as it was a long distance from them. Even had it been closer, it would not have held their attention.

It was a large bull moose who had scraped most of the velvet from his palmated antlers the day before. The velvet had looked like moss growing on sticks, but nearing the rut, the velvet had started to dry and loosen. The bull had hastened the process by rubbing his antlers in willows and other handy brush. Rough limbs cut into the velvet, which then came off in tatters, leaving bright bloody streaks that soon turned dark brown. Thrashing the brush and digging the points in the ground got most of the velvet off. Wet moss and dew on early morning leaves further helped to remove the brown colored dried blood. Now clean, they were a bright gray color, standing out in the setting sun like a flag telling all the world, "His Majesty" is here.

In the next valley down the chain of hills, were two more sets of antlers, one on a huge bull, the velvet still hanging and bloody, his antlers yet a bright red. His companion, a smaller bull, had cleaned his several days before. Already bright gray was turning into tan and even brown in rougher places. The bulls were gradually moving toward the lowlands and into the trees as they no longer needed to protect their antlers from injury. They were now mature and hard. Their instincts were also prodding them to move toward cows who typically stayed in lower valleys.

But none of this registered in the minds of the coyotes, their interests were more local, and on where the next meal would come from. Their travel along the ridge turned up two grouse who were picking up gravel for their craws. Having no teeth to grind up seeds, the grouse has to continually eat gravel so their gizzard can break up seeds and make them available for digestion. Even so, some seeds do not get digested, but are excreted intact to land in a new place, starting a new plant. Many plants depend upon just such a thing to spread into new locations and continue their life cycle. Some plants even require the action of a bird's or mammal's digestion to break down the hull before the seed is able to germinate.

The coyotes spotted the grouse early, and after watching for a few moments, began stalking them. The grouse, intent on searching for the proper sized gravel, did not detect them until the attack began. The nearest was caught, just off the ground, and was brought down in a cloud of feathers. The other grouse, more fortunate, as he had been a few feet further away, had just raised his head to look around. This gave him the needed edge, and was able to climb above the leap of the second coyote. He flew to the top of a nearby spruce, and from ten feet above the ground witnessed the killing and eating of his brood mate. After watching for several minutes, he finally flew away, landing in another small spruce where he intended to spend the night. He had been hatched this spring in a clutch of seven. Besides himself, only three others and the mother hen now survived.

Split among the four half-grown pups, the grouse did little except whet their appetites. After nosing among the feathers for any possible scraps, they continued down the ridge. They had not traveled far before coming upon an animal that was new to them. This one did not run from them, but only ambled clumsily at a gait no faster than a walk. It gave the appearance of something easy to catch and small enough to overpower without danger. Its small head, was low to the ground, and could only be seen by getting in front of the animal. But each time the pups got to the front, it pivoted, keeping its rear toward the enemy. The odd actions were entirely new to them, and being young and inexperienced, were unsure of themselves. They held back, each waiting on the other to make the first move.

While it did not show an impressive set of teeth or threaten with a wicked set of claws, there was an aura of danger. The pups were content to just follow for some distance. As porcupines go, this was a large one. He had grown to thirty pounds during his seven years of life. Porcupines (*Erethizon dorsatum*) are the second largest rodent in North America,

Tom Willard

only the beaver is larger. This one was nearly a foot tall at the shoulder and almost three feet long. Its dangerous tail added another foot. Underfur was now forming for the coming winter, and it would soon be thick enough to protect it from subzero weather. The long guard hairs were tan to yellowish, and only close scrutiny separated these harmless hairs from the extremely dangerous quills among them.

Although the porcupine has a formidable set of typical rodent incisors and strong claws capable of digging and climbing trees, these are not their main line of defense. Claws are used to climb because their principal food is tender branch tips, spruce needles, and bark of spruce, willow, cottonwood, and other trees. Much of their life is spent in trees. Like other rodents, they have to gnaw constantly to keep their incisors worn down. This porcupine had been caught on the ground. In summer they feed extensively on ground plants, including berries in fall, and grasses in spring when they are new and tender. To all appearances, the animal was helpless, and about to become a meal for the pups. But helpless he is not. This was a lesson soon to be taught to the quartet who were quickly building up courage to attack.

The boldest of the pups, the oldest male, with a snarl attempted to get to the front of the porcupine, only to find the prey had quickly turned—his bristly rear was still in his face. While the others held back, pup and porcupine performed a dance as such, each movement of pup brought a countermove from the rodent. Frustrated, the coyote backed off and sat on his haunches. He was confused and getting more aggravated by the minute. At this pause in the action, the youngest female entered the foray. Darting forward, she attempted to grab, what she believed to be a hind leg. No sooner had her nose touched the guard hairs when she felt a slap on her cheek. Instantly the side of her face felt as though it was on fire. Letting out a loud yelp, she jumped back and began shaking her head, trying to get rid of the quickly growing intense pain.

Porcupine quills are as sharp as man-made needles. Little force is needed to embed them deeply in flesh. Not only are they extremely sharp, but their tips have tiny barbs. Once deep enough for the barbs to catch, they are nearly impossible to pull out. Different parts of the body grow different lengths of quills. Those on the back of the head are half an inch or shorter. They grow longer down the sides and on the back and tail, some getting to be three inches long. On rare occasion, larger porcupine quills can measure four inches. The only part not having quills is the underside from chin to tail, and that part of the head forward of the ears.

71

The female coyote could not help but squeal and howl from pain. She tried rubbing her head along the ground and pawed frantically at them with her forefeet. Nothing helped—every attempt simply drove the quills deeper. The side of her head had at least fifty barbed needles slowly penetrating, deeper and deeper. The inside of her mouth had a dozen more and several were protruding from the end of her nose. Another two were piercing her right eyelid and were pointed directly for the eyeball.

The antics of the female put a fright into the others. They backed off, totally puzzled. Only the aggressive male still had ideas of staying with the porcupine, but he was much more reluctant than he had been. Keeping close, but at a respectable distance, he stayed with the porcupine who was slowly moving away. He still had his quills erected, and now the coyotes had some idea that the animal was dangerous.

Making one last attempt to solve the puzzle, the male tentatively reached out with his paw and touched the side of the porky. He was immediately impaled with half a dozen quills that penetrated the pads and toes of his foot. Yiping, much as the female had, he quickly pulled back, shaking his paw. As he had only gently touched the animal, these quills were not deeply embedded and he was able to pull most of them out with his teeth; however, while doing this, he pushed two in deeper. From these, he would limp for several weeks until the quills worked through the toes, and the ensuing infection cleared up.

However, the female coyote would not be so fortunate. In deep pain, she followed her siblings, holding back while they killed and ate a number of lemmings and voles. Her discomfort was such, she could think of nothing but pain. Repeatedly, she rubbed her head against rocks and moss hummocks and anything else she could find in a vain attempt to rid herself of the torture. Nothing helped. She only succeeded in breaking off a few— most were only driven in deeper. Her tongue was, in essence, pinned to her gums in two places. Her fate had already been sealed by the quills in her nose. They were pointed directly toward her brain.

It was now a race between infection and starvation—death would be slow and cruel. In three days the quills blinded her right eye and infection began. It spread into her nose and mouth. Unable and even unwilling to eat, she slowly wasted away and died three weeks later, before the quills reached her brain. The coyote litter of five was now down to three. The porcupine, unhurt by the encounter, was still only a mile away unconcernedly munching on bark in the top of a cottonwood tree. He would spend the winter in this and several other nearby spruce trees.

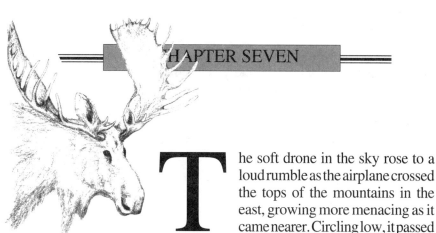

CHAPTER SEVEN

The soft drone in the sky rose to a loud rumble as the airplane crossed the tops of the mountains in the east, growing more menacing as it came nearer. Circling low, it passed over the coyote pups who dodged into an alder thicket, except the female that was punctured by the porcupine quills. She never even heard the sound of the motor, so great was her misery. Passing beyond the coyotes, the plane banked toward a small lake.

The family of wolverines, used to the sound of airplanes, ignored it until it was nearly upon them, flying only a hundred feet about the tree tops. Never had one come this close—the noise drummed loudly in their ears. Fortunately they were near a thick clump of willow, and hid in them while the roar passed overhead. The airplane was watched with apprehension and a good deal of curiosity as it continued for some distance, then banked, and made another wide circle of the area. After several minutes of these maneuvers, the plane made one last arc, cut back on power, and dropped below the trees. Shortly thereafter, no further sound was heard.

At a small lake three miles to the north, the Cessna, equipped with floats, landed and taxied to the shoreline where there was a level spot without trees. By cutting the engine, and at the same time, swinging the plane sideways, the pilot was able to float gently to the bank, coming to rest against the soft moss. Stepping out quickly, the pilot picked up the end of a rope, already tied to the float, hopped ashore, and secured the plane by tying it to a thick clump of blueberry bushes. He was then followed by a man in hip boots, slightly graying at the temples, who carefully navigated the water-slick float.

Hopping to solid ground, he allowed the pilot to get back on to assist a young man from the rear seat. Still in his late teens, the young man confidently stepped on the float and immediately lost his balance. Fortunately, the pilot was still near enough to catch his arm and hold him until he regained his footing. He was lucky to be saved from a cold dunking.

"Careful!" admonished the pilot, "remember what I was saying about you're being a long way from help while you're out here? Starting your hunt cold and wet would not be so good. If you get careless enough to get hurt before I come back next week, you might get into a life threatening situation. Paul, you watch out for your son. Bill, you watch out for your Dad. To be safe you need to look after each other." The pilot continued talking as he unloaded the plane, handing gear to the hunters who stacked it on dry, moss covered hummocks. Between the hummocks was standing water. Trees did not grow this close to the lake, and the men were ankle deep in water as they moved about in the unloading.

"That big bull we spotted was less than a mile south, toward the small stream. If you can't find him, the smaller bull was no more than a half mile east in that large boggy area. Remember, I'll haul out one bull at the price set, but if you shoot the second one, you pay extra."

"This is the best spot for a camp. Just move over there next to those trees where it's dry and reasonably level. I'll expect you to be here, and ready to fly out in seven days. Weather permitting, I will be here on that day, or the first flyable day after that. Do not leave this area! We know where you are and will get you out. Have a good, safe hunt!"

With that, the pilot untied the rope, pushed the plane out while hopping aboard the float, climbed into the cabin, and was shortly taxiing down-wind for takeoff. Reaching the other end of the lake he turned, went full throttle, brought the plane up on step, and shortly lifted one, then the other float off the water and was airborne.

There was a deafening roar as the Cessna passed over head. Paul and Bill watched as it headed east, climbing steadily to clear the mountains. Soon there was silence, itself as loud as the plane had been. Father and son looked at each other realizing they were actually on their own. Slowly, grins brightened their faces. They were alone in Alaska's bush!

The grins changed to outright laughter that quickly subsided into realiza-tion that there was a lot of work to be done. The only suitably level and dry spot was found, and working competently together, soon had the tent erected. Before dark they were settled, gear properly arranged, water hauled and purified, and a latrine area designated.

Father and son had hunted and camped many times before in the Lower-48, but always in areas where there were roads and nearby towns. For the first time in their lives, they were many miles from any other humans. There was no way to communicate with anyone.

Prior to the hunt, they had carefully made lists of gear and food, having been supplied with a rough list by the pilot's air taxi service. This, they amended to suit their own personal needs. Everything had to be selected with the basic knowledge that weight was paramount in importance as the plane could carry just so much. Clothing that is both warm and will keep you dry is necessary. And food enough for the time in camp, plus additional days if the weather goes to pot and the fly out day is not flyable.

Alaska weather in the fall is frequently wet and windy in Gulo's territory. There are times when several days will pass when only the foolhardy go up in an airplane. Wind coming over the mountains can easily blow fifty miles an hour, creating air turbulence that will toss small planes violently about and make takeoff and landing hazardous if not impossible.

These same winds can be dangerous to the outdoorsman if his tent is not up to withstanding them, or he does not secure it properly. Being outside the tent on cold, windy days can be pure misery if the proper clothing is not available. Rain is frequently a companion to wind, heaping further discomfort on the unprepared. Each of these elements on their own can ruin the trip for those with poor gear. And when rain combines with wind and cold, it becomes a survival situation.

Layering clothing is the best way to dress. Heavy coats can be removed and placed in backpacks when walking, then put back on when resting or sitting still. A lot of time is spent sitting and using binoculars to glass open areas for game. Backpacks are a necessity, not only for carrying extra clothing, but for basic survival gear, and for the hard work of the hunt—packing out meat.

Raingear, strong enough to withstand rough usage, is also a necessity. Thin or poorly made boots or coats cannot safely protect. There is no way to replace ripped or torn items when the nearest store is over a hundred air miles away, and you are without a plane to fly to one. Duct tape should be on the required list, as it has held together many a boot, coat, or tent that became damaged.

The most appropriate raincoats are made of Gore-Tex, or other similar material. These will allow a person to move about without getting as wet from sweat as from rain, which is what happens with other materials that do not breath. They are not perfect, but are the best available, although they are expensive. The lack of a hundred-dollar raincoat can ruin a trip costing several thousand dollars.

The Alaska bush is best handled with hip boots as the principal foot wear. Not only do they keep you dry on rainy days, but also when there is a heavy dew on grass and bushes. Most lowlands have numerous areas of muskeg and small streams that need to be crossed if you move about much. Common rubber boots are not tall enough as a rule. Although you may indeed camp in an area that is lacking much muskeg, hip boots will be needed in getting in and out, and in loading float planes. Leather hiking or hunting boots can be worn on those dry days when you plan to be in areas of solid ground. Always bear in mind that rain can come quickly in mountainous or coastal areas. A sunny day can turn to rain in the matter of a few minutes. Sometimes it even seems rain is forming directly above, with you as the specific target.

Food is selected according to likes and dislikes of the camper; however, remember to be edible, you must be able to keep it from spoiling. Perishable foods can be kept cool and fresh for a short time simply by digging down into shaded, wet moss, and placing plastic wrapped foods in the bottom, then covering them up with the removed moss. Moss makes good insulation. It is far better than leaving perishable foods above ground. Sinking plastic wrapped food in cold water in the lake or a nearby stream also works, but you have to be careful that water is kept from contents. This also helps to hold down the odor of food, which is tempting to passing bears. Usually the smell of man will keep bears away, but this is not always the case. Many people hang their food high in trees, but some areas do not have trees large enough for this—some areas have no trees at all. Each camper must make do with what nature has provided.

Food should be concentrated as much as possible to hold down weight, and simple enough to be easily prepared if you want to spend your time hiking or hunting instead of cooking. High energy foods such as candy bars, trail-mix, raisins, and other similar foods are recommended both for the camp, and to be carried in backpack for snacks and emergency use. Cold weather camping will require nearly double the amount of calories a person would burn up otherwise. This needs to be considered when planing for such a trip.

During that first evening, the hunters watched a clear day change, while thin clouds formed in narrow bands above the western hills. Moisture in them turned the sky into indescribable hues of gold, orange, and violet. For long minutes they stood silently and watched as the colors changed one into another. Then the sun fell below the far hills and the display gave way to darkness. They had seen many beautiful sunsets on other trips, but nothing that would compare to what Alaska had shown them this evening.

As the sky darkened, stars relit the night, and far, far away the silence was punctuated by the howl of a wolf. So faint was the call that father and son looked at each other, silently asking the other if he had heard it, or was it just imagination. The lonesome call accented the stillness of the night. Nothing else could be heard, there was no movement in the trees—the lake was glassy calm, dimpled only by trout feeding on insects.

After completing their camp chores, they crawled into their sleeping bags, wanting to be up before dawn. However, this first night, sleep did not come quickly. In their minds, images of trophy bulls were conjured up and fantastic shots made. But it was hard to concentrate on those images as the thought of marauding brown bears attacking them in the night kept coming into their minds. Their ears were tuned to the slightest sound outside the tent. It was some time before they finally fell asleep.

During this evening, the wolverine family moved up the mountain side away from the area of the hunters, not because of them, but simply to hunt the high area. Finding a particularly abundant area of crowberries they stopped to feed, enjoying the sweet juice, then continued up into rocky areas. There, they located smells of prey among dens in the rocks; however, the residents were deep in their burrows for the night. Not inclined to dig in rocky ground, they moved a short distance where another large patch of crowberries was found. Eating, they eased their hunger and spent the rest of the night lying in the open.

As the sun rose, the rocks started to come alive. The wolverines began picking up fresh scents, the same ones smelled during the night. Small game requires individual hunting, each must find their own food, so the wolverines separated, using their noses to guide them.

Gulo worked the flat area above the rocks, finding several dens. She cautiously hunted among them. Picking up sounds of movement and a strong scent at one entrance, she crouched a short distance away and within a few minutes a gray-brown, furry head popped out. Unaware of the danger nearby, the animal left the hole and stood up on its hind legs. At that moment Gulo leaped on it, crushing its head with one bite before it could make a sound. Picking it up, she carried it to a rocky outcrop fifty yards away, stuck it between two large rocks, then returned to the denning area.

Approaching cautiously, she again searched for sounds and smells, and a short distance from the first den found another one to her liking. Setting up her second ambush, she patiently waited, this time for several minutes before her prey emerged. Again she sprang to kill, but this time the animal was able to let out a warning whistle before succumbing to the powerful bite.

Gulo understood what the sound meant, no more marmots would be leaving their dens for a long time. She picked up this kill and went to the location of the first. Tearing into the animal, she fed until it was almost gone, then finding a soft spot, quickly dug a hole and buried the rest. Picking up her first kill, she started back down the mountain side. Uncomfortable out in the open during daylight, she was cautious and alert in her descent and did not stop until reaching treeline. There she dropped her burden.

The hoary marmot (*Marmota caligata*) is a mountain dweller, a vegetarian, and a member of the rodent family. It has a rather large, round head with small, round ears. At this time of year, it was starting to put on its winter coat, a dense underfur covered by guard hairs of silvery-gray. This color changes to a light brown toward the rear and on its short, bushy tail. Fully grown, they can weigh fifteen pounds and even more in fall when they have the heavy accumulation of fat necessary for winter. This animal is a true hibernator and needs to feed well before denning up.

Finding an appropriate spot, Gulo cached the marmot, left a scent mark nearby, and continued on into the trees where she curled up among willows. Garou and Carajou had also been successful in their foraging. Like their mother, they had found nothing until daylight when their quarry became active. They had stayed in the rocky area, and through stealth and ambush, had been able to capture and eat several pikas.

These small animals are *Lagomorphs*, in the order of hares and rabbits, but a different family. Their appearance is about halfway between a rabbit and a rat. The collared pika of Alaska (*Ochotona princeps*) is about one-half pound in size and gray-brown with a lighter gray patch around their neck. The lifestyle of the pika is unique, they actually cut green grass and make hay of it by spreading it to dry. This hay is then stored in stacks near and in their rocky dens, and is eaten during the long winter as they do not hibernate.

The two young wolverines headed down the mountain after they had eaten their fill. Both were carrying pikas in their mouths to cache in the moss among trees. Not crossing Gulo's scent, they found a cool place, stashed the kills, and slept the day away. The family did not regroup until two days later. Carajou and Garou hunted together during this time, but both were becoming more independent. They occasionally separated, hunting alone for a while, then rejoining.

They were now three-fourths the size of Gulo, with Garou the larger of the two. Both were accomplished hunters. Although capable of living on their own, they spent a good deal of time with their mother. Garou, however, was getting short tempered with his family, and no longer entirely at ease around them. His nervousness was because of an instinctive feeling he needed to be alone, a trait that is strong, especially in males of this species.

Garou's longing to leave was further enhanced one day when the dominate male of the area came near and almost got into a fight with him. The near disaster was averted when both Carajou and Gulo joined him, and with a common front, made the male unwelcome. He left, but there were no doubts Garou would have to leave the area in the near future.

CHAPTER EIGHT

The hunters rose before sunrise, and with some small confusion, were able to cook their breakfast, gather their gear together, and leave camp just as it was light enough to walk safely. Although it was further away, they decided that the first try would be for the large bull. Heading in the direction indicated by the pilot, they took compass readings and kept a close watch about them, noting landmarks to help guide their return.

Progress at first was slow. Hummocks in the low area were new to them. After trying to step from one to another, they decided that wandering between them used far less energy, although it added considerably to the distance they had to walk. After getting away from the low area near the lake, the ground rose quickly and walking was easier in spite of hills they now had to climb. They left the hummocks behind and the ground was firm and footing was good. Dew on vegetation was heavy and both were glad they had listened and worn hip boots. The added noise of the boots would have to be accepted as their wool pants would have been soaked in short order without them.

Climbing a small ridge, they found a place giving them a good view of the terrain about the lake and stopped for a while to take it all in. The open area to the east, toward the mountains, was visible as was an especially dark ridge below a rocky area to the north. To the south and west the progress of a small stream was traceable, either by seeing the water itself or the thick growing, taller trees outlining it.

The view from the top of the hill was good. They stayed there for some time, using binoculars to glass open areas and to fix the general lay of the land in their minds. Being experienced hunters, they knew to familiarize themselves with the area. Getting lost is serious business, even more so in the Alaska Bush.

Spotting nothing in the open areas, they descended the hill and continued south in the general direction of the larger bull they had seen from the plane yesterday. Game trails were found deeply worn into moss beneath trees. Occasionally they found other signs of moose, heart shaped tracks and piles of nuggets, but none of these were fresh.

They quickly learned the lesson of going around willow and alder thickets. Taking a detour of a half-mile was quicker and easier than the strain of going directly through dense brush for a hundred yards. Muskeg was found in several places. Once more they were thankful for hip boots. Hunting the bush of Alaska was definitely different from anything they had previously done.

Morning went swiftly and noon found them again on a small ridge. Choosing a comfortable open spot, they ate while glassing the area. It was one of those days when it is great to be alive; the sun was warm but not too hot. The breeze was enough to keep most of the insects on the move, and a second application of repellent on exposed skin stopped even the more persistent ones from biting.

September, before hard frosts, is a time of biting insects. There is the ever present mosquito, but the real villains are flies. Several black fly species inhabit the area: red ones, brown ones, black ones, and especially white-sox. This little black fly has white spots on its legs, therefore the name. Blood brings them in hordes, and butchering out a moose will draw swarms of them around your head. Wind helps keep them away, but it is necessary to keep your shirt sleeves down and buttoned, even if the sleeves get bloody. Repellent on face and other exposed skin will protect those areas.

These flies will land and crawl up sleeves and pant legs to bite. It is imperative all skin they can get to has a coating of Deet (N, N-diethyl-meta-toluamide). This is the only repellent really effective in controlling these tiny pests. Other milder, rub on solutions and home remedies, such as ingesting certain foods or vitamins, work only in a limited way, if they even work at all. These tactics have no place in the Alaska bush.

A large number of bites from these flies can make a person ill, and itching will drive you crazy. Some allergic people have welts for a week or longer, itching all the time, while the welt turns into a red spot similar to a bruise. Imagine a dozen bites or more, all itching intensely, and you can see how an enjoyable outdoor experience could turn into a nightmare. This is no place to be squeamish about putting chemicals on your skin; your body's reaction to the bites is far worse than what Deet will do. If you refuse to coat your exposed skin with this repellant, do not try to experience the outdoors in the north.

The hunters stayed on the ridge for a couple of hours watching for movement, but animals are less active during the middle of the day, and nothing was seen other than a few birds flittering from tree to tree. A large group of robins on migration stopped for a few minutes before moving on. Their red breasts were nearly gray, having been worn and frazzled from their summer's activities. Their next molt, on the winter grounds, would renew the bright red for next spring's mating season.

A small group of gray jays lit in the trees and bushes nearby. Unafraid and curious, they came within a few feet of the hunters and were rewarded for their bravery by having some small crusts of bread tossed to them. They were content to wait for more bounty until a northern shrike showed up to see what was going on. Then, they decided it would be healthier to be elsewhere. The shrike left shortly thereafter, swooping from tree to tree, looking for some small bird or mammal to make a mistake and provide his next meal.

The warm sun took its toll on the hunters. Resting on their packs, they fell asleep. Once, below them, no more than two hundred feet, a porcupine ambled past heading for better pasture. A few minutes before they woke up, six caribou crossed the ridge a hundred yards away. It was a pretty sight to miss, but one they would have only watched as these were cows, calves, and one young immature bull. They were heading south on their regular migration and were out of sight in the rolling hills before the hunters opened their eyes.

Realizing they had a good place to spot game, they decided to stay on the ridge until the big bull appeared, or it was time to head back to camp. Dividing up the area, they glassed, looking for movement or unusual colors. Rocks and stumps turned into bears, logs became bedded moose—bringing smiles on their faces when they realized their error. Soon they got familiar enough with the terrain to identify these places and pass over them.

As the angle of the sun shifted, different spots changed in color and when one place faded into shadow, another would brighten. Even grasses in valleys seemed to shimmer, silvery at times, then a deep, brownish-green, constantly moving with the slightest breeze. Tall cottonwoods towered over other trees, and with aspens, were covered with yellow leaves. Aspen trees were easily identified even from a distance as their leaves, suspended on flattened stems, twisted and turned with the tiniest movement of air. Joining in the yellow display were willows following water courses and edged up into valleys in hills. Alders retained much green in their leaves, but some were beginning to turn into their rusty-brown fall color.

The open, sunny areas were spotted with the always green crowberry, and bearberry leaves that were in process of turning from a velvety green to scarlet. Blueberries could be seen on many nearby bushes as lavender tinted red leaves were beginning to drop. Although not as colorful as maples and oaks of fall in the southern regions, the north does have its own fall beauty.

Late in the afternoon Paul, glassing the mountain side three miles away, found a black spot moving every once in a while. Getting out their high powered spotting scope, they quickly decided it was a good sized black bear, apparently feeding on something. Had they been closer, they would have seen it was gorging on crowberries. The bear was watched until it fed over a knoll and disappeared. It had been a satisfying sight. One they would remember long after the hunt was over.

The shadows were getting long and they were beginning to consider heading for camp when Bill, who had been watching to the east, saw a flash of white. Calling the attention of his father, both concentrated on the location and were soon rewarded by the sight of a large bull moose walking out of the edge of a small opening. His recently cleaned antlers were bright and out of place against the dark background. Quickly aligning the spotting scope on him, they decided it was the big bull they had seen from the plane. It had moved from that location and was now actually nearer their camp. However, they knew the day was too far gone to attempt a stalk. All they could do was to enjoy the sight and hope he would be in the same area tomorrow.

The low angle of the sun struck directly against the bull's antlers making them appear white; however, they were a dirty gray and before long would be stained darker from scraping them against trees and brush. They were tall, wide, and impressive. Through the spotting scope they could count several points on each palm. Brow tines were long with several points on each side. It was a true trophy bull, just about ready to pass his prime. The bull would stand over six feet at the shoulder and fifteen hundred pounds on the hoof. He had already bred three cows this fall and most of his attention was directed to locating and breeding any receptive cow he could find.

It seemed but moments before the light gradually faded and to reach camp before dark they had to leave. Reluctantly they gathered and stowed away their gear, thinking of the bull all the time. With their last actions, they planned the route they would take to try to relocate the bull in the morning.

It was nearly full dark before they reached camp. They stumbled several times during the last few hundred yards. The ground could not be seen well and their boots caught on rougher spots. This brought out the decision to make sure to be in camp before it got this dark in the future. It was simply too dangerous to move about when they could not see well; help was too far away to take such unnecessary chances. No one had fallen this time. They had been lucky. The next time they might not fare so well. After the evening meal was prepared and eaten, father and son talked late into the night, outlining tomorrow's plans and reliving the events of the day.

Unknown to the hunters, they had passed within a few hundred feet of a female black bear. She and her two cubs had found a particularly good stand of blueberries and were leisurely working their way through it. The patch was large and would furnish them good eating for the next few days. The cubs had been weaned in August, but still pestered their mother on occasion. However, sweet berries now held their entire attention.

They had been born in the winter den in late January, only a half pound each, and had been suckled by the mother while she snoozed the winter away. Mother and young had left the den in late May, at first for a short trip outside, but after a couple of days they no longer returned to it. Mother had been bred the preceding June, but delayed implantation had held off the cubs' birth until the following January.

> The black bear (*Ursus americanus*) is a good mother, providing her young with nourishing milk and necessary protection from predators. Not normally an especially vicious animal; however, she is, when her young are threatened.

Late in spring she had met the same male who had bred her. This time his presence was not tolerated. Immediately upon detecting him, she sent her cubs up a spruce tree and then attacked. There was no bluff to the charge. The hair on the back of her neck and shoulders was standing up and her ears were flat against her head. The larger male retreated as fast as he could, realizing his life was in dire peril. She followed only long enough to assure herself he would not return, then came back to the cubs. It was several minutes before she called them down from their perch. She was still popping her teeth and growling as she led them off in a different direction.

Few animals are as formidable as a mother bear with young cubs. They will not hesitate to attack anything posing a threat to them. The male bear most certainly was a threat. Had he been given the opportunity, he would have killed and eaten his own young. This action is frequently the case when the male animal plays no role in tending their young. Many attacks by bears on humans occur when, by their mere presence, a female feels her young are in jeopardy. But if she has the chance, she will silently take them away from danger.

The sow and cubs ate their fill of berries and wandered off into a thicket of willows and dwarf birches. She lay down and her cubs cuddled against her, bellies as round as basketballs. They had no thoughts of nursing, there was no room for more food. For the next few days, the bear family would stay within a few hundred yards, eating berries until they could eat no more, sleeping, then rising again to eat all they could hold.

This same evening, two miles further west, the coyote family had come across an injured caribou calf—left behind when it could no longer keep up with his mother and her small band. It was standing on three legs, head down from pain and weariness.

Three days earlier the caribou herd had been jumped by a small pack of wolves. The wolves had singled out another young one for their victim and had killed him. This calf caribou had escaped by running down a ravine, but his escape was futile as his headlong dash was also his disaster. Jumping one large rock, he had come down on another that turned, spilling him hard. Rising with difficulty, he found his right foreleg useless, broken just above the hoof.

He tried to follow his band, but they quickly outdistanced him and suddenly he was alone. Angling away from the wolves, he headed for the first cover he could find, a small stand of spruce. Movement was so painful he stopped. Panting, the terror of the attack left, but was replaced by another fear, for the first time in his short life, he was alone.

The next three days were agony; every movement brought sharp pains up his swollen leg. Water was nearby, and he drank frequently as his fever rose. There was a plentiful food supply, but he ate little; his conscious being overpowered by the pain of the splintered bone. This was his state when the coyotes picked up his scent.

Keeping down wind, the coyotes slowly approached, the male in the lead, followed closely by the female. The three pups, who were now half grown, brought up the rear. When in sight of their prey, they stopped, and at once knew he was going to be easy to kill.

Slowly the male moved close, then charged, with the female just behind him. Only a few steps to the rear of her were the pups. Hardly able to stand alone, the caribou was easily pulled down and the male clamped down on its throat while the rest of the family attacked his stomach and flank. Before the caribou stopped gasping for breath, his abdomen had been torn open and entrails pulled out. Snapping at one another over choice parts, the coyotes ate while the caribou's legs kicked in final spasm.

They left to lie down during the night, and returned to feed once more in the early morning hours. The following evening they were back, stalking the kill until assured it had not been taken over by another predator; then fed again.

The black bear and her cubs, having pretty well cleaned up the berry patch, left it the same evening. Wandering off in no particular direction, they began again to hunt food, a never ending search by bears. By early morning they found nothing substantial and grazed on sedges that were no longer nutritious. The plant growth had stopped; they were tough, no longer succulent or able to do much more than give an empty belly something on which to work.

The coyotes left the caribou by daybreak. This time going nearly back to their den area before lying down to sleep through the day. They were still traveling when the bear and cubs caught the scent of the kill.

Carefully moving back and forth while down wind, the sow detected the location of the smell and that coyotes had been there, but she picked up no other danger signs. Cautiously, she stalked the dead animal. It was only after assuring herself all was safe she approached it. Quietly she walked about the carcass, frequently checking the air for any danger. She had stashed her cubs before making the final approach, and now, with a low sound, called them to her.

Although they had eaten enough plants to nearly fill themselves, the caribou's flesh was the desert for their night's dinner. It was nearly midday when they finished their meal and the sow and cubs moved off. Not far away they found a grassy spot, out of the rising, gusty wind, but in the open enough to soak up what sun they could.

Clouds were forming over mountain tops and were quickly building into dark masses. By late afternoon, the sky was covered and isolated showers swept across the valley in several places. The bears moved from the open into trees and again lay down, this time under a large spruce which kept the rain from them. The temperature dropped and the night promised to be a wet and cold one.

The coyotes' day had been spent in like manner; at first lying in the sun, and then moving to more shelter as the weather came in. The dark evening got them up earlier than normal. The male was the first to rise, stretch and yawn, and was followed shortly by the rest of the family who went through the same antics. The female touched noses with two of the pups, then trotted after the male who was already heading toward the kill.

Circling down wind, they quickly picked up the smell of the carcass and had started moving to it when the first hint of danger was detected. They froze in position, and all noses came up, drawing in the new odor. Hair rose on their backs as they identified it as bear, and they stayed in place for several minutes. Sensing the bear was gone, they moved slowly to the kill—stopping and checking the air every few steps. Finally, they could see the remains and again froze in position. Long minutes more they waited, searching the area for any movement. Slow step by slow step they moved in—at all times poised for immediate flight. Reaching the carcass without mishap, they began to feed, but nervously stopped frequently to check the wind and search the surroundings for danger.

The bears, having feed till noon, were late in rising, and it was full dark when they did so. Their down wind approach to the caribou easily told the sow that her food had been reclaimed by the coyotes. Sending the cubs a short distance up a spruce tree, she stalked the carcass again. Sensing nothing more than the coyotes, she became bold, and with growls and popping teeth rushed toward them. No match for her, the coyote family abandoned their kill and left the area.

The sow fed for a time before she went back to the cubs, called them down from the tree, and took them to the stolen kill. They spent the night eating. By daylight little was left except skin and a few bones with some bits of meat clinging to them. Leaving, they would return to finish it later; however, foxes found it shortly after they were gone, and by the time the sun was high, the bones were polished. That evening the bears had to content themselves with soft bones and skin. By the time they left the next morning, there was only hair and larger bones to mark the spot.

CHAPTER NINE

On the second day of their hunt, Paul and Bill rose to find the air much cooler and clouds thick, particularly over the mountains. During the night, several rain showers drummed on their tent and wind was high enough to forecast an uncomfortable day. They ate a hurried breakfast, gathered their gear, and checked packs to make sure they had what they would possibly need for the day. Knives and cartridges got more than one check as did their safety items: compass, fluorescent tape, and emergency kit.

Satisfied they had everything, they left camp heading back toward the ridge where the large bull had been seen last evening. Travel was easier this time; they knew what areas to go around and where the best footing was. Reaching the ridge faster than they had the day before, they quickly looked over the area. Spotting nothing, they took off their backpacks and made comfortable places to set. They intended to spend the day, or at least until the bull was located.

They sat near each other, facing different directions, and used binoculars to search openings and thinly grown areas. Satisfied nothing was near, they switched to distant areas to study them. Most of it was too far to go to stalk something, but just the sight of wild game brings the adrenaline up and adds zest that is the actual backbone of any hunt. Paul was the first to spot something unusual, a brown spot that quickly disappeared. He kept his glasses on the area and soon picked up movement. Whatever it was went through a small dip in the terrain. Carefully focusing his binoculars, he decided it could be nothing other than a brown bear!

"Bill, look at that area just below the rocky peak. Then look straight down until you see a large boulder with two smaller rocks below it."
"I've found the boulder, Dad, but I don't see anything else."

"Wait! Now swing to your left until you find a shrub all by itself. Just above it, is a brown bear."

Bill followed his father's directions and soon located the shrub, then looked above it to the brown spot suggested, but there was no movement. He was about to call it a false spotting when behind the blob a smaller one came into view—then a second one. The large brown spot began moving and two smaller ones followed closely behind.

"Bears!" Bill nearly yelled in his excitement. "It's a sow and two cubs! Just look at em! I haven't seen anything like it in all my hunting days!" The bears were moving slowly and appeared to be stopping often with their heads to the ground. "Get out the spotting scope, Dad, while I keep track of them."

Paul removed the large spotting scope from his backpack. With fumbling fingers, he finally got it set up and focused on the bears. The bears were most accommodating, for the most part, staying out in the open and giving the hunters clear viewing. The powerful scope was able to tell them the bears were feeding on something close to the ground. They correctly surmised it was crowberries, as it was doubtful anything else would be plentiful at that elevation. The sow was not exceptionally large, but still a formidable animal. Her coloring, and that of one of the cubs, was a dull yellow. However, the second cub was much darker and appeared to be nearly black at that distance. Bill thought, at first, that it was an adopted black bear cub, only to be reminded by his father that a black bear cub would not be accepted by a brown bear—it would be promptly killed and eaten.

The bear family provided entertainment for the hunters for over half an hour before finally feeding over a knoll and going out of sight. Then they went back to their binoculars, scanning the area, near and far, for anything that was unusual or moving.

Not much later, Bill spotted a small group of caribou moving at the top of a low hill. He was able to direct his father to them, only to have them cross over the hill. It had been a short glimpse and father and son were chagrined that a group of animals had been able to make it up the hill before being spotted sooner. Had they hiked over the area of the hills, they would have found the ground more rolling than it appeared in their binoculars. There were many dips, folds, and valleys. Much more of the area was hidden from them than they realized.

Toward the middle of the morning a faint grunting sound was heard to the east. Although they were unable to pick up its source, it appeared to be moving and coming in their general direction. After some thought, Paul finally stated, "That could be a bull. It's somewhat like I've read they sound, but it sure isn't as loud as I thought it would be. Whatever it is, we should be able to sight it before too long." There was no answer from Bill; he was intently searching, looking for any movement in the trees and brush below. The sounds ceased and their spirits dropped, but still they kept a close vigil.

Minutes went by and just as they were about to give up, Bill cried, "There!" Out of nowhere a black head appeared above a willow patch. "It's a cow." No sooner had he said this than the cow moved out into the open and was followed by a smaller cow. Heads up and alert, the moose stopped, but soon started feeding on shrubs about them. They were no more than two hundred yards away and feeding in their direction.

"Watch for a bull! Watch for a bull!" whispered Paul. "Those grunts had to be a bull!" Nearly holding their breath, the hunters waited, binoculars watching the cows and then swinging to the brush behind.

Again minutes passed, the excitement lessened and disappointment began to set in. Perhaps there had been no bull; perhaps it had gone another direction, or maybe had simply laid down. The cows worked closer and it appeared it was a cow with last year's calf, as the second one was noticeably smaller and somewhat lighter in color. Nearly giving up on seeing a bull, the hunters contented themselves with watching the cows. Paul got out his camera, attached the telescopic lens, and set it up on a tripod. He took several frames, then went back to using his binoculars, refusing to believe there was no bull.

Suddenly he was there. How had he been able to get into the open without being seen? It was as if he simply materialized. Paul and Bill both loudly whispered, "Bull!" at the same instant—no further conversation was needed as they enjoyed the thrill of sighting their first close bull moose. "It's not him," said Paul, breaking the silence. This was not the bull they had seen yesterday, antlers were narrower, palms smaller, and there were only two brow tines to each side. Still it was a beautiful animal, standing with his head alert, looking from side to side. He was a dark chocolate brown with long, tan legs. His antlers suddenly turned white as sun peeked through the clouds, bringing everything about the bull into sharp focus.

The bull angled toward the cows, who had at first looked his way, but then went back to browsing. The hunters simply watched for a few minutes before Paul thought of his camera and again began taking photos.

The sun was again hidden by clouds, and deep disappointment enveloped

BORDERS®

- Returns must be accompanied by the original receipt.
- Returns must be completed within 30 days.
- Merchandise must be in salable condition.
- Opened videos, discs and cassettes may be exchanged for replacement copies of the original items only.
- Periodicals and newspapers may not be returned.
- Items purchased by check may be returned for cash after 10 business days.
- All returned checks will incur a $15 service charge.
- All other refunds will be granted in the form of the original payment.

BORDERS®

- Returns must be accompanied by the original receipt.
- Returns must be completed within 30 days.
- Merchandise must be in salable condition.
- Opened videos, discs and cassettes may be exchanged for replacement copies of the original items only.
- Periodicals and newspapers may not be returned.
- Items purchased by check may be returned for cash after 10 business days.
- All returned checks will incur a $15 service charge.
- All other refunds will be granted in the form of the original payment.

BORDERS®

- Returns must be accompanied by the original receipt.
- Returns must be completed within 30 days.
- Merchandise must be in salable condition.
- Opened videos, discs and cassettes may be exchanged for replacement copies of the original items only.
- Periodicals and newspapers may not be returned.
- Items purchased by check may be returned for cash after 10 business days.
- All returned checks will incur a $15 service charge.

39517941

STORE: 0114   REG: 04/55   TRAN#: 8346
SALE   04/02/2001   EMP: 17802

DEMONS OF STONEY RIVER
    5826536,   QP T   3.74
    14.95 75%PROMOTION
PERIODICAL
    086441132840 04 PR T   3.95

            Subtotal   7.69
            TN 8.25%   .63
  2 Items Total   8.32
            VISA   8.32
ACCT # /S 48061402009S0
            AUTH: 309187
NAME: ALLBRIGHT/JEFFERY

        CUSTOMER COPY

        04/02/2001 08:47PM

Bill. Here he was within one hundred fifty yards of the biggest animal he had ever seen—and it was too small to be legal! The hunting area they were in required nonresident hunters to take only one bull having antlers at least fifty inches wide. The best rule for determining this measurement is to shoot only those with at least three brow tines on one side, which makes it legal even if it does not make the fifty inches.

Although this bull looked to be about fifty inches wide, he had only two brow tines per side. To shoot would be reckless. If it did spread fifty inches, it would be legal, but if not, heavy fines would be in order for taking an illegal animal. Paul and Bill had thoroughly read the game regulations and were not tempted to take the bull. However, they were treated with a long observation of the trio as the moose decided to lie down. They stayed there for a time while Paul took nearly an entire roll of film before the moose decided to move on down the valley.

It was quiet at midday. They ate their lunches, and this time took alternating naps, so that one was awake at all times. Clouds began getting darker and the few breaks in them disappeared. Slowly they became lower, and by noon, the mountain tops were no longer visible. The afternoon and evening promised to be less than comfortable. A quickening of the wind in early afternoon cut short their naps and they brought out their raincoats, which helped keep the wind from chilling them. Visibility was getting lower by the minute. They could no longer see well enough to glass much of the mountain sides.

Paul was about to put away the camera and spotting scope in anticipation of rain when he caught sight of a large white bird alighting in the top of a tall spruce a short distance away. Quickly focusing his camera he was able to catch a rare sight. Thinking he was seeing a snowy owl, he was surprised to find a falcon in his lens. It was an off-gray color with dark uniform spots over his back and wings; its head free of markings. The sight was brief, long enough for only two frames before the bird took off and the rapid beat of its slender wings swiftly took him out of sight.

The gyrfalcon (*Falco rusticolus*) is large, with wings spanning nearly four feet. It lives mostly by feeding on other birds, principally ptarmigan and grouse. Around seacoasts, they live on water fowl and other sea birds with an occasional small mammal. It has a long slender tail and pointed wings, all designed for the speed it needs in catching other birds. Gyrfalcons are predominantly gray in this area, but at times are nearly white; occasionally, a dark brown. These are color morphs (Gr. meaning form, also used in place of phase.) of the same bird.

Because they are not plentiful, gyrfalcons are seldom seen by people. Any close sighting is to be treasured.

A light rain began falling about five o'clock, and with the rising wind, the day was quickly turning miserable. The two hunters huddled together, still looking for their bull. The raincoats they had been wearing to break the wind now served to keep them dry. Camera and spotting scope had been dismounted, placed in water proof bags, and stored in their backpacks. Binoculars were kept inside coats, unless something caught their eye, and then they had to be sheltered by hats and hands to keep water drops from their lens.

Shortly after rain began, their heartbeats quickened when Bill located a brown animal moving on a knoll not too far away. Picking it up by eyesight he declared, "brown bear!" Binoculars appeared from under their coats and Bill said, "Look just to the right of that small spruce on the first hill, he's in that patch of red." Paul was able to locate it with his glasses. After watching it for a short time, he started to laugh.

"Better take another look, son," Paul replied with a large grin on his face.

"Dad, it is a bear! Look, now it's moving…Oh! Bears don't look like that do they?" Bill joined his father in the laugh when it dawned on him that the bear had turned into a porcupine, and was much closer than he had thought. Had it been a bear at that distance, it would have been huge. Nearby porcupines are occasionally mistaken for a bear that appears to be a long way off. Some hunters are even fooled to the point they make a long, hard stalk—much to their embarrassment.

Weather worsened as day progressed—the men were not comfortable. Rain would slack off, with an accompanying drop in wind, however each time their hopes for improvement were short lived. Lulls were followed by a new wave of wind and rain. The sky darkened with the coming night, and they finally decided to return to camp. As they were gathering their gear to leave, they made one last sweep of the area.

It was Bill who picked up on the white spot, nearly passing it over, but quickly bringing his binoculars back to it. He did not recall any rock or white log in that section—he continued to watch it. Within a few moments it disappeared, only to reappear a few feet away.

"Dad, I've spotted a bull!" He directed his father to the spot, and together they watched as the bull came into full view. This was the bull they were after. He was still in the general area where he had been seen before, no more than a thousand yards from camp. He was crossing a long, narrow bog. The opening gave the hunters a clear view of the animal, but fading light would not let them pick out full details of his antlers. However it was easy to tell they were tall and wide, with many points. When his head turned sideways, the number of brow tines made it obvious he was over the minimum.

Once more it was too late in the day to attempt an approach. They began studying the terrain for a stalk and hunt of the area first thing in the morning. Ridges, valleys, and open areas were committed to memory in hopes they could come up on the area with as little disturbance as possible. Swinging back to the bull they found he had been joined by a large cow. Hopefully, she would keep him occupied and he would not leave to look for other companionship. Their strategy planned, backpacks were shouldered. After one last look at their quarry, they headed back to camp.

Once down in timber, they were out of most of the wind. With heat generated from walking, they finally got warm again and made good progress back to camp. They were now familiar enough with the area to move swiftly. Avoiding bad areas of muskeg and alders, they had to travel further, but it was easier and took less time. It was nearly dark when the tent came into sight, and they were relieved to see it. Moving through rough areas in the dark is extremely dangerous; it is easy to trip over roots, sticks, or simply just uneven ground.

Paul and Bill stripped off their wet gear and hung it to dry as best as possible in the close confines of the tent. Lamp and stove were lit and they sat down to relax. Before long, the lamp and stove had warmed the tent and a sense of contented satisfaction came over them. In spite of the nasty weather, they had seen game, and their thoughts were only of the pleasures of the day—not the hardships. Misery of cold wind and rain was already pushed into the background.

The day had been productive; one by one they recalled the highlights. The brown bear; with her two cubs had started out the day, and ending when they finally got to see, although not clearly, the large bull moose that was the object of their hunt. Again, they marveled how animals could seem to suddenly appear out in the middle of a large opening without having been seen getting there—as the caribou had done. The small bull moose brought on a discussion as to telling the age of a bull by the size and configuration of his antlers. The conclusion was that they did not know enough about the animal to come to a conclusion, and that they would have to find the answer after they got back from the hunt.

Paul prepared the evening meal of steak and potatoes. Bill sopped up the drips from the drying rain gear. Food was eaten, and although Paul had believed he had cooked too much, it was all gone when they were through. Activity and cold had used a lot of calories, and they were able to eat much more than they would have at home.

Bill cleaned up after the meal, during which time his father teased him about seeing bears with quills. Bill knew it would be a long time before he heard the last of that, and hoped he would come away from the hunt with some sort of tale on his father, otherwise it would be brought up every time the hunt was mentioned. But these things make up the fun of the trip. It was not long before the two men were warm inside their sleeping bags and fast asleep.

Nearly two miles to the north, a young silver fox was busy in a grassy bog hunting voles. His thick fur, glistening with water drops, kept him oblivious of wind and rain showers. His two litter mates, both of the red phase (morph), not far away, were also filling their stomachs with microtines. Later, they would make several caches of these small rodents after they had eaten all they wanted.

The coyote family was about the same distance to the west, spending the night hunting in various directions. A snowshoe hare and a grouse filled out their nightly fare, along with a complement of voles.

The wide ranging wolverines located the spot where the injured caribou had been killed. Finding all the meat and offal gone, they used their powerful jaws to break the large bones that were left. They ate the marrow from these, and consumed as much of the bone itself as they wanted. Finding nothing else, they continued on their way, leaving only bits of bone and a few tufts of hair on the ground.

Wind rose steadily during the night. Although rain was light at times, mostly it was heavy and drumming loudly on the shaking tent. Several times it awoke the hunters, but knowing their tent was well made and tied down properly, they quickly returned to sleep. But not before the thought, "I hope it lets up by morning!"

Some distance up the valley, under a white spruce whose limbs brushed the ground, lay the black bear sow and her cubs. Snuggled tightly together, they slept, ignoring the wind singing through tree tops and rain soaking everything outside their cozy bedroom.

CHAPTER TEN

There was no sun the next morning; daylight came in a slow, dingy manner. Clouds were only a few hundred feet above the ground; in places there was fog on the ground. It promised to be a wet, nasty day. The only improvement was the wind had dropped. But at thirty-eight degrees, even the light wind felt cold. The hunters buttoned up to shut out the elements as best they could, but after a hundred yards, they had to unbutton as body heat began to build up. They knew it would not be long before their sweat would soak their undergarments. Their progress was steady and quiet, marked only by occasional swish of a willow branch brushing against hip boots.

Nearing the area where the bull was last seen, Paul stopped. In low voices they made plans, and their decision was to stay together. With low visibility, it seemed the wisest thing to do. They would follow a low ridge, one on each side, and watch the valleys. Only a few steps would be taken at a time, then stop and scan; a few more steps, and again stop to look. Progress would be slow as they believed the bull was nearby. They hoped to see him first and to move fast would give the advantage to the bull. For nearly two hours they hunted, seeing and hearing nothing but an occasional jay. Even the jays were quiet because of weather.

Coming to the end of the ridge, they stopped, deciding they were probably past the bull. The best thing to do would be to cross to another ridge where the trees were thicker. Possibly the weather had moved him into the shelter of the spruce's thick limbs.

Crossing over took half an hour, entailed wading of a boggy area, that in some places, was nearly to their knees. Paul thought this was a time it would have been easier and faster to have skirted the muskeg. The shortest distance is not always a straight line when walking in Alaska.

After climbing the second ridge, they stopped to catch their breath, found a large, smooth rock, and sat down. Pulling out binoculars, they glassed nearby, then switched to the areas further away. Satisfied that nothing was visible, Bill pulled a candy bar from his pack, broke it in two, and gave one part to his father. Quietly they sat, allowing their open coats to slowly let out the sweat that had built up from the climb. Timber here was thicker and they would have to move even slower than before. The wind dropped to only a slight breeze. It was crossing the valley in front of them, fortunately directly into their faces.

Long minutes were spent watching the valley and hills beyond until finally they were cooled down and rested. Then they arose and resumed the hunt, this time angling back toward their lake. By noon, they found a good spot where they could sit and glass a large open area. They stopped to eat and relax. After eating sandwiches made before leaving camp, Bill took a nap while his father kept alert, exchanging the duty when Bill woke up. Their spirits were dropping by the minute as almost nothing had been seen all day. They had now hunted back to within half a mile of camp.

Finally, leaving their noon stop, they began to slowly hunt toward camp. Following another ridge, they had gone only a few hundred yards when suddenly a cow walked out of the timber into the open valley below and in front of them. She could not have been over two hundred yards away. The hunters crowded behind a small spruce, parting the branches just enough to watch the cow. Knowing the rut was getting into full swing, the chance of a bull being nearby was good. It was only a few minutes before a spot of light gray was seen moving through the willows behind and to the right of the cow. It seemed an eternity, but at last, the animal stepped out from the cover—their disappointment was immediate. This was a small bull, probably not more than four years old and having a spread around forty inches.

For some reason, the young bull hung back and did not come near the cow. The cause becoming apparent when to the left of the cow a small tree started to shake violently. Grunts, like they had heard the day before, came from the area of the shaking tree. The hunters knew there was another bull interested in the cow. A limb broke with a loud snap. In a few moments a huge, dark brown animal stepped into the clearing.

The new bull trotted toward the cow while the small bull, still off to one side, held his ground. Stopping, the big bull's mane stood up on his neck and he turned his antlers from side to side. In this way he was showing their size to the young bull and sending out a challenge to him. Taking stiff legged steps toward the cow, he showed his intent to the young bull, who quickly realized he was totally out-matched. The youngster sidled away, his eyes never leaving the newcomer. He moved quickly into the alders, stopping only once to look back, and left the arena to his master.

This was their bull! Two hundred yards away stood the largest animal they had ever faced. His body was nearly black, but even in poor light, its antlers stood out like beacons. Although they were starting to turn brownish from fighting brush and small trees, they were still a dirty gray. Palms were wide and tall. Each sported numerous points, some small ones at the top, those on the sides were at least a foot long. Brow tines were also palmated with several points on each side, and each point was over six inches long. This was truly a trophy bull!

"Let me get a good rest for my rifle. I can get him from here!" said Bill, excitedly.

"No!" answered his father, "he's not going anywhere and we can go down the other side of this ridge and get a closer shot. This is the time to be calm. We need to be sure of a clean kill, Bill. There's no reason to try it from here."

Reluctantly, Bill agreed. Together they backed up, keeping the spruce tree between them and the moose. When out of sight they moved to the back side of the ridge and quickly followed it, keeping it between them and their quarry. Judging when they had gotten to the right place, they quietly moved back to the top of the ridge, once more keeping behind a tree.

Peeping through the branches, they relocated the bull, now less than one hundred yards away. At this distance, Bill could easily keep his shots within two to three inches; there would be a clean kill. Waiting patiently, they stayed behind the spruce until the bull and cow had their heads turned away, then Bill and Paul moved forward to a small rise in the ground. Bill placed his backpack on it. He then rested his rifle on the pack, found the bull in the scope, and took several deep breaths to settle down his nerves.

"Wait until he turns to show his side. Don't hurry." whispered his father. "You know the point of aim, just behind the shoulder, just below midway of his chest. Take your time and squeeze; make sure you don't jerk the trigger."

It seemed forever to Bill. Actually it was only a few minutes before the bull turned and presented a clear, broadsided shot. Bill settled his crosshairs on the spot and was surprised when the gun went off. The boom of the shot was immediately followed by a smacking sound that was almost an echo, but too fast for an echo. The bull didn't move other than to look in the hunter's direction. The damp air and trees had muffled the shot, and all was eerily quiet. The men watched the bull who simply stood and stared back.

"I missed!" said an astonished Bill.

"No you didn't! Shoot again!" his father replied.

Once more Bill shot. This time the bull took a few steps forward, then stopped. A third shot rang out and the bull, taking one more step, fell, his left antler digging into soft, mossy ground. One of his hind legs kicked in spasm, then all was quiet. The cow had already left the area, trotting into the trees, but her departure had gone unnoticed by those on the ridge.

Bill turned to his father and let out a deep breath. Grins spread on their faces. Paul held out his hand to congratulate Bill on his first moose and said, "Now the hard work begins!"

They wormed their way through the willows to the bull. In spite of cool weather, they were sweating as much from excitement as from exertion. It was huge! The largest animal they had ever taken was a small bull elk. This made that seem like a mule deer. Cameras were removed from packs and photos taken from several angles. Using timers, Paul and Bill were able to photograph themselves with the bull.

Paul removed a small tape measure from his pack, and with Bill holding the other end, stretched it between the points of the widest tines. "Sixty-one inches!" Paul stated, "and maybe another half. This is a great trophy, even if it's not one for the record book, it is a terrific one for your first bull! Let's measure across the palms." Again the tape was pulled tight, across the left then the right antler palms. One was thirteen inches and the other an inch wider. There were seven tines on the left palm, eight on the right. The shortest point was three inches, the longest on the sides of each palm measured fifteen inches.

The brows were palmated. There were four points on the left, one measuring nearly seven inches. Those on the right side were shorter, but then there were five points, none under four inches in length. Measuring and counting completed, they stood back and again looked at each other with smiles and sparkling eyes.

"Now it's time to get to work" said Paul.

Bill volunteered for the messy job of gutting the animal and Paul held up the hind leg while Bill made the first cut, opening the abdomen from chest to pelvic bone. After rolling up his sleeves, he reached inside and pulled out the viscera that had not come out on its own. Using his knife, he cut the diaphragm and quarts of blood poured out, filling the abdomen and overflowing onto Bill's hip boots. Standing in the gore, he reached inside the chest with one hand, his knife in the other, carefully turned to avoid cutting himself. He located the wind pipe and esophagus and severed them. His shots had all been through the lungs and they came out in bits and pieces. Bill realized the bull had been dead with the first shot, but still glad he had made the follow-up shots. He was relieved the moose had died quickly.

Bill cleaned out the chest as best he could after removing and setting aside the heart. He then pulled out the intestines, being careful to cut around the anus and remove it, along with the bladder, so their contents would not taint the meat. With his father's help, they pulled the gut pile away from the carcass. Using their boots, they scraped away as much of the blood and gore as they could. By this time, Bill was tired from bending over, and sweat was dripping from the end of his nose. His hip boots were covered with blood as well as his hands and arms. He stopped to wipe off what he could with damp moss covering the ground.

While Bill rested, Paul began skinning. It was not long before he had to stop and sharpen his knife. Moose skin, he learned, was much tougher than the small deer he was used to working on. Bill soon joined him, and with one pulling while the other used his knife, the skin was removed from the side and then was tugged out of the way.

They spread a tarp and began tossing chunks of meat onto it to cool. By this time, it was late afternoon. Bill took both packs back to camp, leaving their unneeded gear, and returned empty to start packing meat to the lake. Before evening Bill had two packs of boned meat at the lake and decided it was too late to make any more trips.

Near camp, the meat had been put into game bags on an area where there were a lot of spruce needles and moss. The place had been selected for dryness, and there were small spruce trees surrounding it. From these trees, small ropes held a tarp in suspension over the bags, well above the meat. In this manner, rain and sun were kept away. Cold air could circulate underneath the tarp and among the bags, which were not touching each other. Bags would be turned at least once a day so cool air could get to all the meat. This time of year, the meat would last for many days without spoiling, as long as it was kept dry and away from the heat of the sun.

The tired hunters ate a large meal and talked over the events of the day, reliving the excitement. They were thankful it had not rained in spite of the chilly dampness and hoped it would hold until they were able to get in the rest of the meat. Sleep came early to two weary men.

They did not leave camp until full light the next day. Arriving near the kill site, they slowed and made a cautious approach, going first to the place where they had originally spotted the bull. From that point they watched the carcass for a full thirty minutes before deciding nothing had disturbed it, and that it was safe to finish cutting it up to pack back to camp. Regardless of their being sure the kill was undisturbed, they were still apprehensive as they neared it, stopping several times to look and listen. They had heard many tales of people who had walked up on a carcass that had been claimed by a brown bear and had been sorry for their carelessness.

They had worried overnight that something might carry off or gnaw on the antlers, but this was not the case, and they decided that the first thing they would do would be to remove them and carry them some distance from the carcass. For this purpose they had brought a small saw in a scabbard, one they had used often on deer.

The head was pulled into position and Bill began to saw the antlers off. However the tough skin slipped about on the skull and the saw could not cut it. This was solved by using a knife to cut and pull back the skin so the saw could bite on bone. The saw worked for a while, but then they found it was too short, and it kept binding and pinching. The heavy head could not be twisted into the right position for the saw strokes. They finally decided it would be easier to use the hatchet they had at camp. Removal of the antlers would have to be delayed.

Both cut chunks of meat until Bill was able to make up a full pack, which he took to camp, returning with the hatchet. Being careful not to chop into the antlers, or to break the skull apart, they were able to remove and carry them to the top of the hill, well away from the carcass.

Boning and packing the meat was completed by early afternoon. On the last trip, the antlers were tied onto Bill's back pack. The pack also had the last of the meat. With antlers, it weighed at least seventy-five pounds. Young and strong, he strode off with his burden, thankful this was the end of it.

But the homeward trip was not to be uneventful. Antlers snagged on limbs and pulled him sideways. Once nearly unbalancing him. They rested every couple hundred yards, but even Bill was getting tired before they were half way to camp. It was in timber, while following a game trail, he stumbled, his toe catching on a protruding root. Falling face down, he hit the ground with a resounding thump, the heavy pack nearly knocking the wind out of him.

Paul had been bringing up the rear and saw his son go down, but was not able to stop his fall. He was up to him within a few strides. By that time, he heard Bill start to laugh, and his fear changed to relief. Helping Bill to sit up he asked, "Are you all right?" but got no answer except a silly grin from Bill who simply shook his head.

"Are you sure you're okay?" He repeated.

"I think so, Dad, at least I don't hurt...very much."

Bill touched the side of his chin and felt a stinging, then looked at his fingers, but there was so much moose blood on them, he didn't know if any of it was his. Paul looked at Bill's face and saw a scrape with a small amount of blood oozing out.

"Looks like you skinned your chin, but I guess you are all right otherwise. We've been pushing too hard. We'll stay here until we are rested. Be thankful you didn't get hurt bad; this could have been serious. You might say, we've learned another lesson." Paul sat back. They rested until their heart rate returned to normal and sweat began to dry on their faces. Then Paul stood and helped his son get to his feet, staggering under the weight again on his back. Hopefully, they could make it back to camp without further trouble.

The trip on to camp was uneventful, and the rest of the afternoon and evening was spent in leisure. Although it was cool, they sat by the lake for a time, relaxing and enjoying the quiet. A flight of ducks passed overhead, their wings sounding loud in the stillness as they circled the lake before splashing down. Toward the mountains, several ravens were seen flying to their roost, croaking to one another on the way. As the sun set, once again, it put on a display of colors they would remember for a long time, but never able to describe in words.

It was still three days before the airplane would pick them up.

CHAPTER ELEVEN

Three foxes found the hunters' kill the first night. Since they had carried off only a few scraps of fat, their presence had not been noticed by the men. They returned to the kill the second evening, and again ate their fill. They were carrying off more chunks of fat and meat, to be cached some distance away, when the approach of another animal drove them off. The second arrival of the evening was the male coyote. After checking the area thoroughly, he proceeded to fill his own stomach.

The foxes had to watch from a distance and when the coyote left in the early morning, they returned to the carcass to eat and carry off a few more bits and pieces. They were mostly interested in fat that would give them the necessary calories to ward off oncoming winter's cold.

The morning sky grew lighter, but so slowly trees seemed to just appear out of the dark. There was no sun. Everything looked fuzzy and damp. Clouds of yesterday were still hanging low, and once more there was fog and light rain showers. The hunters slept late, restoring energy used in packing their moose to camp. After eating breakfast, and between showers, they checked the meat cache, turning the bags, allowing cool air to get to all sides.

Weather did not improve as the day progressed; light rain at times pelted the tent loudly, sounding far worse than it was. By late afternoon, restlessness had set in. The hunters, tired of reading and sleeping, decided to put on rain gear and hike to the kill site to see if anything had found it. It would be icing on the cake if they could bring home the skin of one of the predators that would be attracted to it. Paul still had a tag, and it could be used on black bear, wolf, or another game animal.

The hike to the ridge was a wet one. Again they were thankful for good rain gear and hip boots. Looking soaked, but actually dry on the inside, they quietly climbed the ridge overlooking the gut pile. Peeking over the top, they easily located the white bones standing out plainly in the gloom.

Staying on hands and knees, they closely checked everything in the valley. It was apparent that something had been there. The leg bones were not in the same position in which they had been left. However, nothing was feeding now, and being uncomfortable on their knees, they stood up and crossed the ridge.

They sat just below the point where they had shot the moose, and got as comfortable as possible, pulling their coats and rain gear tightly about them. Their seat was just below the skyline of the ridge and in front of a small clump of blueberry bushes. The bushes would break up their outline and make them nearly invisible, unless they moved. The damp breeze fortunately, was coming to them from the carcass, but that also put it directly into their faces, quickly numbing cheeks and noses. Dividing the chore of watching into the wind brought some relief. They stayed on while the sky darkened with evening's approach. The rain was generally light, but at times rattled on their raincoats. However, the miserable evening was brightened by a silver fox that came in early to get his evening meal.

The fox appeared nervous, raising his head frequently, but did stay for several minutes before leaving. He seemed disturbed, and left without carrying anything away. All of the fat and loose chinks of meat and offal had been either eaten or carried away by others. If he wanted more, he was going to have to stay there to eat it. The two hunters had left camera and spotting scope at camp as they had not wanted to take the chance of getting them soaked. It would have been too dark for good pictures anyway. They had to content themselves with watching the fox through their binoculars.

Shadows deepened and rain refused to let up. Wind dropped at times, but would then renew itself, sucking more heat from their already chilled bodies. Just as they were talking of returning to camp, movement was spotted at the carcass. Stiff fingers clumsily dug out binoculars. In the dim light they could make out a wolverine tugging on a leg bone that was larger than itself. Dropping the bone, the animal hopped to the other end of the carcass and started chewing on something there.

"It's a wolverine!" said Paul, "I never dreamed we would see one!"

"Your shot, Dad!" said the young man. But, the father said nothing, and just watched through his binoculars.

"It's too dark to shoot now. He's too small a target. I would hate to wound it." Paul finally replied. "Let's just watch till dark and come back in the morning. Maybe we can get a shot at him then."

103

Abruptly the wolverine left and for several minutes all was quiet; then suddenly it reappeared. The animal seldom was still for more than a moment or two, jumping from one part of the carcass to another. Finally it settled in one spot for several minutes, gnawing meat left on the neck bones. It was tempting for Paul to shoot, but he was able to keep his desire in check and it paid off as a movement at the rear end of the carcass caught their attention. There was another wolverine!

"Two!" said Paul. "That's unusual, wolverines are loners."

No sooner than the remark was out when a third one appeared. They were treated with the rare sight of watching three wolverines at one time.

"It has to be this year's litter," said Paul, "adult wolverines aren't normally together in the fall."

They watched for several minutes before concluding that one was larger than the others, surmising correctly that this was a female and the mother of the other two. Suddenly the largest picked up a leg bone that was bigger than she was, and carried it into the brush. She was quickly followed by the others.

Gulo did not like to stay at a kill too long at a time. This was her way of getting food and taking it where she felt safe to eat. Going only a couple hundred yards, she stopped. The three of them finished off their evening meal with the leg. They spent the night gnawing on it, and finally cracked the bones to get at the marrow. Morning would find them back at the carcass.

The hunters returned to camp after the wolverines left, hoping they would be back tomorrow. The evening's excitement lasted long after supper. They hoped the weather would clear; they were getting tired of almost constantly being damp and cold. But their gear was standing up to the test, nothing had ripped or tore, and they were as dry and warm as they could expect in this kind of weather.

They rose before dawn, ate a fast breakfast, and as soon as it was possible to see well enough to walk, they left, hoping the wolverines would be there—or at least come to the gut pile. Weather had cleared considerably, and the morning light showed only a few clouds in the sky. Wind had also dropped, but then, so had the temperature, and they noted thick frost on everything near the ground.

At times stumbling in dim light, they hiked to the site, making as little noise as possible. They arrived at the ridge and peeked through the spruce tree, but could not make out for sure just where the carcass was. They had gotten an early start; the valley was still in deep shadows. Once more binoculars came to their aid and the bones were located, appearing just as they had left them the evening before.

No animal was seen. It did not look like anything had been there during the night, although a coyote and the silver fox had come and gone after filling their small stomachs. A feeling of disappointment came over them knowing their time was getting short; but they settled back, got comfortable, and contented themselves with the solitude and beauty of the morning.

Thick clouds were hovering high above the mountain tops, but elsewhere there were only a few scattered, thin ones and a lot of blue sky was showing between them. Edges of the mountain clouds grew brighter and soon were rimmed in gold while their centers stayed a deep purple. As the rising sun lit the sky, shadows in the valley gradually disappeared and the bones became visible without binoculars.

Suddenly everything became bright and clear as the sun topped the clouds. The stillness of the morning was overwhelming; nothing moved. It was so quiet, it seemed they could hear their own heartbeats. A raven passed overhead making no sound except a faint swishing as his wings beat against the air.

As the sun rose higher, their hopes fell; daybreak is the best time to find something on a kill. Once a flash of movement at the carcass made their hearts skip a beat, but it was just a jay that was soon joined by several others. Silently the birds picked at the bones, getting beaks filled, and carrying bits into trees to cache in various nooks and crannies.

The morning crept on and the temperature rose. The sun, striking the hunters, warmed them and soon they were nodding, relaxed in its comfortable heat. Father and son shook their heads, trying to keep alert, but the peace and quiet was too much and both finally dozed.

Only moments after their eyes were closed, Gulo and her kits arrived at the bones and promptly began chewing on the large ones that hadn't already been carted off. These were joined, ribs to back bone, and too cumbersome to carry away.

The minutes dragged by—the hunters breaths came slow and even while the wolverines sated their hunger. Neither of the men stirred when a few gusts of wind came over the ridge behind them and traveled on down the hill. Heat held their scent above ground and at first above and past those at the carcass; but, then the breeze slowed and the faintest of all scents reached the nose of Garou. He turned quickly in the direction of the humans. Both of the men were still unaware of the activity below them. They were sleeping, while at the carcass was the reason they had so carefully stalked to their present position.

Gulo, then Carajou, both alerted by Garou's alarmed posture, raised their noses to test the air just as another touch of scent was brought to them. All immediately turned and disappeared into the nearby willows. They were gone in a second and only the jostled willow limbs gave sign of their passage as two yellow leaves slowly drifted down.

None of the wolverines knew what they were running from, but the new smell was one of danger, and they were too wary to stay and find out what it was. They quickly moved away from the area, not really frightened, but they had eaten enough and the edge had been taken off their hunger. They discreetly left, heading in a direction away from which the scent had came.

Paul awoke with a jerk, glanced quickly at his sleeping son and shook his head, disgusted with himself to realize he had been so lax. With his binoculars, he looked over the carcass and came to the conclusion that all was well—he had missed nothing. He did not know how long he had been asleep. His watch could only give him an approximate time. He guessed no more than a half-hour. "Oh well, it was too short a time to have missed anything," he thought, "if anything had come in to feed, it would still have been there." A puff of wind then arrived from his left and further assured him that they still had a good chance of seeing something. He let Bill sleep, but was wide awake and watchful himself.

Bill woke up a short time later, grinned sheepishly at his Dad, and rubbed a cramp in his neck. "How long did I sleep?" he asked.

"Less than an hour. I even dozed off for a time myself, but so far as I can tell, nothing has come by. All is quiet" answered his father.

When the sun was high, they dug out mashed sandwiches and chewed on them slowly, trying to make them last a long time. The inactivity was beginning to get boring, and they had all afternoon yet before it would be time to head back to camp. Conversation was sporadic and always kept low. The sound of a human voice is alien in the bush, and the quiet of the day gave them the idea their voices could be heard from a long distance.

They tired of trying to sit still. After lunch, both decided they had to get up and move around. There were some openings in the valley behind them, so they sneaked back over the ridge, then traveled just below its crest until the ridge petered out. Not much could be seen in this valley, so they followed the trees to the next ridge and cautiously crossed it. Below them was a small pond created by a beaver dam. Around the pond was a large area of muskeg, treeless, for the most part, grassy with willows, dwarf birch, and sedges.

Spotted here and there were clumps of black spruce, scraggly and stunted. As the ground rose and dried out, alders took over, then birch and aspen trees, and finally, white spruce. A few sharpened stumps of birch and aspen were seen, reminders of the food beavers needed. But no new cuts were visible. The beaver dam looked old with many sticks in it hidden by new growth of willows and sedges. The beavers had built it, then left the area when the food supply diminished.

They left a pond that was habitat for other creatures. But gradually, in years to come, the pond would fill, the dam would be gone, and the water would revert to a small stream coursing through the valley. Trees would sprout along its banks, until again a beaver found it to his liking and built another dam, cutting the trees for it and for food.

Having worked up a sweat in the heat of the day, they found a shady spot and sat, deciding the change of scenery was refreshing, and this was a good place to wait for evening. It was doubtful anything would come to the moose kill in this heat. It was nearly sixty degrees. Most animals would be napping in the shade somewhere.

A new portion of the mountain was now visible to them. The rest of the afternoon was spent watching it. Several caribou were seen high and far away, but none looked to be big bulls. Everything had small antlers, a least for caribou. Being used to seeing the small antlers of whitetail and mule deer, some of these antlers did appear to be huge. But they had studied pictures of caribou before the hunt, and knew these were probably cows and calves with maybe a yearling bull or two.

The sun was well past its zenith when Bill saw movement just above timberline, and focused his binoculars on the area. Trotting into view was a wolf! And behind him, over the hill, appeared another, then more came into sight! Describing the location, he was able to direct his father to them. Both watched the pack trot slowly across the mountain. They were too far away to pick out details, but they moved along in a string, and the men were able count thirteen in the pack. It was led by a dark, nearly black wolf, and followed by one that looked to be nearly white. The others were mostly gray, but among them was another black, and two that were white.

"What a sight!" exclaimed Paul. "I never realized there could be so much difference in their colors."

"That one at the tail end looks snow white, doesn't it?" said Bill. "I wonder what they are doing way out there in the open?" And no sooner had he said it, than the wolves bunched, milled about, then spread out and began laying down. All except one, that stood apart from the others.

Soon a yelping was heard—half bark and half howl. They realized it was the standing wolf sounding off. One of the others then stood up and joined him. For nearly a minute, the hunters were serenaded in a most ancient manner. This was not the long wail they had heard the first night, but still it was exciting and they held their breaths, the better to hear the song.

The wolf pack rested for nearly an hour with some getting up now and then to stand and stretch, then find a more comfortable place and lie down again. The sun was beginning to get low when the black wolf got up and started walking slowly down the hill. Behind it, the others casually rose to their feet and headed the direction the leader had taken. Three of them still lay for a time until the others were nearly out of sight, then they arose and quickly trotted after the pack. Soon all were hidden in a valley. They were headed in the direction of the hunters.

"Well, another great memory for us, Bill. It would have been nice to have been close enough for pictures, but then I guess we have the photo in our heads. It's not something we'll ever forget."

"I know I sure won't! Let's get back to the moose kill. Who knows, maybe the wolves will find it and give you a chance to fill your tag" replied Bill.

"No such luck, Son, that is just asking too much."

They rose, stored the gear they had removed from back packs, then retraced their steps back to the stand they had at the moose kill. They moved slowly over the ridge and into position, after checking it out thoroughly, then again settled down for a long wait. It would be nearly two hours before they would have to leave for camp.

Shadows lengthened and the air cooled noticeably. Coats were donned, and as evening wore on, were zipped up to hold in body heat. The valley dimmed, and they became more alert with anticipation. Surely the wolverines would show up before time to leave.

Suddenly, a dark shadowed moved—they sat up straight, the better to see over some intervening bushes. But there was only deep shade and although they watched closely, no further movement was seen.

"I could swear I saw something," whispered Bill.

"So did I," answered Paul. "Wolverines are small, keep watching."

Then a shadow seemed to emerge from the tangle below them and move toward the kill. It was several feet into the open before it stopped—both men were quick to get their glasses on it.

"Black bear!" whispered Bill. "Get him, Dad!"

Paul slowly put down his binoculars. The bear was in plain sight and under fifty yards away. He lifted his rifle just as slowly, not wanting the bear to catch any movement he made. Snugging the stock against his cheek, he peered through the scope and picked up the black form. The lens magnified and illuminated it. Even in the dim light, the bear was seen clear and sharp.

Paul's finger slowly tightened on the trigger, but then the bear began moving further into the clearing. Again it stopped, this time rearing up on its hind legs and looking intently at the moose bones. Then it lifted its nose and sniffed the air while turning its head from side to side. Paul knew it would drop again to four feet so he waited, not wanting to take the chance it would move just as he fired. He held the crosshairs dead center and waited for the right moment. Then the bear was heard to give a low grunt and they saw it drop down on all fours.

The silence was shattered as Bill nearly shouted, "Cubs! Don't shoot!"

The startled Paul lowered his gun and stared at the bear. Just behind it were two cubs. They had stayed under cover until the mother called them out, wanting them near her as she approached the kill.

"Boy, that was close!" said Paul. "I almost pulled the trigger!"

Luckily the bear had not heard them and continued across the narrow valley, stopping every few steps to smell and listen. Her attention was riveted to the area before her. She knew there was great danger for her cubs, but the odor of rotting meat and guts was appealing; she did not want to pass it up. Very cautiously, and slowly, she made her way with the cubs hanging closely to her rear.

It took her nearly fifteen minutes to travel the few yards. Upon reaching it, she stopped and stood up again, looking and listening, trying to pick up any danger signs. But all was quiet. The only smells were the offal and small predators that had already fed at the carcass. None of these scents were dangerous, as long as she kept the cubs close. She began to feed on the remains. The cubs joined her and were happily gnawing on bones as she cleaned up the entrails.

Paul and Bill were engrossed in watching the tableau and failed to seen the beautiful sunset lighting up the sky. They tried to take photos with a telephoto lens, but the light was so low they would find later that their attempts had been useless.

As dark arrived, they quietly gathered their gear and moved up the hill to leave, just as a wolf howled. It was close and the bear was seen rising again to stand erect. They heard her let out a low woof, and the cubs got so close to her they became invisible. She stood for only a few moments, long enough to hear several other wolves join the first one. The sow dropped down and moved quickly away from the sound of the wild dogs. She had no intention of trying to protect her food from a pack of wolves when she had two cubs to defend. She and the cubs were in the brush and out of sight within a few leaps.

It was too dark for the men to stay and see if the wolves were coming in or simply passing by. From the location of the howls they were not where they could smell anything, but that was no guarantee they would not find the kill. The wolves soon quieted and the men knew they had to leave or they would be stumbling through the trees in the dark. Reluctantly they quietly left the ridge and headed for camp.

The plane was due the next day.

CHAPTER TWELVE

Paul and Bill prepared and ate the evening meal while chattering of wolves and bears. The day had been one of boredom at times, and then real excitement. After eating, realization the hunt was all but over hit them—their mood quieted noticeably.

"You know, Dad, if we packed tonight and got everything ready to go, we could sneak back to the kill for a couple hours, and still make it back to camp before the plane could get here."

Paul mused for a few moments, then smiled and said, "Let's do it! He can't fly through the mountain pass until well after daybreak. It would be noon at least before he got here. There is a good chance something would come in soon enough to skin it and get back to camp."

They gathered strewn gear, putting it into duffel bags, leaving out only things they would require for the morning's venture. Cooking utensils were cleaned for the last time and stowed; tomorrow they would do no cooking. Cold cereal and sandwiches would be their food for the day. It was late when all was finished; the tent looked more bare than it had since being set up. Crawling into their sleeping bags, they talked quietly until past midnight when finally they fell asleep.

Once more the day dawned sharp and crisp. It had turned much colder with clear skies; the lake was edged with a thin ring of ice. Frost covered trees and ground, and all the world was glistening. The hunters were well away from camp long before the sun rose, their way lighted by the whiteness of the trees and ground. Crystals of ice shattered from limbs and grass as they moved toward the ridge, and their boots became coated with clinging shards of diamonds.

They were in place before the sun made its appearance. The valley was white, quiet, and serene. The bones were hidden under frost, but with difficulty, they could make things out with aid of their binoculars.

Nothing had fed since frost had formed, none of the red meat could be seen, all was evenly coated. Somewhat disappointed, they settled themselves while crystals on boots and clothes melted with body heat, they watched the sun slowly top the mountains. Its rays danced through the frost, reflecting in every direction—it was so bright it hurt their eyes.

Quietly they waited, not speaking, eyes watching. Far away they heard a magpie's chatter destroy the silence. Time slowly dragged on and a breeze came up the valley, at first, just a light puff, then another until there was a slow movement of air from lowlands toward mountains. It crossed between them and the carcass, taking their scent up the mountain with it. Frost fell from the trees as their limbs swayed in the wind. Its chill numbing noses and cheeks of the watchers on the hill.

More minutes passed. Suddenly, as if by magic, a wolverine was there, standing nervously by the rib cage. They never saw it leave the brush, it simply appeared in the open. No words were spoken, but the son squeezed his father's arm. Quietly and quickly, Paul eased his rifle into position, his heart pounding loudly in his ears. Getting comfortable, he put the sights on his quarry and started to squeeze the trigger. The wolverine made a sudden move and Paul eased pressure on the trigger.

Paul had to wait. Garou had moved to where he was half inside the ribs of the moose, and he made a poor target. But he did not stay long. Backing out, he moved to the right with Paul's rifle following him.

Again he began to squeeze the trigger and once more Garou moved, this time nearly standing upright and looking off into the willows. Hurriedly, Paul put the crosshairs on his chest, then fired...just as Garou dropped back to all fours.

The crashing noise came the same instant Garou felt something hit his back causing an intense burning sensation. His reflexes kicked in and he was away from the open and into the willows in a split second. Gulo and Carajou were arriving at the scene just as the shot sounded, and all three left the area as fast as they could run.

Keeping in the willows and other brush, they were never seen again by the hunters. They were nearly a mile away before they stopped their headlong flight. Gulo and Carajou sniffed at the blood on Garou's back while he started licking at the wound. His skin had only been grazed. Although he would have a scar, he was fortunate none of the muscles had been injured. After a few moments, in which most of the blood flow was stopped, they continued to move away from the area. They would not return to this part of their territory for many days.

Disgustedly, Paul laid his head down on his gun, knowing in his heart that he had missed the shot of a lifetime. Bill said nothing. After a few moments, they got up and walked to the bone pile. Silently they looked over the area and made circles around the carcass looking for any signs that the shot hadn't been a miss. Finding nothing, neither blood nor trail, they headed for camp, satisfied that the wolverine was either unhurt or had only a minor wound.

"Well," said Paul, "a wolverine is a tough trophy to get and I'll probably never get another chance. Weren't they a beautiful sight? We have some great memories from this hunt. We know there are three wolverines still here; maybe someone else will get to see them some day."

Arriving at camp, they made sure all was ready for the pick up, ate lunch, and had no sooner finished when the plane came into view. Hurriedly they took down the tent and began carrying gear to the lake's edge.

The pilot circled, checking the direction of the wind, before making a smooth landing and taxied to the camp site. Cutting the engine he coasted to the shore, hopped out, and tied the plane to some shrubs.

"How was the hunt?" he asked, and was immediately bombarded by both hunters. Laughing at their excitement, he learned of their success, and failure. Within a short time, he had them loading meat and gear.

The heavily loaded plane used a lot of water getting airborne. Circling, they pointed out the location of the kill, hoping to see something feeding on it, but only white bones were visible. Although they did not realize it, bones, hide, and all would be gone in only a few days.

The wolverines were far away. Nearby, a brown bear, hearing the plane, stopped and watched it. The occupants of the plane didn't see him.

CHAPTER THIRTEEN

arou led the wolverines away. The burning in his back, a constant reminder that this place held danger for them. The only stops during the first hour was for him to lick his wound and clean off the blood. Finally, at the far western end of their territory, at least five miles from the moose kill, they stopped and lay down in a willow thicket.

The day was spent sleeping, Garou frequently cleansing his wound, thereby keeping flies from laying eggs in it. Had he not been able to reach the wound, the possibility of fly eggs hatching into maggots would have compounded, and even this minor wound could have turned into a life threatening injury. By night, it had scabbed over and dried into a hard crust. Most of the danger from flies was now past.

Each day there had been less sun, on days when there was any sun at all. Many fall days were cloudy with frequent rains. Aspen, birch, and cottonwood trees, that had recently been a brilliant yellow, were now nearly bare with only a few stubborn leaves still clinging to their branches.

In the open areas, blueberries had fully ripened and were sweeter than ever. Their leaves were reddish, tinged with blue, and many of them had already fallen, carpeting the ground beneath.

Large patches of bearberries were fiery red on the hillsides, contrasting with the deep green of crowberries and lingonberries. Sun, breaking through the clouds, would strike first one patch of color then another, highlighting each as if saying, "Look how beautiful this spot is, and this spot, and this spot."

But this most colorful time of the year is short lived and a hard freeze one night, followed by rain and high winds the next day, brought a sudden change over the valley. Leaves were whipped from trees and bushes.

Within hours almost all were bare and drab, the color gone for another year. Even blueberries began to drop at their sweetest moment only to rot on the ground. But the hardy crowberries and lingonberries would stubbornly hang on, long after snows covered them.

Fall was a short thing. The days became more dark than light, and cold snaps were sharper and lingered longer. The first snows this fall had come with the first cold periods, but always, they had quickly melted, lingering for only a few hours or a day at most. Except mountain tops; there, early snows stayed and the white crawled slowly down their sides. They refused to give up the snows when they came until at last they were completely covered, brilliant white, and bold in sun—cold and foreboding in dark. Winter had arrived.

The brown bear that had been so rudely treated by his mother the previous June, when she had found a mate, had located a rock with a small hollow beneath it. This he enlarged, digging until he had a hole some four to five feet back into the mountain side. It was well above treeline. After his excavation work was done, he carried in many mouthfuls of dried grasses and other plants to form a crude bed. He had instinctively done all of this when the weather had first started turning cold; however, he had not used it until the first heavy snowfall. Prior to that, he had been gorging on berries and anything else he could find.

When deep snow arrived, he entered the den and stayed for a day, then left to wander nearby for a short time. He repeated this action over the next few days until another storm hit, and he went into the den to stay for the winter. He had stopped eating the last few days. When he finally entered the den, he did so with empty intestines. He would not eat again until late May the following year. Snow built up around the den quickly and soon it was no longer visible. The snow covering would insulate him from the harsh winter. The bear became more lethargic. As he entered estivation, his breathing and heart rate slowed, and his metabolism dropped to a low point where he would be able to sleep the winter away without food or water. The thick layer of fat put on by his heavy feeding would have to sustain him for over half a year.

The black bear sow had gone though similar actions. She had selected a den site at a much lower elevation than the brown bear. A short distance below timber line, she found a place where two spruce trees had blown down in a wind storm and were laying across each other. Crawling under this, she had done much as the brown bear, digging out a hollow spot, then bringing in leaves and grasses until she had made a comfortable bed.

She had been successful in raising both cubs through the summer and fall, and all of them had thick layers of fat built up by constant feeding. The cubs had been weaned in August, quickly adjusting to a diet of grasses and berries, carrion, and small mammals. The berry crop this year had been good, and they were well prepared for winter. They entered their den just shortly before the brown bear, and snow had already formed a roof, sticking to the limbs of the downed spruces above them. By the time heavy snow came to this lower elevation, the den was completely invisible, and the bears were snug and warm, the cubs cuddled tightly against their mother.

Black bears estivate like the Brown bear, but this is not hibernation. Estivation is a state where the animal is only in a deep sleep. Body temperature drops only a little, as does respiration and rate of heart beat. Although lethargic upon awakening, animals that estivate can be awakened. They often wake up on their own, sometimes even leave the den for short periods. Animals that are true hibernators, go into a state that could almost be called suspended animation. They have a body temperature only a few degrees above actual freezing, take only a breath or two a minute, and their heart beat is almost unnoticeable. The hoary marmot and the arctic ground squirrel are true hibernators and can be handled at those times without waking up.

Ground squirrels of desert regions of the Lower-48, hibernate in summer when plants dry up and there is little or no water available. This has been called estivation, meaning hibernation in summer; however, it is a true hibernation and the word estivation among some in the scientific community has come to mean, a lethargic sleep, not a true hibernation. There are some in this field who will argue this point. It is my contention hibernation means a deep sleep that renders the animal to an almost unconscious state, and that estivation means a lethargic sleep from which the animal can be awakened with a little effort.

But Gulo and family would not be sleeping away the winter. They would be hunting. Although some times would be lean, they were highly successful predators and winter would not bring much hardship. They will dig several snow tunnels, and during the harshest weather, spend a good deal of time in them. Their habit of caching food when it is plentiful, and they had done a great deal of this during the good times of autumn, would give them a backup food supply for those times when the hunt was not so successful.

The foxes made even more caches than did the wolverines, the coyotes less so. But anytime a cache was located, it was fair game for the finder, no matter whose cache it was. The fox was better at this than the others;

however, many caches were never used, and the food stored in them simply turned into dust and enriched the ground.

The coyotes, foxes, and wolves are all accomplished hunters and starvation would not be a major factor during this winter as hare and grouse populations were high. Chances were good that many of their young would live to see spring, baring accidents or disease.

Caribou moved in from the north. Although there were many who had kept moving through the area, there were several small bands still around. They would move in and out of the area several times during winter. Storms and snow would push them from one place to another, and they would furnish the carnivores a large part of their diet.

Following caribou from location to location are wolves. At least one pack of twelve would spend part of their time in this area and another pack of seven would come through on occasion. Packs are seldom far from caribou herds.

Caribou make up the principal part of the wolf diet in areas where they are plentiful, with moose furnishing a large part of the balance. Although the coyote is occasionally able to kill a caribou, it is usually the ill or lamed who becomes their victim. A healthy adult caribou is another matter. Coyotes and foxes help clean up kills of wolves, who tend to leave for another hunt while there are edible scraps left. Those carcasses of caribou that have died for various other reasons, supply all predators with easy meals whenever they are found.

Surprising, the wolverine is able to hunt and kill as many caribou as they do. Their large feet and light weight allow them to travel over deep snow where the caribou flounder. Caribou found in deep snow by a wolverine is almost certainly a dead animal.

Frequently weighing not much more than a coyote, the wolverine has a tenacity unmatched by almost all other animals. Once they have picked out a victim, they follow it with their distinctive loping gait until the prey is worn out. Then they jump on its back, digging in with claws that are as sharp as a feline's. There they hang on, biting into the neck until the animal goes down; and it is killed. In this way they are able to kill and eat a caribou that can outweigh it as much as ten times. Very few animals in this world have the ability to do this.

Pain to a wolverine simply makes it more vicious—being hurt will not make it break off the attack. Not so coyotes or wolves, who will back off if they are getting bit or being hurt by whatever they attack. Pain simply enrages a wolverine and will make him fight harder, while the wolf will turn and run away.

117

Carnivores rarely attack one another. Meetings are usually handled by both animals pretending the other is not even there. There is little profit in trying to eat something that has the ability to hurt back. There are many exceptions however, particularly when there is a great size difference or one is obviously injured.

Brown bears will kill and eat black bears, but catching one is a rare thing. Also the large old males of the bears will eat young bears, even their own. However this does not happen with great frequency as the mother bear is a formidable opponent. Although she may be considerably smaller then the male, she will defend her cubs so ferociously that males will usually back away.

Possession of a food source causes most confrontations between predators. Even then, common sense usually prevails, and the larger or more ferocious dominates the situation. Nothing is going to drive a brown bear off a kill other than a much larger bear. Even then, the larger might not try unless he is particularly hungry or aggressive. Most food confrontations are quickly settled with the smaller or least aggressive leaving the area. Even the wolverine has more sense than to try to protect a kill from a large bear or a large pack of wolves. However, it will stand its ground against coyotes, small bears, or even two or three wolves, and would be safe in doing so. A lynx would quickly leave a kill should a wolverine show up.

With coming of fall, animals grow dense fur, usually so thick even strong winds cannot get down to the skin. Little body heat is lost because of this. They are capable of living comfortably at temperatures well below zero. Fall and spring rains are shed by the long guard hairs and the underfur does not even get wet.

Snow is less of a problem and is a help at times. Wolverines dig long snow tunnels for their use in winter. Other animals, outside their dens, allow snow to cover them when laying down and thereby conserve body heat. Bear dens are almost always covered by snow, keeping intense cold of winter outside. Snow is a good insulator.

Unique among animals is the hollow hair grown by members of the deer family such as moose and caribou. Air inside the hair forms a highly efficient insulation barrier for the animal. When their skins are made into garments, the hair breaks off easily and they have to be handled with care. No other animals of the north have this hollow hair, although there is a general misconception about polar bears. It does not have hollow hair, as thought by some, even though they spend a lot of time swimming in just above freezing arctic water. Polar bears carry a thick layer of fat, as well as dense fur protecting them from cold. Water cannot get to the skin through this fur. None of the bears have hollow hair, despite what you see on TV's "nature programs."

Plants have long since gone through their annual cycle, growing quickly in spring, flowering and seeding, then stopping growth in midsummer to replenish the food supply in their roots. In this way they are able to live through the long dormant season of winter. Annuals also flower and seed quickly. Although they die each fall, they must go through reproduction in time for their seeds to mature before winter. Seeds also need to store food; they have to be able to sustain themselves until the following growing season. Many plants arriving in Alaska from warmer climates are able to flower and seed; however, their seeds are unable to live through the long, cold winter. Their flowering is a one time thing.

So winter arrived in Gulo's world; each animal and each plant prepared by Mother Nature to survive until spring when they would be able to reproduce again and replenish the earth.

CHAPTER FOURTEEN

As winter wore on, Garou became more restless; something was not right in his life. Each day he was less content to stay or to hunt with his mother or sister. His lone hunts became more frequent. There were times when he did not rejoin the others for several days. One day in late November, he left to hunt toward the west, and, although it was not a planned thing, he simply kept going past the boundary of his mother's territory.

He traveled for two days, stopping several times to rest. Another time just long enough to stalk, kill, and eat a spruce grouse. Although the food was not enough to fully satisfy him, he did not linger to hunt the other grouse he knew to be nearby. His traveling urge had taken control. Not understanding it, he simply complied and the miles flew behind him. Occasional scents came to him from the marks left by other wolverines; each giving him the signal that he must travel on. Being young and not yet completely grown, he was not capable of taking over an occupied territory.

The second day found him in a long valley with ridges left scattered about from the last retreating glacier. There was a small area of foot hills to the south, their upper reaches barren of trees, being above the line where they could grow. The territory was much like that he had just left. Feeling at home, Garou began making side trips, checking for odor of any male wolverine's marks. He traveled in a long oval, picking up smells of a female at the western edge. On the northeastern part, another female. Nowhere were there signs of a male.

Content that he was alone, he began marking what he now considered his new home. Garou claimed an area roughly thirty miles long and twenty miles wide, stretching from foothills in the south out into a wide valley. There was a major stream coming down from the foothills. It was well populated with mink, weasels, muskrats, and several beaver families. This stream, and several smaller ones, joined the larger streams in the valley, finally emptying into a small river further away. The valley was well populated with hares and grouse, and the foothills contained large numbers of ptarmigan.

Garou gave no thought to his good fortune in finding such a desirable area vacant. Had he known the fate of the male who had been the previous tenant, he still would have been unconcerned. His primitive brain was not capable of reasoning out the consequences of the former occupant having been killed by a trapper. Over the past few years the trapper had been flown in by a friend, landing his deHavilland Beaver airplane on one of the larger lakes. The airplane, equipped with skis, lands on ice in late winter, ice that is several feet thick. To save transporting them in each trapping season, the trapper had left a snowmobile, his traps, snares and other gear, in a cache at the lake.

Garou quickly settled into his new home area, spending much of his time traveling around and through it, leaving his scent marks everywhere. He learned the places where certain prey was more likely to be found. The more familiar he became, the easier hunting was. No thoughts came to him of Carajou or Gulo; that part of his life was gone. He was content to live in the present, enjoying his solitude, which would be his lifestyle from now on.

No longer would he associate with other wolverines other than at mating time. Chance encounters with females would be brief. A male in his territory would be met with aggression. If the newcomer did not leave immediately, he would attempt to drive him away. If the stranger did not leave, a fight would follow, the looser leaving to look for another home.

Garou had found the only open territory for many miles; and he was content in being alone. His predecessor had left it two winters previously, but not voluntarily. The old male had lived there for over five years, breeding the females whose territories intermingled with his. He had even crossed into two of the adjoining male areas and bred females there occasionally. One of these excursions had precipitated a bloody fight when he was caught by the resident male.

The old male had been marking his area at the western edge one summer when the tantalizing scent of a female had came to him, blown by an unusual western breeze. His approach to her was a cautious one, not at all as he would have done in his home locale. There, he would have boldly followed the scent with little hesitation. But now he was in unfamiliar territory. He had smelled the marks the resident male had often left in this area. These smells were known to him as well as the knowledge that there was danger involved. His presence would not be tolerated, especially with a breeding female about. The old male had slowly approached the female, finding her in full estrus. Forcing the foreplay, they were soon copulating. He stayed with her for a full day before the other male arrived on the scene.

The smell of the copulating pair was picked up by the resident male when wind shifted, now coming from the southeast. He had been over two miles away when the first whiff reached him. The smell of the invading male enraged him, standing hair up on his neck. Immediately he headed in their direction, plowing through willow thickets and crossing a small stream. His temper rose with each jump. He didn't pause until he was within sight of the mating pair. Still down wind, his presence was unknown. It was not until he was within a few feet of the distracted invader that he was seen.

He struck the shoulder of the old male, who had just enough warning to roll with the blow. Only in this manner was he able to avoid the powerful jaws that were searching for his neck. The momentum of the charge carried him beyond the old male, allowing him the opportunity to get upon his feet and face his attacker. Snarling and circling each other, the old male was ready for the fight. However, being out of his own home area, he had the feeling that all was not right. There was no overpowering desire to continue the fight.

He took a few tentative steps backward. This only precipitated another charge and they met head on. Each tried to get his teeth into the neck of the other. As they were well matched, the struggle only caused lacerations to their shoulders and heads. Tufts of fur were torn out before they backed away from each other. More circling and snarling followed. Again the old male attempted to back away from the fight.

This time he was able to retreat for several feet before being charged again. Again neither was able to gain advantage. After loss of considerable more hair, they again backed from each other and the old male retreated several more feet. This time no charge came, so he slowly backed into a dense thicket. Here the advantage was his and he continued, keeping his face to the other wolverine until so far in the brush he could no longer see him. At that point he turned and beat a hasty retreat toward his own territory.

The local male turned his attention to the female who had been calmly standing by. Sniffing her, he began to be caught up in the desire to copulate. After a sharp nip on her shoulder, almost as if to chastise, he rubbed against her, starting his own mating ritual. Although having coupled several times with the old male, she was still in estrus, and within a short time she was mating with the local male. The invader was quickly forgotten by both. But, he had already passed his genes into the female. Part of the litter she would bear in spring would belong to him.

The old male never left his own territory again. It was a year and a half later that he finally encountered the trapper. Although the human had first came into his area the previous year, the old male had avoided him. When young, he had caught the smell of a man shortly before being shot at, the bullet striking a tree just past him. He never forgot the crack of the projectile as it past over his head and the rolling thunder immediately following. It was joined in his brain that the two were tied together—smell and sound. When he detected the man's odor, he left the area and hunted in another part of his range. The trapper never saw his sign and had no knowledge of the wolverine's presence. He left the area before the old male returned. The wolverine had waited until the detestable smell was gone.

The following year, when the trapper returned, the old male was more bold and did not move so far away. Even then, the trapper was nearly ready to leave before the old male finally came close to the trap line while chasing a snowshoe hare. His tracks were seen by the trapper. From then on, he kept his eyes open and his rifle ready. Expecting his trap line to be raided, he knew that without heavier snares and traps, which he did not have with him, he could not hope to catch and hold a wolverine, and would therefore loose many of his trapped animals.

The old male kept some distance away. It was not until the last week of trapping season, he happened upon a muskrat caught in one of the sets. Such an easy meal was not to be passed up. As the trapper's scent had been kept down, he did not realize the danger. After eating the rodent, he continued his hunt and soon found another trapped animal. This time one of his relatives, a pine marten. Relative or not, he was eaten, and the old male continued hunting, now actually following the faint smell of the man. Finding two more sets and eating the bait in them, he finally left the area, well satisfied with his day's hunt.

The raid was found by the trapper the next morning, bringing curses of frustration. He knew the wolverine would return. He had to either quit trapping for the year or kill him. Since it was another week before he was to be picked up by the airplane, he decided to reset his traps and see if he could catch the robber in the act and end the problem with his rifle. It meant picking up part of his traps in other areas and concentrating on this one section. He would have to run it every day and sit in ambush in areas where he had a field of fire covering several traps. If he had brought heavy duty snares, he knew he could have taken the wolverine with one of them. But with only light snares available, holding an animal as strong as a wolverine would be impossible.

His chance of getting a shot was poor; however, it was the only chance he had. For the first three days he drew a blank, although again several of his traps had been torn out and the catch eaten. Concentrating his attention to this area, he spent a lot of time sitting and watching.

His persistence was rewarded early one morning before sunrise. He spotted movement near one of his sets. The scope of his gun verified it was a wolverine, and when the animal stopped for a moment, he fired. He had been resting his rifle on his backpack and the hold had been steady. After the recoil he brought his scope back down to the trap and was rewarded with the sight of a dark, unmoving object on the snow.

Elated at his good fortune, the trapper moved to the animal and found he had killed his robber. Although the high powered rifle had made a large hole in the skin, it was low down and would detract little from its value. Examining the old wolverine, he found a large, prime fur worth more than the furs the wolverine had destroyed. The trapping season had been a good one. He would be glad to get back home.

Skinning the animal, he found several scars, but none to lessen the value. The trapper ran the rest of his line, taking his catch back to camp to finish scraping and stretching them. The airplane was due in three days. He began making plans to pick up his traps and snares so that he would have them properly cached and ready for use the next season.

The day before the airplane's planned arrival, he had all of his equipment back in camp. Some distance from the lake, in an area of thick trees and brush, he made his cache, and covered it with a plastic tarp. Over this, he placed spruce limbs and other brush. When finished, it was nearly invisible; one would have to come close to realize it was man made, and that it contained something of value. It was doubtful if any human would be around while he was gone, but it was necessary to hide his equipment from being spotted from the air. No oil was used on the traps, allowing them to slightly rust would only help hold down man odors. Oil would give them a smell that would alarm his quarry when he returned next year.

Bad weather delayed the airplane's arrival for two days. Finally the drone of the four hundred fifty horsepowered engine was heard and an uneventful landing was made on the snow covered lake. The plane was quickly loaded with the season's catch and the gear to be removed. The prized skin of the wolverine was shown to the pilot and the tale of obtaining it related, with some embellishments as to the hunting prowess and shooting ability that had been needed. Knowing his passenger, the pilot grinned and gunned the engine. Lifting easily from the snow, they climbed toward the east and headed for the comforts of home.

The land was vacant of a male wolverine through the following summer and winter. The trapper again returned, this time with heavier snares borrowed from a friend. But there were no robberies and the trapper lost no pelts. His take was smaller this season, and it came to mind, he should let the area rest for a while. There was a drainage several miles north he had been watching. It had not been trapped for at least five years. It seemed like a good idea to leave this one alone for a while and try the new location.

The following winter Garou moved in. There was no trapper to break the serenity. Finding an abundance of snowshoe hares, spruce grouse, ptarmigan, and other game, he spent a comfortable winter. Three times he dug snow tunnels, living in them for a few weeks at a time. These were much shorter than the one his mother dug for her natal den. Although he had no caches of his own in the area, he found a few, courtesy of foxes who lived within his range. He had become an accomplished hunter and could have gotten along well without them.

Most of his food was furnished by small birds and mammals, but in December he came across an old cow caribou. Her advanced age and poor teeth brought her into the winter in poor condition, As winter wore on, she became thin and was unable to maintain her body heat. Garou's persistence on her trail easily got him within attacking distance and he jumped on her back. His cat like claws dug in and he clamped down on the back of her neck. Her attempts to shake him off were in vain as Garou held on stubbornly, all the time tearing into her neck. In her worn down condition, she was unable to stay on her feet and Garou dispatched her by chewing down to her vertebra, finally severing the spinal cord.

The caribou furnished many days of food while Garou denned nearby in a small hollow scooped out from beneath a spruce. Without bears to bother him, he was not going to allow anything else to have a part of it. Only twice were some foxes able to sneak in for a few morsels, coming in after Garou had moved away to lie down. It was not in his nature for him to simply stay nearby to guard his kill all of the time.

Garou started on the entrails, followed by the rest of the meat. As the animal had quickly frozen in the winter cold it took a lot of gnawing however his sharp, powerful teeth and jaws were well up to the job and presented no insurmountable problem. Bones were eaten as well as meat. Garou's jaws easily ground them up. Even the heavy leg bones were crushed and consumed.

The neck of the wolverine is larger than its head and the extra size is due to heavy muscles giving his jaws far more power than other predators his size. Bones a wolf could only gnaw are easily broken by the wolverine and the marrow is eaten as well as the bone itself. He even ate most of the skin, chewing off some hair, but swallowing a good deal of it in the process. This caribou had no tallow left on it, having used up the small amount of fat she had in trying to keep warm. This dropped the food value of her carcass considerably, but as Garou had been feeding well on smaller animals, it was of little consequence.

CHAPTER FIFTEEN

Winter was a cold one. All the lakes had frozen in October and snow had come along at the same time. By late November, snow was over two feet on the level and deepening each week. Garou's large feet was an asset. He was usually able to stay on top of the snow, breaking through only in the soft areas.

Many other creatures of the north have some means to help them handle these conditions. The long legged moose has a large hoof, but not nearly large enough to stay on top of snow, unless it is hard packed. However its long legs allow it to walk through snow that would bog down others. Caribou have large feet, bigger for their weight than moose, but they still break through snow that is not hard crusted. They compensate for this by doing most of their winter traveling and feeding in open areas. There, wind keeps snow blown away from ground plants and lichens that are their sustenance.

Wolves and foxes have large, hairy paws. Ptarmigan have feathers on its feet. With its light weight can walk on top of the softest snows. Snowshoe hare is known for his oversized, furry feet keeping him mobile in winter.

The coyote of the north is relatively new to the area and has not yet developed large or furry paws, and is at a disadvantage when compared to the others. However, without doubt, in a few hundred years their feet will change as there is no modern animal more adaptable than has been the coyote. It has changed and thrived when many other animals have become rare or even died out. The world has been changing constantly since it was formed and life that has not been able to adapt has become extinct. Today's world is changing much more rapidly due to the influence of man. It is more critical than ever to be able to conform quickly. Those that cannot, will not survive.

By January, though still not fully grown, Garou had become larger than his mother. Being a male, he would eventually nearly double her weight, but that would come gradually. He would not reach his peak weight for several years. His added weight gave him even more strength and endurance. Once he got on the trail of his prey, he kept on it until the prey became exhausted and gave up. Not blessed with speed, he simply kept up a steady lope and his endurance eventually got him within attacking distance. He used this tactic when stealth failed him. Snowshoe hares ran from him just fast enough to keep ahead. However he never stopped and soon he would get closer before the hare moved out again. Each time he would get still closer, until finally, with a burst of speed, he would have the hare by the neck.

January and February brought more heavy snows till it seemed that there would be so much it would never be able to melt again. A warm spell passed through the area in February followed by more cold and then thaws and a refreeze that left a hard crust on the snow. This was a boon to predators who could now run easily over the top of the snow while the caribou and moose broke through with every step. Most caribou stayed out in the open where it was windswept, but some tried to travel to other locations. These animals frequently bogged down in the deep snow, quickly wearing themselves out. Rarely are they trapped, but later pay the price when their reserves run low and they are unable to move enough to find adequate food. Those that conserve their fat are the ones that live through the winter.

Moose, more fortunate with their long legs, still had many problems. Having to move considerable distances to browse, they used up prodigious amounts of energy plowing through the deep snow. Feeding on tips of willow, birch, aspen, and any other ground cover plants they can uncover, they need thirty to forty pounds daily. Sometimes it takes more energy to get to the food than what they get out of it. Fat reserves are quickly used up during times of deep show. Those that enter the winter ill prepared are the first to die. This means calves first, then older bulls. Cows and young bulls enter the winter in the best shape to survive.

March brought warmer weather, but this is the time when those who have used their reserves finally succumb. If not caught by a predator, they simply lay down and die, finally too weak to eat, even if food is available. They are usually covered by snow within a few days and their carcasses are found and cleaned up by scavengers in the spring.

Heavy snows of this winter killed most of the moose calves and many older adults. This was not a rare occasion. In the whole picture, not much would be changed. This is a normal phenomenon in nature. Almost no deaths in nature are easy or painless, a fact that few humans realize or want to admit. Nature is not a Disney movie where animals live happily ever after.

Garou passed the winter in relative comfort, staying inside his snow tunnels during the worst times. During those periods, he slipped out only for short hunts or simply to rob one of his own caches. Several times the wind howled out of the north bringing heavy snow that seemed to arrive sideways instead of from the sky. Visibility would drop to a matter of feet. Birds and mammals would find various places to get out of the wind as their survival was at stake. Only by conserving their fat levels could they maintain their body heat until they could again get out to forage for food.

Storms lasting several days were hard on some creatures. More than a few did not survive them. But, most wildlife of the North is well adapted. Usually those that do not survive the hard times are the ill, weak, or injured. Most have special ways of contending with the harshness of winter. There are those that estivate, such as bears, those that hibernate, such as marmots, and those that store food, such as pikas. Some smaller birds even have the ability to estivate at night, conserving their energy until they can feed again the next day.

Gulo and Carajou stayed together during the winter, although there were many periods when they hunted separately and did not actually see one another for days at a time. They passed the winter much as did Garou, easily capturing grouse, ptarmigan, and hares. Carajou grew steadily. Before the end of the winter, there was no obvious size difference between herself and her mother.

In early January the females had come upon a cow moose and her bull calf of the year. The pair had been spending time in willows along the stream, but had used most of the browse and would soon need to move on. Then came a time when winter abated somewhat, and there was two days of warm weather. Snow softened, then a strong wind howled once more out of the north and below zero temperatures returned. Soft snow had again crusted over. They had trampled down the snow where they were feeding, but now, with food gone, they had to move into the deep snow. The cow led the way, breaking through the crust with every step. The calf followed closely behind taking advantage of the path made by its mother. Progress was slow and demanding. Before they had moved a half mile, both were breathing hard.

Finding a small thicket of willows, they stopped to browse, regaining their strength for a time. Again they ate what was available, even stripping bark from several trees and eating it. By the time they left the area, they had eaten limbs nearly half an inch in diameter. Such forage has low food value, doing little more than filling their stomachs.

Their next move was longer. Finding only small patches of food, they wandered, becoming more exhausted each day. This was their condition when Gulo and Carajou came upon them. Catching their scent, the wolverines stayed down wind and moved slowly toward the moose. Movement for them was easy, their large furry paws spread their weight on the crusted snow and did not break through.

It was late in the day and the sun had long since gone down in a display of pastel pinks and lavenders, caused by tiny ice crystals in the air. Mountains had even taken up the colors and the snow reflected them until the sun was so low they all faded away. With the dark came stars, so many as to be uncountable and seeming to light up the world all by themselves. But mostly, it was the brightness of the snow that lit up the area. Sitting on a rock at the top of a small nearby ridge observing the scene was a snowy owl.

The silent bird watched as the wolverines closed in on the moose, using anything sticking up from the snow as cover to conceal their approach. They made no sound. They seemed to float over the snow while the unwary moose kept nipping tips from the willows. Their hunger and weakened condition had taken away the edge of their normal alert-ness—the wolverines narrowed the distance slowly and steadily.

The owl watched as the wolverines found a small depression in the snow and nearly disappeared from sight. The bird was just able to see the tops of their backs as they worked through some blueberry bushes and into a thicket of willows and small spruce trees. There they stopped, heads working from side to side trying to find a hole through the vegetation to catch sight of their quarry. Then the sharp, snapping sound of a broken limb destroyed the silence. Although they could not see the moose, they now knew exactly where mother and calf were feeding. Sneaking to the left, they came to a small rise, and cautiously peeking over the top, spotted their prey.

Gathering their legs beneath them, they moved as one, disappearing over the rise. The owl again stretched to see, but this time the wolverines were out of sight. Quickly losing interest, it returned to watching for prey for its own meal.

Gulo and Carajou moved as close as possible, but ran out of cover before they were near enough to reach the moose on the first charge. Breaking out into the open, they were seen by the cow almost at once. The moose hesitated for a moment until it dawned on them that these two small, furry things were actually intent on attacking them. The cow moved first, bucking against the hard snow, then trying to get on top of it. The effort was futile as she immediately broke through the crust and begin lunging to get away.

The young bull was slower to start his escape, and less successful than his mother in moving through snow. He had gotten no more than thirty yards when the wolverines were on him.

Gulo leaped upon his back, digging in with the claws of all four feet. She quickly moved to his neck and sunk her teeth in as deep as they could go. Wrenching her head, she was able to tear open the skin and rip away part of the meat. The small bull reared up, attempting to throw her off, but Gulo only dug in harder with her fangs and claws. In full panic, he fought the demon on his back, but was not able to dislodge her, nor was he able to make much progress in reaching his mother.

The cow had been able to move some distance down the stream's edge where she stopped and turned. Seeing her calf had not been able to follow she started back to him. Hair on her neck stood erect and ears flattened against her head. Returning on the trail she had made, she got within a few yards of her calf and was met head on by Carajou. The wolverine was not in the least cowed by her menacing stance.

Shaking her head, the cow moose made a few feints, and even reared up to strike with her forefeet; however, the dancing animal in front of her refused to back up. The cow found herself gasping for air. Her condition and the attempt to get away had taken most of her strength. Slowly she backed up then turned and left. This time she could not protect her young.

When the cow moved far enough away, Carajou turned to the fight her mother was having with the young bull. Gulo had already torn open a large hole in his neck when Carajou also jumped on his back. The added weight was too much and he fell while both wolverines attacked his neck with great ferocity. Tearing and ripping, Gulo was able to reach the spinal cord and his struggles ceased. For several minutes they moved about the fallen animal, biting and growling, until fully satisfied that he was dead. Only then did they stop to rest and lick the blood from their claws and each others muzzles.

Abruptly Gulo left the scene, climbing the small hill over which they had charged the moose. She looked about, smelling the air and checking for danger. There was nothing, even the rock on which the owl had perched was bare and nearly invisible against the dark sky. She then loped about the kill site, crossing the stream and climbing another ridge on the other side. Slowly she patrolled the area until she was satisfied they were alone, then she returned to the moose.

Carajou had already began feeding. Ripping into the soft flank, she was well on the way to filling her stomach. Gulo joined her and both were biting and tearing at the still hot flesh. They would feed well for many days—if they could protect the kill.

When they had eaten all they could hold, they began tearing off large chunks of meat. These were carried over the hill, where they cached them. Several times each of them performed this act, finding snow banks where they dug down deep, packed in the food and then deftly filled in the hole. Finally, tired and full, the need for sleep became overpowering and they moved off. After making shallow nests in the snow, they curled up and were soon sound asleep.

As night progressed, clouds moved in, the light breeze stilled, and snow began falling. By the time it was light again, the two were covered and invisible to the world. The snow covering had kept them cozy and warm, and with the contentment of full stomachs, they had slept soundly. They had no knowledge of the fox family who had scented the kill and moved in, filled themselves, then carried off several small chunks torn from the carcass to be eaten later. The foxes had prudently left the area before the wolverines woke up and returned to their kill.

Each day Gulo and Carajou fed heavily on the moose. They were gluttons in this time of plenty. Up wind, and well away from them, the foxes hung about, patiently waiting until the way was clear before moving in to feed. By now the carcass was frozen solid and getting a full meal required lots of gnawing. But the predators' sharp teeth were well up to the challenge, and each day the moose seemed to melt further into the snow.

On the fourth day Gulo and Carajou were feeding in full light and, stomachs again distended, were about to leave when they got the feeling they were not alone. Peering around, they finally spotted the cause of their unease. It was the large male wolverine of the area, and he was slowly approaching. Both the females advanced toward him and he stopped, suddenly unsure of himself. He was being faced by two snarling, mad wolverines. Although both females were many pounds lighter than the male, their ownership of the downed moose gave them the advantage, especially since there were two of them. This was the male who had bred Gulo and was the father of Carajou. However this was not the breeding season and his presence was not wanted.

The male turned sideways, walking parallel to the kill, asking to be accepted, but his course was matched by the females who were showing more signs of agitation all the time. Turning, he retraced his steps, only to be once more followed by the females who were snarling and definitely in a bad mood. The male sat down, perplexed at the reception, and both Gulo and Carajou slowly started toward him. They were determined, and seeing the two snarling demons getting ready to attack, the male decided retreat was in order and did so. The females followed him for a hundred yards, snarling and growling all the way, stopping only when they felt they had taken care of the problem.

Quickly they returned to the kill, sniffing it to assure themselves that all was well. They patrolled the area for an hour before returning to finish feeding. When full, they moved away to lay down, but this time they did not move far. The appearance of the male wolverine was still in their minds and they had no intention of sharing their bounty with him.

Their presence kept the foxes away for a day, but by that time the wolverines had forgotten the incident and returned to their habit of moving several hundred yards away after feeding. The foxes were again able to feed. Before all of the moose was gone, the coyote family had also located the kill and had been able to sneak in for a couple meals.

By the end of the week the small bull had been reduced to scraps of skin, skull and a few other large bones. Most of this was eaten by the wolverines. When they finally abandoned it, there was only part of the skull and some hair left. After clean up by smaller animals and birds in spring, there would be no clue left of the incident.

CHAPTER SIXTEEN

The pair of foxes that had six kits born to them the preceding spring were still in the area. Although they had had a good year, there were only three left. One, a runt when born, never did do well, finally dying of undetermined internal malformity within a month of being weaned. He had not been able to hold his own, either at mother's teats, or in fighting for food the parents brought to the litter. Another was too bold and went exploring one day, leaving the protection of his family. He was killed by the female coyote that lived with her family nearby. The other one to die had attempted to cross the Stony River during a time of high water. The kit had drowned when he had been caught by a floating branch and held in the middle of the stream until his strength failed. These kits had been of the common red phase.

Red foxes (*Vulpes vulpes*) have three distinct color phases. The common red phase is a rusty-orange color with white markings. White is on the lower part of the muzzle, following the under belly to the rear. There are occasional foxes with dark underneath, but these are invariably the silver or cross fox morphs (phases). The tip of the tail is white and this mark is rarely absent, even in the darker color phases.

Of the surviving kits one was red and the other two were silver. The silver effect is produced by black hairs interspersed with white. They had the other white markings common to all foxes. The family had not produced the cross fox, a color phase similar to the red, but with a dark band down the back and across the shoulders, forming a cross. All three colors are possible within one litter no matter the coloring of the parents.

Color morphs are common in some mammals, notably bears and foxes. Brown bears have colors ranging from a straw-yellow to black. Different sections of the state have different colors that predominate; however, the full range of colors can be found everywhere.

In brown bears, there are several striking colorations. In the interior, the silver-tip grizzly is the norm. It is from this coloration that the bear got its original name of grizzly—grizzled meaning gray. The tips of the guard hairs are white, giving the bear a shimmering, silver sheen. Another beautiful phase is the brown bear that has light brown to yellowish hair on most of the body, but with the face and legs a dark chocolate brown. This bear is commonly called a Toklat grizzly. On the Kenai Peninsula, Alaskan Peninsula, and Kodiak Island, the most common color is a straw-yellow over the entire body. Among these color morphs is the brown bear that is all chocolate; even at times so black it can hardly be told from a black bear.

Black bears have more color phases than any of the bears, and possibly of any other mammal in this hemisphere. In Central Alaska, it is a solid, glistening black, rarely having the white spot that is usually found on a black bear's brisket. In Southeast Alaska, there are two colorations found nowhere else. The glacier bear is a smoky blue. The kermode bear is an off-white, but with the normal black nose and foot pads. It is not an albino. In the Lower-48, black bears also have the reddish-brown color phase that gives it the name of cinnamon bear. At times, it is also erroneously called a brown bear. Black bears of that area have a whole range of shades of brown, some even appearing to be red. The white patch on the chest is the norm.

The black, black bear could be called a melanistic phase, but the kermode (the white, black bear) is not an albino. Melanism is when black overpowers the normal coloration of an animal. The red squirrel and many other animals having another predominate color, frequently are melanistic which means they are black. The leopard and jaguar both have melanistic phases and appear coal black, but upon close examination, the rosettes (spots) are visible. True albinos lack any pigment at all and its eyes are pink, as are foot pads, nose, and claws or talons.

The fox family was still in the general area of their natal den and feeding mostly on small mammals. This had been a period of abundance. They were wintering well, and the kits would soon strike out on their own to set up their own family units. Much the same could be said of the coyote family. Their three pups were healthy and would soon be out on their own. The two families had met often during the winter, but for the most part had ignored each other.

Their hunting territories overlapped, but when one found the other nearby, one or the other simply turned away, avoiding any conflicts. During periods of poor hunting or bad weather, they relied on their caches or simply went hungry for a few days. Both families benefited from the kills of wolves or wolverines when those animals were fortunate to pull down a moose or caribou. A large part of these kills were eaten by bigger predators, but the coyotes and foxes also got their share of them.

There were two packs of wolves that hunted through the area from time to time, but they paid little attention to those predators living here. They followed the caribou from place to place, killing those easiest to catch— occasionally taking a moose when the situation presented itself. They left their kills when the bulk of the animal was consumed, frequently leaving behind a lot of nourishment for foxes, coyotes, and wolverines. Wolverines, able to crush the heavy leg bones, were usually the last to leave the scene. When they did, nothing remained but tufts of hair and fragments of bone. These would be used by smaller creatures, voles and lemmings gnawed up bone scraps for their calcium content and hair was used by them, and by birds, for nesting materials.

Wolves are efficient predators, living mostly on caribou. One pack of twelve averaged killing a caribou every three or four days. When caribou were not available, they killed a moose about every six to eight days. Any caribou was fair game, although they usually took the one easiest to catch. The young, the ill, injured, or the old who were run down and weak were relentlessly weeded out. It is much the same for moose, but more cows and calves were killed than bulls. Usually when an animal was singled out, they stayed with it until it was run to ground and killed. Then feeding commenced while the creature was still breathing its last.

It was on a cold January day when Gulo and Carajou spotted this pack heading down a tributary of the river. They watched closely as the wolves moved away. Before they got out of sight, a cow moose and her nearly grown calf got up in front of the pack. The chase was on and the wolves pursued the moose into the forest of spruce. The wolverines then went on their own way. Wolves were no longer of any interest to them.

The snow was somewhat soft and both prey and predator were breaking through the thin crust. The moose were making good progress, and at first were able to maintain the distance from the wolves, however they made the fatal mistake of trying to cut across a small frozen lake. Breaking through the snow, their hooves found little traction on the ice and it was not long before the cow fell. The calf was able to maintain its footing and soon disappeared into the spruce trees across the lake. Before she was able to rise, the cow was surrounded by the pack. She lived for many minutes while the wolves tore out her entrails and began eating her alive.

The pack stayed nearby for several days until the major part of the moose was gone. Some softer and smaller bones were eaten, but for the most part, bones were simply gnawed clean. They moved on when the easiest meat was gone, leaving bones scattered about.

The fox family found the kill nearly as soon as the moose went down, but stayed a considerable distance away until the wolves left. They were first to move in on the picked carcass, but had not been there long before being driven off by the male coyote. After he had eaten and left, they returned and found enough to satisfy their hunger. The wolverines did not locate the kill until the foxes and coyotes were through with it, but within two days they cleaned up the heavy bones and also left the area.

CHAPTER SEVENTEEN

Temperatures seemed to moderate in March and dry snow of midwinter was replaced by wet flakes that clung to branches, bending them under their weight. Snow was soft on the ground during sunny, warm days, crusting over again when the sun went down. Buds on trees and shrubs were swollen, preparing to burst as soon as they became warm enough. Everywhere things were preparing for spring that would shortly be upon them.

Owls that had migrated south in fall were now back and had already begun raising their young in the nests and hollows left for them by other birds. Owls do not build their own nests, but simply make use of what is already there. They prefer hollow trees where they lay their eggs without bringing in any nesting material. Their white eggs hatch earlier than any other bird to take advantage of the new crop of Microtines and hares that will soon to appear on the scene.

In higher elevations, marmots were awakening, but were still mostly inactive. The pika had survived the winter by eating the hay they had cut, cured, and stored the preceding fall.

The brown bear sow, bred last June, had given birth to two tiny males each weighing less than a pound, only one five-hundredths of the size of their mother. They were born hairless, and after a brief cleaning by the mother, began suckling and the sow went back to sleep.

Although bred in June, the fertilized eggs had been kept viable in her womb (uterus) without growing. This is called delayed implantation. The eggs do not attach to the mother's womb, but divides for a short time, forming a blastocyst. They float in the embryonic fluid until she dens up in October or November. At that time, they become attached (implanted) to the uterine wall and begin to develop normally. The young of this sow were born in the last part of February.

Delayed implantation is not all that rare. In addition to bears, the weasel family and some other animals also have this ability. It is much like a bird that lays eggs in her nest, but does not start to incubate them until all her eggs are laid. The eggs do not begin to develop until she starts sitting on them. In this way all of them hatch at the same time, usually within a few hours of each other. However this is not a set rule. Some birds start incubating their eggs with the first one laid and the chicks are hatched in succession as a result. The owl is a good example of this.

The wolverine's cousin, the ermine (*Mustela erminea*), also known as the short-tailed weasel, had turned to snow-white for winter except for a black tipped tail. His close relative, the least weasel (*Mustela nivalis rixosa*), also turns white in winter, but his one to two inch tail does not have a black tip. Both of them live in the Stony River area. As spring approaches, their winter white gradually turns to summer brown, leaving some permanent white markings.

The ermine has a soft, beautiful fur and is in demand for fur garments. However, the pelt is small as the animal weighs less than half a pound. The least weasel is much smaller, seldom over a couple ounces. For their weight these weasels are of the most vicious animals on earth, capable of killing prey many times their own size, just as is the wolverine. Their long, slim bodies allow them to follow voles and lemmings into their tunnels. These mammals are their principal food; however, they are also capable of killing animals as large as the snowshoe hare.

Joining weasels in spring coloration change are hares and ptarmigan. All turn white in fall, some keeping dark spots, then returning to brown and white colors in spring. These color changes are necessary for survival as they are active on the snow all winter long. Their winter white makes them nearly invisible on the snowy background, especially when they do not move. The predators, both bird and mammal, can easily spot a dark animal, but a white creature on snow is another matter. The ptarmigan uses the snow to hide in, as well as on. When being chased by predators, they will actually dive from the air into snow drifts, burying themselves until the danger is past.

Down in the lowlands, along the streams, mink were already mating. The mink (*Mustela vison*) is in the same family as the wolverine and also has delayed implantation, however it is a brief one. Their breeding takes place early, in February and March, but instead of a long delay in implantation and their young being born the following year the delay is a month or less. Young are born in April and May.

The marten (*Martes americana*) is also of this family, the *Mustelidæ*, but is a tree dwelling member. They breed much like the wolverine, the actual breeding taking place in the summer, followed by up to nine months of delayed implantation. The young are then born the following early spring. While the mink is just now breeding, the marten young is being born, having been conceived the preceding summer.

Still in this family, ermine (also called the short-tailed weasel) has delayed implantation similar to the marten. However his tiny relative, the least weasel, does not use this biological function. They have a gestation of only a little over a month and may produce more than one litter a year; in good times, up to three. It is interesting that among members of the same family, their reproduction can be so different.

Gulo and Carajou stayed together in the same area during winter, but one warm day in February, Carajou began traveling south. She wandered for nearly two weeks, finally finding her own territory in a spruce covered valley just north of the Bonanza Hills. This is an area of spruce trees with cottonwoods following the water courses whose banks are clogged with thickets of willow, dwarf birch, and berries of several varieties.

Her area, like Gulo's, also backed up against hills whose tops were treeless as the climate and elevation would not support them there. Thick stands of spruce became steadily shorter and more open the further up the hillside they grew, until suddenly there were none. These hills became higher the further south they went, finally rising abruptly into ridges that eventually turned into low mountains.

Carajou spent the first few months traveling and marking her new home. She crisscrossed it many times until every hill, valley, and rock were imprinted in her brain. By the end of summer, she knew the territory so well she could head direct to safety, should she be threatened. Without having the ability to think, Carajou registered all around her. She would never be lost or in doubt where she could find certain prey or a place of safety.

All mammals have this ability as do the birds. Perhaps birds are even more highly developed in this, as they know every limb on every tree in their home area. This is so detailed in some birds that if limbs or bushes near their nest are destroyed they may not be able to find the nest again. The loss of the limb or bush changes the area from a place they know to a place they don't. Their primitive brain is not capable of relating the change to the past. And so it follows that one must not disturb the area about nests as well as the nest itself. Not all birds are this sensitive, but there are many that are.

Carajou set up her range inside the home territory of a large, old, and dark colored male. His domain extended to the west nearly twenty-five miles and close to the shores of Whitefish Lake, one of the larger lakes in this part of Alaska and, much used by those flying in to hunt or trap. His range followed the valley to the east which is hemmed in by low mountains in the north and Bonanza Hills to the south.

Just beyond the edge of his eastern boundary was another prime location for float planes, Telaquana Lake. His area was almost exclusively drained by small streams flowing north through a valley to the Stony River. However, Whitefish Lake itself drains to the west into the Hoholitna River. Both eventually empty into the larger Kuskokwim River that flows on to the southwest finally arriving at its destination, the Bering Sea.

The male had been here for over six years, having been run out of an area to the south and west when he was not yet fully grown. At the time he had been too young and too small to control the area he had chosen and was driven out by a larger male. Finding this area nearby, he had settled down, and was not contested for the first two years. By then, he had grown to forty pounds and had little trouble in holding on to his home.

The male learned of Carajou a few days after her arrival, but as she was not in or near estrus, he was uninterested and did not attempt to follow her trail. Their paths crossed several times over the following months. Only once did they actually see each other, and they experienced only slight interest. After only a few moments, both went their separate ways.

At the end of June, Carajou came into heat for the first time. The distinctive odors she emitted were blown about by the wind, and for the first day or so, it went undetected by the male. He was too far to the southwest. Then, for some unknown reason, he turned toward the east and began traveling generally toward the female. He first became alert to her scent when he was still several miles away and from that moment on, his direction was no longer erratic.

The male followed the odor trail through willow and alder thickets, crossing small streams and upper reaches of Mulchatna River. This stream reaches the ocean far to the south of the Kuskokwim River, at Dillingham, but at this point it was small as it was not far from its origin, the Bonanza Hills.

It was only a short swim to cross the stream and its cold, swift water did nothing to dampen his ardor. He climbed the far bank and continued on his quest, finding the scent stronger the further he progressed.

Nearing treeline, he crested a small hill and stopped. The odor was strong now. His nose unerringly picked out the direction. His eyes followed his nose and quickly detected movement among the thin spruces in the valley below.

Carajou had come upon a porcupine. She had recently eaten and without hunger driving her, was not aggressive. Her mother had usually ignored porcupines and Carajou was tempted to do the same, but now her curiosity had gotten the best of her. She tried to confront the animal head on, but he would not have any part of that. The porcupine kept his back turned toward her with his quills raised in a menacing fan, the center of which was a tail loaded with deadly barbs. She was in the act of reaching out with a paw when the male made a noise behind her and she whirled to face him.

Carajou would never know how close disaster was to her. The appearance of the large wolverine had saved her from a mistake that, in the least, would have been painful. The smell of the male destroyed all interest she had in the porky. After drawing in his male scent, she coyly turned and ran down the valley.

The male followed closely behind her, aroused and excited. Carajou was also excited, but being new to this experience really did not understand why she acted as she did. The porcupine was forgotten and it ambled away, moving as fast as stubby legs would carry him. Over the hill, he would find plants to his liking and he would stop to feed, also forgetting the meeting with the dangerous wolverine.

Carajou's flight was short lived. Down in the valley was an area where a small stream watered thickets of willow and stunted cottonwoods. Among them she halted. There the courtship began; however, as she was in the early stages of estrus, copulation would come later. She was inexperienced, but the male had bred many females over the past several years and the breeding would go successfully.

He stayed with her several days, copulating many times, until she went out of estrus. Then, both lost interest in each other and the male went on his way. His instinctive needs were fulfilled and Carajou would give birth to her first family the following March. The male had performed his function in life, but her's would continue through the time the young were raised and capable of taking care of themselves.

Carajou's summer was mostly uneventful, hunting was good and she filled out until she was almost as large as she would ever be, nearly twenty-five pounds. She shared her territory with several other predators. There were numerous foxes and a few coyotes, but they avoided getting close to her. Carajou would have killed any fox she could catch. The same would happen to any coyote; however, she did not go out of her way to actually hunt them. They were not her regular prey, and besides being difficult to catch, they would put up a fight. There was other food that put up much less resistance.

Carajou had picked up the scent of a male lynx on two occasions but never sighted the animal. Not plentiful in this area of small trees and thin vegetation, lynx prefers deep timber and thick brush. However, they do live here and do well when there are lots of snowshoe hares, their main diet. They become scare when there are few hares as they have a hard time living on other fare.

Carajou's summer travels crossed the trails of a black bear sow with a single yearling. She had picked up their scent several times, but instinctively turned away and never got too close. This was basic survival instinct, a bear with young is not something around which to get careless. The wolverine deftly avoided any contact, always finding somewhere else to hunt.

There was a huge brown bear who considered this his home. Although he and the wolverine met once in a while, they simply ignored each other. Carajou had been fortunate to always hear, see, or smell the bear before they got too close together. She knew he was dangerous and would gladly make a meal of her if she was foolish enough to give him the opportunity.

When winter arrived, Carajou was in good condition. Her fur was long and luxurious and the underfur dense. She would have no trouble keeping wind and wet away from her skin. While wolverines never become fat, she was at least on the plump side, which would help her through any lean times she might encounter. The two fertilized eggs in her womb became implanted, and their cells began to divide. Carajou was early in having young, as many female wolverines do not have their first litter until after the age of two. However her tender age would not bode well with the young who would arrive in March.

The first litter of wild animals usually are fewer in number than with those who have had previous litters. The new mother is not experienced and even the fewer numbers is a strain on her. Survival rate of the young is low with the new mothers. But the winter progressed with Carajou feeding well and the eggs developed normally within her womb.

143

CHAPTER EIGHTEEN

G arou's first summer alone was one with times of good and times of stress. He had become well settled in his new territory when spring arrived. During this time he had no contact with any others of his sex. However he had cut the trails of several females without getting close to them. He knew the females were not a hazard to him, and that their presence in his home area was nothing to be alarmed about.

One day in late April, Garou was busy working an area where voles were abundant. He had nearly eaten his fill when the scent of another wolverine reached him. This smell was definitely not a female, and hair on his neck began to rise. Although still weak, the odor was strong enough to give him a direction, and he began moving that way.

Garou moved cautiously and stopped frequently to look around and to test the air. His course took him to a small, swift stream. He followed along its bank to the edge of treeless muskeg. The open area stopped him and he spent several minutes listening, watching, smelling, and waiting.

Garou's reluctance to enter the clearing was fortunate, as shortly the object of his concern appeared on the other side. The newcomer was light in color and blended well with the grasses of the muskeg; however, his movements betrayed him and Garou caught his sight when he broke out of the willows and into the sunlight. A low growl rumbled in Garou's throat, but not loud enough to be heard by the intruder. The hair on his neck and shoulders came erect and fire snapped in his eyes. A rage came over him that took charge of his entire being. This was not to be tolerated, his home was being invaded!

The intruder had been traveling cross wind until coming to the stream. There, he turned down wind and directly toward the area where Garou had been feasting on voles. Traveling into the wind was not a smart move; however, this was the best direction available to him. Two days previ-

144

ously, his own territory had been invaded by a much larger male wolverine. He had fought valiantly and had inflicted damage on his invader, but was overmatched and lucky to get away with his life.

The fight had taken place near a fast-moving stream. Just as he was about to be fatally gripped by the throat, he had fallen down a high bank and into the water. He was able to swim to the opposite bank which was low and smooth. Jumping quickly from the water, he entered dense willows and was out of sight before the conquering male realized what had happened. The large male hesitated, not wanting to jump down the steep bank into the water, and the hesitation was just long enough for the youngster to disappear.

The fight was over. The large male had his new territory, and now had no further interest in the former occupant. Garou's invader had been driven from his home and he had to look elsewhere for territory.

The big male turned to lick his wounds, none were serious, but were bleeding. The flow had to be stopped. His nose bothered him more than the cuts on his body; his right nostril was torn open, and blood was bubbling with every breath. But within a few minutes, blood clotted and starting to form a crust. The cuts he could reach were licked clean, and those he could not simply crusted over, quickly forming a barrier to infection.

The young male had traveled several miles before he stopped to take care of his own wounds. His right ear was shredded. His left fore foot had been bitten so severely, he was unable to put his full weight on it. There were numerous cut on his shoulders and face. These he cleaned as best he could, but most of them already had dried blood sealing them. His flesh was severely bruised beneath the cuts, from powerful bites.

He rested for the balance of the day and when he got up to resume traveling, found every muscle in his body was stiff and sore. He moved slowly at first, but was able to get up to half speed after the first mile. The rest of the night, he traveled, stopping only once when he found a colony of voles. With several of these, he was able to ease his hunger.

He bedded down at sunrise and spent the day sleeping, trying to recover from his injuries and weariness. Afternoon found him up and again traveling, still slowly, especially the first couple miles. This was his physical condition when he appeared on the far side of the muskeg, where Garou waited.

Upon coming abruptly into the sunlight, the newcomer stopped, tested the air, and found nothing as Garou was down wind and his scent was traveling the other direction. He moved slowly, favoring his sore foot, keeping to the edge of openings. Garou waited, motionless, and concealed, no more than twenty-five yards away, directly in his line of travel.

The limping male nearly walked into Garou before he saw him—Garou was biting into his neck before he could react. Rearing on his hind feet, he spun about in a defensive reflex action. The movement was fortunate as it lifted Garou from his feet and tossed him to the side. Before he could recover his feet, the invader was running and nearly out of sight in thick blueberry bushes. Snarling, Garou took out after him and was able to catch him within a short distance. The injured wolverine was not able to move fast enough to get away, even with a lead.

Thoroughly beaten only a couple days before, the newcomer had no intention of trying to stand and fight again. He was in no physical condition to do so. Garou, being young himself, was not experienced enough to take full advantage of the situation and a running fight ensued. They bit at each other viciously, neither getting the upper hand. But each time there was a chance the injured male would break away and run, until Garou again caught up with him.

They fought in this manner for nearly a mile. By that time both were noticeably winded. They were still beside the small stream and the traveler finally dove in and swam to the other side. Again his antagonist hesitated, Garou was tired and, since the other seemed anxious to leave, he did not immediately follow.

Garou paced up and down the bank of the stream, growling while the adrenaline subsided. Then he lay down and tended his wounds until he was rested. After cleaning off the blood, he rose and waded into the water and, on the far side, picked up the scent. Loping along the trail, he followed it for some time, finally deciding his enemy was gone and the danger past. The injured male would have to find another territory to take over. He was fortunate to have survived the past few days.

Garou was fortunate the young male had been injured when he arrived. Had he been healthy, the fight would have been more even. It was possible that one of the two would not have survived. This could easily have been Garou. As it was, he had successfully defended his home and his courage, already well developed, was bolstered, and any future incursions would be met with even more determination. But summer would pass without him being tested. The only other wolverines he met were females.

146

That summer he tracked down each of the three females who lived in the area, usually picking up their scent from long distances. During the first encounter, he was extremely nervous and unsure of himself; however, he did act aggressively and with a good deal of bumbling around finally completed the sex act and impregnated the female. She had already had several litters and her patience and cooperation in the courtship had a good deal to do with its success.

In August, he found the other two females. With a good deal more assurance, he spent several days with each. Both were fertilized, and went their way with Garou forgetting them in a short time. Of the three matings, there would be a total of seven kits born—a successful year for the young male.

With fall's arrival cottonwood and aspen trees turned yellow once more and crowberries ripened, along with another bumper crop of blueberries. Bears fed heavily on the berries, storing up fat for the winter. Down in the valleys, beavers busily cut and buried limbs in the bottom of the lakes and streams for winter food.

Snowshoe hares began to turn white and ptarmigan lost more and more of their summer plumage. Garou made many caches in September. They were all of the preparation he would make for winter, other than growing thick underfur and long guard hairs to protect him from snow and cold.

Winter passed peacefully; the trapper did not return this year. Although many planes passed overhead during hunting season, none had landed near him. The main caribou herds returned to feed on the open mountain and hillsides. During winter, Garou developed into an efficient killer of them. Although he was still not heavy, he was powerful and aggressive—this was all he needed. His first opportunity to develop this new skill came with a young male caribou.

It was early winter, there had been soft snow falling for the past two days, and it was already deep on the ground. Garou's large feet did him little good as the snow was simply too soft to support his weight. He had been plowing through it for hours, finding only a few voles to ease the hunger pangs in his stomach. Irritated at his lack of hunting success and tired from the deep snow, he climbed to the top of a large boulder. As it happened, the rock was beside a well-traveled game trail used frequently by moving caribou.

Garou had been on the top of the boulder only moments when a movement caught his eye. Coming down the trail, directly toward him, was a caribou. Garou crouched down in the deep snow covering the rock until only the top of his head was showing. As he watched, the caribou stopped, pawed the ground and lowered his muzzle into the snow. He cropped some dried grass and, finding little else, moved on. The wolverine was motionless as the animal approached, unsuspecting of the danger awaiting him just a few heart beats away. A light breeze was blowing, but it was crossing the trail at this point and there was no way for the caribou to pick up the scent of the wolverine.

As the young caribou passed by the rock, he was only a few feet away and just below Garou's level. The bull was totally unconcerned until the snow exploded and Garou was firmly attached to his shoulders. Panicked, he started to run, but the demon clinging to his back held on and began biting into the back of his neck. The pain only added to his fright and made him run all the harder. The weight of the wolverine and the shock and pain soon stopped the animal, who by then was panting and weakening fast.

Garou, sensing his prey's vulnerability, began tearing great gobs of hair, skin, and meat from his neck. It was not long before the caribou fell. Once down, the wolverine finished him off in short order and stood back, panting himself from the effort.

When he caught his breath, he circled the area looking for danger, but found none. He returned to his kill and licked the blood from the caribou's hair. Again he checked the air for smells and looked about for any movement, then turned to the kill and began to feed. Garou had made his first major kill without any help from his mother or sister.

Weeks later, in the dark of late winter, he found another caribou having a hard time. With every step, he broke through the lightly crusted snow. Garou had been able to catch up with him and leaped upon its back, riding it down and making another kill. During the rest of his life, he would actively hunt caribou and frequently would be successful. Although caribou were several times his own weight, once he was able to get on them, they had little chance in getting him off. His sharp claws and teeth, complemented by his determination and strength, were more than enough to kill animals of this size.

Garou was well fed during the winter. Along with the two caribou he killed, he found two more that died of other causes. One was an old cow that had simply died of old age, her teeth were worn down to the point she had difficulty in eating and had not been able to fatten up enough to last out the winter. Basically, she starved to death. The other was a bull injured during the rut. The combination of infection and again, lack of fat, had made him too feeble to withstand the cold. Supplementing the caribou were snowshoe hares, ptarmigan, and spruce grouse, along with many voles and lemmings.

Spring found the wolverine heavier, and with an attitude that would make him a formidable opponent to anything that was anywhere near his own size. The only thing that would make him back down now, would be a full-grown bear or a pack of wolves. He was extremely strong with heavily muscled legs and a thick neck, larger than his head, that contained muscles to give his jaws power far beyond others of his size. No longer would he have any doubts as to his ability to defend his territory. Over the next two years, he would be challenged twice. Each time the fight would be short with the encroaching male quickly leaving the area.

This spring he also made his first kill of a moose, although it was newborn. He found the calf where the mother had left it while wandering off a short distance to feed. Garou had simply stumbled upon the young animal as they have almost no odor when young. The opportunity was so sudden, he was able to kill the calf before the mother knew he was in the area.

Upon hearing the commotion, she came to defend her baby, with the mane on her neck erect and ears laid back. Garou backed off only a few feet, facing the irate cow. She sniffed her offspring but did not realize it was dead. Then, she charged the wolverine; however, he was agile enough to avoid her, dancing to the side when she got too close. Garou refused to leave and the cow stood her ground near the calf, occasionally making short charges.

Garou tried sneaking up to the calf; however, the cow met him before he could get to it. The two animals continued to circle and charge each other for several hours as the cow refused to leave the calf. Finally Garou got close enough to the calf to grab its leg and tug on it, but was able to move it only a few inches when he was again charged by the cow. This time, however, instead of dodging away, the wolverine leaped on the cow's head. Startled, she reared back and swung her head sideways, dislodging him. The act terrorized the cow so that she backed away, and Garou sensing the advantage, immediately charged her. This time the cow lost her courage, turned and ran off a short distance.

Garou broke off the attack, returned to the calf, and tore open its flank skin. By this time the cow returned, but did not crowd the wolverine. She stood off and watched her young being eaten. She remained for a time, but finally gave up and walked away, leaving Garou to his meal.

149

Gulo took no notice of Carajou's departure in the spring. They had each gone their own way so much there was not even a sense that something was missing. Dispersal of young was so natural to her there was no feeling of loss, she simply kept on with her own life.

Dispersal of young is necessary or else inbreeding would result, causing a limited gene pool. If unrelated genes are not introduced, mutations begin and deformities result. On occasion, this can be good, but that is rare. Usually, inbreeding causes an inferior animal incapable of living productively. Those slow, have poor hearing, sight, or smell are at a disadvantage and among the first eliminated. There are many slight defects brought on by inbreeding making an animal less able to cope with its environment. Survival of the fittest is an actuality in nature.

There were few lean times for Gulo. Her territory had sufficient game to kill and she was a successful hunter. This spring was a time of ease as Microtines were plentiful and so were hares. Hares were especially abundant, having reached the peak of their population cycle. The next season, however, would find them in a sudden crash and predators of the area would have to hunt much harder for their sustenance.

The few lynx in the area would have a particularly difficult time as they hunt hares almost exclusively. Lynx do not have a good nose and they use it little in hunting. It is a sight hunter. While their nose is below par, they do have exceptional eyesight, particularly under low light conditions. They spend almost no time smelling out voles and lemmings. These animals make up a small part of their diet. Lynx depends mostly upon his eyesight and short, quick attacks.

Gulo had one lean period in early spring, before the newborn of the small mammals arrived. For various reasons her hunts happened to result in few substantial meals. For once, she was hungry. At the end of several days of poor hunting, she happened upon the same large porcupine that had caused the death of the coyote pup the preceding year. Had Gulo been well fed, she most probably would have ignored the porcupine, however with her stomach empty, its appearance was a matter for immediate attention.

Gulo approached the prickly creature cautiously, but with obvious intent. The porcupine immediately turned its back to her and raised its quills, giving it the appearance of being much larger than it was. Gulo had prior knowledge of the animal, having killed and eaten them more than once. Although she had never been slapped by the tail that was laying on the ground, somehow she understood its danger and danced around the rodent, keeping head to head with it. The porcupine tried in vain to turn quickly enough to keep its back to her but was only partly successful. The wolverine had to move in a bigger circle but was much more agile and had little trouble keeping nose to nose.

Gulo made quick darting movements, attacking its face which was free of quills. Quills do not begin until near the ears. These slashing attacks to the head were disconcerting and the porky moved and turned about as fast as possible to avoid them. However, the wolverine was simply too fast and within moments the porcupine's head was bleeding from several bruising bites. This finally resulted in the rodent going into shock and Gulo was able to get in a crushing bite to the head. With this bite, she tossed the animal and it lit partly on its side. Gingerly, the wolverine flipped it on its back and carefully tore open the soft underside that was free of dangerous quills.

Gulo fed slower than she would have on any other animal. Still, she got a few quills in her paws. The porcupine was fat and grease coated the wolverine's muzzle and paws. When full, she left the carcass and retired to a blueberry thicket that was just now beginning to bloom. She cleaned herself as best she could and was able to pull out most of the quills. Some refused to come out and she bit them off, leaving the pointed barbs embedded just under her skin. These would cause her discomfort, but eventually they would either work their way out or be absorbed.

The wolverine is one of the few animals that is capable of killing and eating porcupines without getting stuck with hundreds of quills. Of the weasel family, both the wolverine and the fisher are able to do this.

The fisher (*Martes pennanti*) has a home range in the northern part of North America, however not so far north as Gulo's territory. Fishers are found in Alaska only in the Southeastern Panhandle and their range is eastward through Canada. They reach ten to twelve pounds, much smaller than the wolverine, and are usually a dark brown with a golden sheen on shoulders and head. Being in the weasel family, they are ferocious for their size as are all of the *Mustelidæ*.

The porcupine was large and had enough fat for Gulo to come back to finish it off after several hours of digesting. The extra calories in the fat more than made up for the lack of substantial food over the past few days. Gulo stayed with the carcass until she had consumed it all. But due to the quills, she did not eat the skin.

Gulo was once more bred by the same male of previous years. This time he fertilized four eggs. She would have an above average number of young in the next litter. The meeting lasted for several days as usual, with Gulo getting bad tempered as she went out of estrus. Without the proper smells, the male began loosing interest in her and they went their own way.

The brown bear sow that had driven off her "teen age" son the previous June, when she went into estrus, emerged from her den with two small cubs during the last week of May. The sow was lean and thin, but the cubs were chubby and full of energy. They spent the first few days close to the den with the sow suckling the cubs between their playful romps in the snow. She was personally not yet interested in eating, although the cubs were demanding of her milk.

She had gone into the den fat, weighing over five hundred pounds; however, the long winter and the drain of the cubs had brought her weight down to well below three hundred. She would gain weight slowly until the cubs were weaned. Then, she had to put on as much fat as possible to sustain herself through the next winter.

Finally they left the den area and wandered down the mountain side, the cubs following as best they could, sometimes floundering through the softening snow, and at times joyfully sliding and rolling down steep slopes. Mother frequently joined them and occasionally they would climb back up a slope to enjoy a second or third slide down it.

Reaching lowlands where most of the snow was already melted, she began searching for early growing plants. They would be her diet for several days until she got her digestive system operating again. The cubs were totally uninterested in plants, spending their time playing with each other and trying to get the sow to lie down so they could get to her nipples. Usually they were successful. As the days passed by they grew quickly. By late June, they were active, round balls of fur, fighting and biting each other. Their mother was patient with them and sometimes actually joined them in play. When she had other interests, her manner could be brusque and the cubs would get cuffed when they became too mischievous.

The end of July found the cubs many times their birth weight and were eating plant and animal matter along with their mother's milk. Several times in early spring, the sow's exceptional nose picked up the scent of decaying flesh and they had fed on animals that had died during the winter. She also killed three newly born moose calves when they were found a short time after being born. Caribou migrated north to have their calves or she would have killed and eaten a number of them. Wolves followed the caribou to their calving ground and were taking their share of caribou calves.

One sunny, windless day, she and the cubs were grazing on a hillside. They were relaxed and the cubs were chasing each other as mother filled her paunch with succulent vegetation. The warm sun had a calming effect on the family and they were totally at ease. The sow was paying little attention to the cubs, even though they were making a good deal of noise, growling and attacking one another in mock combat. All were unaware of the boar that was stalking them from the far side of a thicket of willows.

This boar was the father of the cubs, although he did not know it. It would not have mattered as all that concerned him was food, and one of the cubs would make a good meal. He was mindful of the female however, realizing she would not hesitate to attack if she spotted him. The boar was over eight hundred pounds and would weigh nearly one thousand by the time he went into the den in early November. A huge animal, he still wanted no part of the much smaller female. He lay behind the willows waiting for one of the cubs to stray away from its mother and closer to him. It would have to be just right for him to be able to kill the cub, pick it up and run before the female could react.

Just then an errant puff of wind ruffled the hair on the back of his neck and traveled on, directly to the sow. She immediately let out a loud "woof," spun to face the boar and rose on her hind legs to try and locate him. His odor was familiar to her—there was no doubting the danger of the situation. She called the cubs to her. Picking up on the mother's agitation, they quickly responded. Cowering behind her, they also stood on their hind legs, trying to understand what was the danger.

Realizing he had been discovered, the boar rose up on his back feet, possibly to show the sow how big he was, but mostly so that he could see better. The sow was growling and popping her teeth, working her saliva into a froth that coated her lips and dripped from the point of her chin. The boar answered with his own popping, but he no longer had any heart to press the situation and dropped to all fours, turned and began walking away. This was all the sow needed. She immediately charged, whereupon the boar began running as fast as he could.

Mother bear followed for only a short distance as she would not get far from the cubs. She stopped and watched till the boar crossed the valley and topped the ridge of the next hill. She rose again to stand at full height, trying to spot any further movement, but found none and returned to the cubs who were now crouching in the grass trying to be as small as possible.

She sniffed them to further assure herself they were all right, then took them off in the opposite direction of the boar's departure. The family traveled for over two miles before stopping, then lay down in a dense willow thicket where she allowed the cubs to feed on her swollen nipples. Within an hour the incident had been forgotten and the cubs were sound asleep, lying tight against their mother.

By mid-August, the cubs were weaned and the mother was eating everything she could find in a desperate attempt to get as much fat on her body as possible. With the cubs no longer a drain on her system, she was putting on weight fast. With the abundant crop of berries, she would enter the den in excellent condition. The cubs also were voracious in their feeding, sleeping only as they had to, to allow their full bellies to digest.

It was one of those times when the bears had laid down between meals that Gulo nearly blundered into the midst of them. It was also one of those calm days when scent was not traveling far before it rose on the heat thermals.

The wolverine was close before she realized that bear scent was on both sides of her. She spun about instantly, just as the sow rose and gave a loud roar. The sound was more than enough to give her all the incentive she needed—she ran as fast as she could. Fortunately there were thickets of willow, dwarf birch and blueberries in her path. She plowed through them, disappearing almost immediately.

Gulo was many yards away by the time the sow was moving. The bear followed for only a short distance as the wolverine made her hasty retreat. The sow could see the shaking bushes that marked Gulo's departure, and she watched until all movement ceased and the offending scent dissipated. For several minutes, she stood, teeth popping, until assured the danger had passed. Then, she returned to the cubs and moved them away from the area, traveling until she felt they were safe.

Gulo traveled for a distance before she slowed. It had been a close call. Although she was a courageous animal, she was also intelligent enough to know when to run. Once the adrenaline was gone, she slowed, finally stopped, and after catching her wind, moved off to hunt. The bears were quickly forgotten.

Birds began to migrate as hours of daylight grew shorter. Great flocks of robins came through the area, stopping for only short periods, their once bright red breasts now a rusty gray, worn and weathered from summer's abuse. The spring mating season would find them decked out in new feathers, the gray again red.

Once, more than a hundred sandhill cranes passed overhead with long legs stretching beyond their tails, and just as long necks on the other end pointing the way. Their rasping calls faded as they climbed higher, heading for the mountains to the east.

Ducks of many species dotted lakes, stopping to feed and rest, but never for long as they had thousands of miles to travel before they would reach their winter home.

Snow finally arrived, along with bitter cold; however, thick fur of the mammals kept them warm. Even those that did not den up were warm and dry. Gulo began making snow tunnels with the first heavy snow falls, but the early ones were short. She used them for only a few days before moving on. It was as if she was practicing for the large one she would construct in late February in anticipation of the new family that would arrive in March.

CHAPTER TWENTY

In January, snowshoe hares began dying. Gulo had little trouble finding dead ones for food. The cycle for hares had reached its peak and nature was now weeding them out. Their huge numbers had brought on a stress they could not handle. Diseases spread among them as their food became scarce. Bark was eaten from saplings and sprouts as high as the hares could reach, working higher with the help of each new snow. Snowfalls quickly covered the dead but Gulo's keen sense of smell easily found them. She grew fat and round from the plentiful supply of food. And, the fertile eggs in her womb began to develop.

Her natal den this year was long and deep, nearly forty feet in length. The den cavity itself, at the end of the tunnel, was also larger than usual. For some uncanny reason, she had built it to hold a larger family. She filled the den with leaves and grasses and made a cozy nest so that there would be a warm, comfortable place to bear and suckle her young.

Gulo's labor pains began in March, almost the same date as the litter of Garou, Carajou, and the unfortunate Glutt. The birthing went easily. She was an old, experienced female and the four new born came without difficulty. They were healthy and began suckling soon after they were born. Gulo had them clean, warm, and feeding in less time than she had the three in her previous litter.

Dead and dying hares gave the wolverine plenty of food. Many were found near enough that she had to spend little time away from the kits. With Gulo well fed, they had as much milk as they could hold and grew fast and strong. Their eyes opened and the baby fuzz turned to fur. Within a few weeks they had been weaned. They easily changed from milk to a diet of hares that were brought to the den by mother. Not long after that, they began to follow Gulo on her hunts for food, tripping over each other as they tried to keep up. They were noisy and a nuisance, but Gulo was able to find enough food in spite of the handicap.

Slowly the kits developed their hunting instincts and by July were making kills of their own. All four had survived to this point; however, one did not make it through the month. He ventured alone into the open on the mountain side one late afternoon, lured there by strange new scents on the breeze. His curiosity was his downfall as he had no more than topped a small ridge when a golden eagle spotted the movement and swiftly dove on him. Although he outweighed the bird, the kit was immediately killed by the powerful strike.

The eagle perched on his body, talons buried in flesh, his eyes scanning about looking for danger. For several minutes, he simply watched the area, then turned his eyes to the dead wolverine kit. Cocking his head from side to side he eyed the animal closely, then began to tear at the skin. Within moments raw flesh appeared and he began feeding.

Before twilight fell, the eagle was so full it could hardly fly, but by making a running start he was able to take wing, and with slow, powerful beats rose in the air. He made straight for tall cottonwood trees along a small stream and there lit on the top branch and settled down for the night.

Before dawn the next morning, the scent of the kill came to the nose of a coyote and though the smell of wolverine was strong, the aroma of blood overcame her fears and she approached. Cautiously, she neared, poised to flee at every step, until finally assured that all was well, then she touched the flesh with her tongue. Quickly she looked over her shoulder, muscles still tensed, but all was quiet. Gradually she relaxed and began feeding on the remains. It was gone by full light, and the coyote headed downhill, in the same direction taken by the eagle.

The next disaster to come to the family was during the following month when the first of the caribou began returning to the area. The old wolverine spotted one of the first to arrive, traveling an old, traditional caribou trail. Gulo, having killed caribou before, lay in ambush, with her kits beside her. Patiently, she waited until a young bull got close enough, then sprang to his back. The boldest of the kits also leaped on the bull that by now was bucking and running, trying to shake them from his back. The other kits followed closely behind, nipping at his hind legs.

The caribou ran frantically, paying little attention to where he was going, trying to rid himself of the pain being inflicted on his neck and back. His headlong flight was total panic—and directly into a tree. The abrupt stop caused Gulo' to loose her grip and she also struck the tree. She hit it a glancing blow and was knocked to the ground where she landed with a resounding thump. She was stunned for a moment but the young one was not so fortunate. He was thrown to the ground and the caribou fell on top of him. Gulo was able to regain her feet and attacked the caribou's throat before the animal could regain his senses and rise. The other two kits leaped upon its back and the caribou was quickly dispatched. The fate of the other kit was unknown to them. They were absorbed in feeding and his disappearance went unnoticed.

Once filled, the animals moved from the kill, laying together some distance away to digest their large meal. They cleaned their paws and each other's faces and finally, contentedly fell asleep.

Over the next few days the wolverines fed on the carcass, not concerned that one of them was missing. Finally they got to the point when they found the remains of the other kit. He had been unable to get from under the caribou and had slowly smothered. Had he gotten free, he would probably have died as several ribs were broken and had punctured one lung. Gulo and the others smelled the dead sibling, recognizing him, but not fully understanding. They did, however, soon leave the carcass. For once failing to eat all of a hard won kill.

The remaining two kits were female, each nearly identical in coloration to their mother. Both stayed with Gulo until late November when one went hunting one day and never returned.

She dispersed north and traveled nearly fifty miles before she found unoccupied territory to her liking. The last female was the youngest of the litter. She stayed with Gulo through the rest of the winter.

January snows covered the area in deep drifts and some caribou became easy prey when they wandered in from the open, wind blown areas. Gulo and her hunting partner were able to kill a cow one morning when they caught it floundering in soft, but crusted snow. They could move faster on top than the cow whose hooves had broken through. The animal was brought down within a short distance as it was too worn down to put up much of a fight. Gulo and her kit fed on the kill, then moved off to sleep. They had food that would sustain them for many days.

They had nearly cleaned up the carcass when, early one morning, their presence was detected by a pack of wolves. The wolves approached from down wind and Gulo and the kit had no indication that any danger was near. The pack numbered thirteen and they spread out, slowly stalking toward the feeding wolverines.

The pack had cleaned up their last caribou kill several days before and that last meal had only been a snack for their large numbers. Since then, they had been hunting unsuccessfully and all were hungry. The first scent they picked up had been the bloody carcass, quickly followed by the odor of wolverine. Normally, they would avoid contact with wolverines however their hunger, bolstered by their large pack size, made them curious enough to see if they could take over the kill.

Silently the pack advanced, using trees and brush to conceal their movements, their large feet keeping them on top of the snow. The wolverines failed to detect them until a movement caught the eye of the kit. She whirled just as the pack charged from only yards away and the whole world in front of her appeared to be nothing but wolves. She leaped into the low branches of a spruce tree near the fallen caribou and quickly pulled herself up, claws digging in and tearing out small bits of bark. The kit didn't stop until she was near the top of the tree.

The first indication of trouble came to Gulo when she caught, out of the corner of her eye, the kit's frantic leap for the tree. In that instant, she heard the wolves in their rush toward her. Had she jumped for the tree at that moment she would have been able to get above the charge of the wolves. However immediate flight was not in her personality and she turned to see the danger.

She had little time to get set before the pack was upon her—she met the first wolf head on. Gulo was able to clamp down on the wolf's throat and her fangs penetrated and ripped open the jugular vein. Shaking her head she threw the wolf down, let go, and turned to face the rest of the pack. There were wolves all about her by this time. One grabbed her hind leg, effectively pinning her down, and two attacked her neck. Unable to move, still she was able to get one more wolf by the throat, biting down and crushing its wind pipe.

She refused to let go of the wolf's throat but there were simply too many others. Their weight pressed her into the snow and she was unable to move. Four of them had her in their jaws before one was able to get to her throat and shut off the air. It took several minutes before she died, her chest working frantically to pull in oxygen, but the passageway was no longer open. All this time the other wolves were fighting to get to her and those who did, bit and pulled on her body. Two legs were broken and she was disemboweled before her heart stopped beating.

Gulo was dead.

She had put up a courageous fight, but had been overwhelmed by numbers. Two or three wolves could have been handled, but thirteen was too many. The pack did not fare too well in the encounter themselves as two of their number were dead and several had severe cuts inflicted by Gulo's claws. She had clawed one in the face, gouging out an eye, blinding the wolf on that side. The pack had paid for the attack, their bravado costing them dearly. The gain had not been worth the losses and injuries they sustained.

The kit in the spruce had witnessed the killing of her mother from the swaying tree top. She was safe from the wolves where she was, and had no intention of leaving her perch as down below several wolves circled the tree watching her. But food was more important and they returned to the caribou.

The wolves worried the torn body of Gulo for some time before finally tearing it apart and devouring it. The scraps of caribou they found were quickly gone. There had been just enough to whet their appetites.

The Alpha female sniffed the dead wolves, looked up the tree at the kit, and then headed down the valley. Most of the wolves followed her, but some held back a few moments, looking for any food that had been missed, then they trotted off to join the pack. Soon all was quiet again.

It was over an hour before the kit came down from the spruce. She was tense and cautious as she went to the bits of bone and fur that was once her mother. She nosed about the area for only a few moments as her need to get away was strong. Then she left, heading the opposite direction the wolves had taken.

The kit was now on her own, but she was nearly full grown and capable of taking care of herself. Gulo had been the owner of this territory and since she was now gone, there was no longer a need for the kit to disperse. She would remain to claim the area where she had been born.

CHAPTER TWENTY ONE

Garou fathered more than thirty kits by the time he was six years of age. Many of these had not lived to maturity. This is the way of nature. Some of those that lived to breed—died shortly thereafter from many causes. Animals, seriously injured or becoming ill in the wild, do not have a good chance of survival. There are no doctors, hospitals, or medicines. Even their own kind does nothing to help them. Nature ruthlessly weeds them out, leaving only strong and well adapted to carry on.

Garou was nearly fifty pounds in weight when he went into his seventh winter. He was past middle age for a wolverine, as few live in the wild beyond the age of ten. Those held in captivity in zoos, given good medical care and proper diet, have a longer life span. Some will live beyond fifteen years. But, wild animals get no medical care, and there is always something that will eat them if they get disabled. Although he was starting to show some signs of his age, Garou was still a healthy and powerful animal.

This was the winter the trapper decided it was time to return to the area and his old trap lines. He was flown in, along with his traps, snares, snow machine, and other equipment when trapping season opened. It had been late in the day when he arrived at the frozen lake. It was dark by the time he had his tent set up. Trapping gear was left outside so it would not pick up any more man smells than necessary. He would have to spend most of the next day finishing up his camp. He was in no special hurry to get his trap lines set out. The season was long enough to get what he should take. He had always been careful not to over-trap an area.

His pilot was not one to push things and had not taken off for the trip through the mountains until he was sure the weather was good enough. Flying through mountain passes is dangerous unless the weather cooperates. There are pilots every year who press their luck and try to make it through when visibility is bad. The lucky ones survive. The others end their lives by crashing into mountains they didn't see until their last moment.

Within a few days, the trap lines were out and he established a daily routine he would follow until the season ended. He was familiar with the area, and his traps and snares were successful from the first days. He spent a lot of time fleshing out furs and drying them so they would be in good condition for sale. The season went well as the area had been untrapped for several years so there was an abundance of fur animals. The number of pelts grew steadily. The daily catch did not start to dwindle until the end of the season was near.

Garou had done most of his hunting at the other end of his territory this winter and had cut the trail of the trapper only twice. Each time he stopped to examine the smell, but as it was new to him, paid little attention to it and went on his way. He did not attach any special danger to the odor, but as it was something unfamiliar he did not try to follow its trail.

The trapping season was well over half gone before he again came upon the trail of the trapper. This time, there were other faint odors more familiar to him associated with the man smell. These were smells of food, and he followed the trail for some distance. Soon he located a trap containing a mink. The animal had died immediately when the conibear trap had snapped shut, crushing its chest. The frozen animal was pulled from the secured trap, and he went only a few yards before stopping to eat it.

The mink made only a small meal and Garou continued down the trapper's trail. The next trap was empty and still unsprung. Smelling the bait, Garou pawed at the metal, still curious about it, when suddenly it snapped shut on him. He leaped back from the sharp pain, hitting the end of the trap's chain. His paw was caught. The trap was for small animals, and when he gave a hard jerk on it, he came free. The paw was skinned and bruised and he put it down gingerly on the snow. Pain and anger flooded his brain. He grabbed the trap in his teeth and shook it. Rearing back, he felt the restraint of the wire tying the trap to a small tree. He jerked until the wire broke and Garou fell backward, the trap still clamped in his teeth.

As he moved off, the wolverine carried the trap with him, the chain and broken wire marking the snow beside his own prints. He was some distance away and off the trail of the trapper before he dropped the trap. Garou continued, no longer interested in following the trapper's scent. His sore paw slowed him down at first but most of the pain went away after a while and he moved toward the east. A mile away he stalked and killed a spruce hen filling out his meal for the day.

The trapper was not far behind Garou. An hour earlier, he might have caught sight of his robber. Arriving at the mink set, he found only hairs to show that the trap had caught one, and numerous tracks told him who had taken his prize. He reset the conibear and returned to the trail he used to follow his trap line. Ahead of him were the wolverine's tracks. He knew that if the animal kept on the trail it would find and rob every one of his traps.

Reaching the site of the next set, he found only more wolverine prints. The trap was gone. There were signs the wolverine had been caught in it, as on the snow were long dark hairs he knew were not from small mammals he had been trapping. The loss of the trap was not surprising. He looked about for it, believing it would be nearby. Not finding it, he began to follow the wolverine's trail and soon saw where the chain had drug through the snow. He was sure the animal was making off with it, and a few minutes later, found the trap nearly buried in snow. Placing it in his backpack, he followed his own prints back to the trail.

"Well," he thought, "I've got my trap back and he's left the trap line. Maybe getting bit by the trap taught him a lesson. Maybe he won't come back." But he was sure this was wishful thinking. This had happened to him before. Every time a wolverine started raiding his traps, it did not stop until something was done to stop him. He had nothing in his pack strong enough to handle a wolverine. He finished running his line and returned to camp. There he got out his extra heavy duty snares and put them in with his gear. If the robber came back, he would be prepared to handle the situation.

Garou did not return to the area for over a week. The trapper believed he was gone for good. His traps were not being robbed and there were no tracks of the wolverine crossing the trails he traveled. However, he continued to carry the strong snares with him.

It was only chance that Garou came back to this area. He had not followed the trapper's line far enough to learn that it could furnish food for him. When he again happened onto the man's tracks, he began to follow them. His brain connected the man smell with the mink he had eaten, but this was not a conscious thought. Connected also was the trap closing hard on his leg and when he came upon the first trap, he stopped.

This time, instead of reaching out to touch it, he gave it a hard slap. The trap hit the end of its chain, triggering it and the jaws snapped shut. A loud, metallic sound of steel on steel rang in his ears. He was so startled he jumped straight into the air, much like a cat does when suddenly frightened. However, unlike a cat, he did not run. He watched the trap, almost expecting it to move, but it did not. He approached it again, smelled it, found the bait and ate it. Again he struck the trap. This time there was no noise, except the rattle of the chain when it hit the end. His curiosity satisfied, Garou once more took up the man's trail.

The next trap was located. This time it was holding another fur for the trapper. Garou pulled the small animal into two pieces before it came free of the trap and he quickly ate both parts. The trapper had lost his second mink. The connection in the wolverine's brain was getting more strongly reinforced and Garou headed down the trail. He was now alert and looking for the next trap.

Trap number three was empty and Garou gave it a hard swat with a front paw. The trap sprang into the air, again clanging loudly. This time he was prepared for the noise. When it came, the reaction was less, although he still jerked back. He found the bait, ate it, then went back to the trapper's trail. The wolverine had found a new food source. He followed the man's scent, robbing traps of dead animals and tripping those that were empty and eating their bait. Only when he was full and satisfied did he leave to find a place to lay up and digest his hearty meal.

CHAPTER TWENTY TWO

On his line the next morning, the trapper came to the place where Garou had entered the trail. After the first three traps, the man knew the wolverine had learned to rob. There was nothing to do but kill him, or quit trapping. Nearing the end of the line, he found were the wolverine had left it. From then on, his sets were undisturbed. In those left, he had taken a mink and two marten. These were quickly skinned, and he put the pelts in his pack. He also kept the carcasses, carrying them with him. He went back on his line instead of cutting across the hills toward camp.

On his way, he kept his eyes open for good places to set his heavy duty snares. Returning to one spot, he stopped and got one from his pack. He took no care to hold down his own scent. He wanted the wolverine to smell him. That would help lead him to the trap he was setting. He firmly anchored the snare to a three-inch tree, formed the loop, and suspended it at the proper height between two sticks. He put one of the marten on the ground then blocked access to it by limbs and sticks, forming a makeshift stockade around it. He left only the snare's loop in the opening, forcing the animal to enter by sticking his head through the noose.

Stepping back, he looked over the set, made a few adjustments, and continued on his back trail. On the way home he made the other two sets, each similar to the first. Now he was prepared. When the wolverine returned, he would not have to go far before he came across one of the snares laid for him.

He was tired when he reached camp, but with the small take for the day, he had little to do but think of what else he could do if the snares did not work. He would not check them the next morning as that would be too soon for the wolverine to return. He would run the trap line that went another direction tomorrow, then check the snares the day after that.

The trapper knew his animals well, Garou was too full to feed again that night or even the next day. He didn't head for the trap line until long past the early sunset. Garou picked up the trail about the same point where he left it the day before. Knowing he had found food in that direction, went back the way he had came. He found two traps, both empty, which he enjoyed tripping, and ate the baits. The next stop was the first snare left for him.

Garou picked up the odor before he caught sight of the set. This was different from the others, and he approached with a little more caution. The first thing he saw was an animal lying on snow that was torn up and littered with sticks. In the middle of the debris was a fox and it was cold and stiff. Buried in the thick fur around the fox's neck was the wire snare that had been meant for Garou.

Nearby the snow was tinged with pink where the marten carcass had lain. It was not there, having been tossed several feet to the side by the fox's frantic attempts to escape the tightening loop. The more he struggled, the more it had tightened and had quickly cut off his air. The catch on the loop prevented it from loosening. There was no escape.

Garou had no idea the fox had saved his life. It had smelled the bait and stuck his head in the hole, the noose silently tightening about his neck. The fox picked up the marten and backed out but the noose was already snug and it cinched down. Dropping the marten, he fought the snare which got tighter with every jerk. His air was cut off and his efforts became weaker until he could no longer fight. Within minutes he was dead.

The fox's sibling had found him shortly after that and had stayed for some time waiting for him to get up. He fed on the marten, occasionally nudging his silent liter mate. Finally he gave up and left the scene, taking the rest of the marten with him.

Garou did not know what had happened, but was glad to find this large meal waiting for him. He was going to get fat and lazy if food kept being as easy to get as it had the past couple of days. He fed on the fox, then tried to carry off what was left, but the snare was still fast to the tree. Jerking harder and harder in frustration he finally was able to tear the body from the head and carry it away. He buried it in a snow bank only a few hundred yards off the trail. Then he left to lay up again; he had no need to follow the trap line any further.

The trapper had high hopes, even after he passed the first snare and saw it untouched. He went down his line checking, and when necessary, resetting his traps. His take was getting smaller each trip, and he was glad the end of the season was near. He had done well, but was getting tired, and was thinking of his bed at home, a long, hot shower, and good home cooking.

He was disappointed when the second snare was undisturbed, and became more so when there was no sign of the wolverine anywhere along the trail. As he neared the last snare, he hurried forward. Seeing the area torn up, he grew excited. When at last he stood at the set and read the signs, he knew that he had missed catching the wolverine. Not only that, the wolverine had been well fed in the bargain.

He reset the snare, all the time thinking he now had a good chance of getting him. The wolverine knew the trap line had food for him, and this one spot had been better than the rest. He looked over the area before he left and made doubly sure the snare was secure to the tree. He checked the rest of his line and returned to camp. There was no doubt in his mind, he would come back in two days and have a wolverine pelt.

The next evening found Garou headed for the place where he had eaten the fox. He was so sure of himself by now that he approached with little caution. This time the sticks were sticking in the snow, but there was little odor and most of it was where the fox had been. There were blood stains on the snow and nothing else.

He stuck his nose into the hole in the sticks but there was nothing inside, only the faint scent of blood. He didn't get in far enough to get the snare over his head. He backed out, again saved by another animal. During the night a marten had entered the hole, slipping in under the loop, and had drug the bait out and eaten most of it. What was left, had been cleaned up by a passing raven.

Continuing down the line Garou tripped the traps, eating the bait. Twice he found and ate animals that had been caught. Nearly full, he was almost ready to quit and leave when he came upon the middle snare. Garou was unconcerned of the danger. He had been feeding too well without any hint of trouble for several days and was totally unaware of the snare.

Smelling the skinned carcass inside the sticks, he stuck his head in the hole. It was further back than he wanted to go, but the smell was too tempting and he stretched his neck until he got his teeth into the bait. He pulled back, dragging it with him, and suddenly found something grabbing him by the throat.

Instinctively he pulled against the cable and the noose tightened further.

Rearing backward he pulled as hard as he could, but the snare held, and only tightened more. He could no longer breath, still he grabbed the cable in his teeth, biting and chewing with all his strength. The grip on his neck did not let up.

His chest worked in and out, but no air entered his lungs, and his eyesight began to fail. The night was turning darker and stars danced in front of his eyes. He bit on the wire, chewing and gnawing until, suddenly, his muscles began to relax and all of his great strength left him. Garou lost consciousness and his chest heaved a few more times, then moved no more. Inside his chest his heart continued beating for some time, but soon, even it was stilled.

By morning the body had become cold and rigid, and shortly after the sun rose above the mountains, the trapper came down the trail. Arriving at the first snare he again saw a torn up area. And again was disappointed. It held another fox, but this one was uneaten and he removed it from the wire and placed it in his pack. He wondered if something would foil him again and the other two snares would not have the wolverine. However he saw the dark spot on the snow before he got near the second snare. Again his hopes rose. He was sure it was the wolverine, and nearly ran the last few yards.

He stopped a few steps away, admiring the animal, glad that he would loose no more of his catch to the wolverine. He was sad and glad at the same time. Sad such a beautiful animal was dead, but glad that he had stopped the thefts from his trap line, as well as having an expensive fur to sell.

CHAPTER TWENTY THREE

Carajou had raised both of the kits in her first litter. This was some what unusual; most first time mothers were too new to the world to be able to handle emergencies. The death rate of young born to first, and even second time mothers, is much higher than with one who has had several litters. They make too many mistakes, leaving the young for too long a time, or leaving them in a poor location. So many things can happen that even the smallest lapse of care can be fatal.

These first two were males, and by the following January, both had dispersed. They traveled for long distances before they were able to find a home territory. In this way the gene pool was forever changing and keeping the offspring healthy and strong.

Her second litter consisted of three. Of these, only one was still alive the following spring. They had made it through the summer and fall, but when the kits left the care of their mother, one tried to settle in an occupied area. The fight with the resident male was a fatal one for him. The other was killed and eaten by a pack of wolves. She had been caught out in the open, unable to find cover to protect her rear. The six wolves attacked, coming from all directions. They were more than she could handle. Although she was able to kill one of her attackers, she went down under the rest of them.

Her fourth summer was one of lean times. The hare population crashed and there had been an excess of rain in the spring. This reduced the number of new birds and other food animals. She had gone into estrus, but had not been found by the local male. He had been occupied at this time with another female many miles away. Normally she would have come into estrus again later in the summer; however, the stress of the lean times changed the chemical balance in her body and she failed to come into heat a second time. This year she had no young.

Carajou had six offspring still living by the time Gulo and Garou were dead. She never saw her mother or brother after she and Garou left the natal area. Their lives had been solitary ones. Garou had been alone almost constantly, staying with females only when he was breeding them. The females were alone, only after their young left. Then they spent a short time with a male while being bred. They were alone again until the arrival of the next litter. This is the nature of wolverines, and they were content in the way they lived.

Carajou lived long for a wild wolverine, reaching the age of fourteen. By this time her teeth were worn down and some were missing. Two of her canine teeth had been broken and she was reduced to feeding almost entirely on lemmings and voles. Her speed diminished and she no longer had the quick spring that could easily catch a hare or bird.

In winter of her fourteenth year she fed less and less. The times were hard and her body would not do what she asked of it. There were many times when her stalk of prey failed. They seemed to be able to avoid her easily and she became slower yet as her food supply diminished.

Winter had been especially cold and the snows were deep. Carajou rarely made snow dens any longer. The energy required to dig was beyond her abilities and she slept out in sheltered places, curling up in drifts or beneath the snow covered limbs of spruce trees.

The blizzard of January found her in such a place and the wind howled over her, dropping snow upon her sleeping form. The day turned into night and still the wind blew and the snow followed the wind around trees and rocks, forming ridges and drifts that became many feet deep in places.

Carajou slept, moving little, reluctant to disturb the snow covering that insulated her from the bone chilling wind. Two days later the wind finally dropped, snow stopped, and clouds disappeared. Sun shown brilliantly in the cold, white world. Magpies and gray jays began to move about, quickly followed by bustling chickadees, all hurrying to find food before their bodies used what reserves they had.

Dawn had been cold and so quiet the rare call of a bird seemed obscene when it disturbed the stillness. The sky was cloudless, and other than the slow progress of the sun, nothing moved. Tree limbs were frozen in place and only shadows changed the shape of the landscape. The sun, never high, soon dropped below the western horizon, and still nothing moved. The snowdrift where Carajou lay became lit with starlight. Later the rising moon cast shadows of trees across it. And nothing moved.

An old saying among guides says "bear hunting is hours of boredom punctuated by moments of sheer terror." This is true in all nature.

The life of a wild animal is much the same day after day. Their life revolves around eating or being eaten, with occasions of mating thrown in. The predator is ever alert for something to eat; the prey is ever alert to keep from being eaten. This is nature in its purest form.

Prey animals instinctively hide from predators. Predators instinctively hunt their prey. Young are not taught these things by parents. The young of prey species hide without the mother communicating this to them in any way. How could she convey such an idea to them?

Predator young can be seen stalking, pouncing, and play killing their siblings long before they ever observe their parents hunting. Watch a domestic kitten stalk and attack a string or toy, when that kitten was taken from its mother at weaning time.

Man is intelligent and has altered the earth simply by his being here. This alteration has had a tremendous effect on nature. It must be understood that we are managing wildlife simply by these changes. We are destroying the habitat for some and creating it for others.

There are those demanding we leave animals alone. But this is an impossibility. We are here, and for good or bad, the world is no longer the same. Animals cannot move to another place when their home is taken; that other place is already a home to others.

Since we are managing wildlife, either directly or indirectly, we cannot leave them alone. Predators such as bears, wolves, and others have been eliminated from some areas. We therefore have to take that predator's place or the balance of nature is upset. Without predation a deer herd, or other prey species, will quickly destroy its food supply. This has happened countless times. It is many years before the land will again support more than a very few deer.

When emotions are brought into play, the deer we want to save from the hunter or other predator is humanized. The Bambi Syndrome is, if you want to put a name on it, let the beautiful creature live a long life of love and happiness; let it dine

171

on an unending supply of succulent food and never feel fear, pain, or suffering.

But, please come into the real world. There is hunger, pain, and suffering in nature. Where is the food when it is covered by deep snow or has been browsed so high it can no longer be reached? Where is the freedom from pain and suffering when there is no one to give aid or medical treatment? Without proper food an animal uses up his reserves and becomes weaker. The extra effort needed to find food requires more food and a vicious cycle begins. Very shortly it cannot effectively process the food it obtains and its fate is sealed. Painful diseases, predators, or hypothermia eventually ends the suffering.

Minor injuries, that to a human seem inconsequential, are major tragedies to a wild animal. A broken leg to us is an inconvenience; to an animal it is a slow, painful death most of the time. The predator cannot catch its food and the prey cannot keep from being eaten—sometimes while still alive.

Nature is harsh, cruel, and unforgiving. There is nothing man can do to change it. We must learn to work with nature as it is, not try to make it into something it cannot be. Humanizing wild animals is the surest way to cause problems. Biologists need to be able to manage wildlife without politics and emotions. They make enough educated mistakes without having to deal with people who are ignorant about nature.

No one truly understands nature and how everything from microorganisms to the largest creatures interact and depend one on another. We have come a long way, but the journey has just begun. Possibly the most detrimental thing to our learning has been the humanization of wild creatures.

The human mother feels deep pain at the loss of a child. The trend in recent years is to equate wild animals with man. This is humanization and has caused all sorts of complications. The wild mother rarely shows anything more than rudimentary protective instincts. Stories of them staying for days by the side of a dead offspring are nothing but myths. Most animal mothers leave dead young behind and resume their normal activities within minutes. Some wild mothers are known to eat their dead; fathers frequently are killers of their own young.

Only man can think and reason. Only man can put his thinking into words and convey a thought to another. Some of the more intelligent animals can learn somewhat complicated actions by repetition and reward. But not one of them can intentionally teach another animal to perform the action.

Since God placed man above the creatures of the earth, it is necessary to come to the fact we are also different from them. Animal do not think as humans think. Only man has the ability to ponder and resolve problems. God endowed man with intelligence and emotions and set him apart to "rule over the fish of the sea, the birds of the sky, and over every living thing that moves on the earth" (Genesis 1-28). It is our duty to learn all we can of nature so that we can be the steward that is our destiny.

172

Glossary

Afterbirth—See placenta.

Alpine—Usually meaning altitudes near and above 5,000 feet, however it also takes in that habitat that has alpine weather, plants, and animal life. Alpine in northern regions, such as Alaska, can be at sea level in the arctic, slowly rising in elevation the further south you go, and gets to altitudes well over 8,000 feet in the Colorado Rockies.

Anal Glands—Glands in or near the anus. Many mammals have these and use them to mark and define their hunting or home territories. They are well developed in the Mustelidæ (weasel family) and Canidae (dog family). Your family dog has one on each side of its anus and this is what dogs sniff when they greet each other. The skunk (a member of the weasel family) has anal glands so well developed they can spray a highly offensive liquid.

Antlers—Antlers are not horns and horns are not antlers! Antlers are grown only by members of the deer family. They are shed annually and regrown. They are composed of the same substances as bone. Horns are not shed and are composed of keratin, the same substances as hair, finger nails or hooves.

Baculum—This is the penis bone common to many mammals and is a different size and shape in all.

Barren—In the context of animals, it means without or unable to bear young. In the context of the earth, it means little or no plant growth.

Blastocyst—This is an embryo in the earliest stages. See implantation.

Browse—The leaves and tips of small limbs of trees and shrubs. An animal that lives on this food is called a browser. Most deer are browsers.

Cache—A place or store of hidden food.

Calving—Having a calf. A calving area is where females go to have calves.

Carnivore—A member of the Order: Carnivora. Most carnivores live on meat.

Carrion—Dead flesh, usually in some state of putrefaction.

Catkins—Without getting into detailed scientific terms it is basically the inflorescence (flower) of plants in the willow family (Salicacæ). Everyone should be acquainted with the catkin of the well known pussy willow.

Clutch—Used in this book in the context of birds, here it is a brood of chicks or nest of eggs.

Craw—A bird's crop, where food is temporarily stored before digested in the gizzard.

Cross or Crossbreed—See Hybrid.

Cycle—This is a succession of recurring events. As it pertains to nature, it is the highs and lows of populations of mammals and birds. The microtines (i.e. voles and lemmings) and the lagomorphs (i.e. snowshoe hare) are highly cyclic mammals.

Delayed Implantation—See implantation.

Dispersal—Going different ways. Nature uses dispersal of young so inbreeding does not result.

Domesticated—Tamed to live and breed for the benefit of man.

Dormant—Not active, in a form of suspended animation.

Estivation—Being dormant. (Also can be spelled Aestivation).

Estrus—The time when a female will accept the male, the time of ovulation (when her egg or eggs are mature).

Gene—DNA coding for determining traits that are passed on through generations.

Gizzard—A bird's stomach where food is ground for digestion.

Graze—Grasses and grasslike plants. An animal that lives on grasses is a grazer.

Guard Hairs—Long, bristle-like hairs that overlay the soft, dense underfur of many mammals.

Herbivore—Animals whose main diet is plants.

Hibernation—Beyond estivation and dormancy. The body temperature drops as well as metabolism and the animal is in such a deep sleep they cannot be easily awakened.

Horns—See Antlers.

Hummock—Usually meaning knolls or hills, however in this book the hummocks are more like mounds, one to two feet high, up to several feet across, and are built-up layers of dirt, roots, mosses, and other plants. They are usually in low lying areas and frequently in wet, boggy places. It is easier to meander between them than take the shorter distance straight across their tops. Some can be soft and sometimes you must jump to get to the next one. Either that, or step up and down continuously.

Hummocks are common in Alaska, and, although they are sometimes difficult to travel through, they do provide convenient places to set and rest, as long as they are dry. I have never found them in places where there are few mosses.

Hypothermia—When the body temperature lowers. The first symptom is shivering. If the body is not warmed it progresses until euphoria sets in. Some people have felt warm and taken their clothes off. Death soon follows. Being immersed in water or having wet clothes accelerates its progress drastically.

Hybrid—The young of parents of two species. They must be closely related, but true hybrids are rarely fertile and normally do not have young. The most common example of this is the mule, the result of a jack (a male donkey) breeding with a mare (a female horse). Crossbreeds are the young of parents of the same species and they are fertile. The most common example of this is the dog, all dogs come from a common ancestor, the wolf. The different breeds of dogs are a result of selective breeding, but still they can be crossed, and fertile young are produced. The mating of a dalmatian and a great Dane is called a cross, not a hybrid. However these two terms, hybrid and crossbreed, are frequently interchanged, even in the scientific community.

Implantation—The act of the fertile egg or blastocyst attaching itself on the uterine wall. Delayed implantation is when the egg is fertilized and has divided to a limited point when it is called a blastocyst. It then floats in the embryonic fluid, being sustained by it for a period of time, from one to eleven months, before it attaches itself to the uterine wall. It does not develop during the blastocyst stage, it is dormant at that time. Development only occurs after attachment to the wall and it is fed by a link to the mother, the placenta, a system of blood vessels.

Imprinting—This occurs immediately after birth or hatching, and is common in the animal world, probably more so among birds but in mammals as well. Basically, it is that the newborn identifies itself with the first large live object it sees, smells or hears—its parent under normal circumstances. A caribou calf will always identify itself as a caribou and will join other caribou. It will also identify its own mother from the other caribou from its first moments. There have been instances of birds, hatched by humans, never seeing their biological parents, that have imprinted on the first human they see upon hatching, and from then on identify itself as human and follow that person around.

Mammal—All animals that have mammary glands with which they feed milk to their young.

Marking—In the animal world, this simply means delineating an area or territory as being their home range or feeding area. Different animals mark differently and some do not mark at all. Usually marking is done by various scent glands but also by urine and feces.

Metabolism (Metabolic rate)—The rate at which an animal converts foods into energy. An animal that has a high metabolic rate burns energy fast and needs large amounts of food to sustain itself. The masked shrew (Sorex cinereus), common in North America, has an extremely high metabolic rate and needs to eat nearly constantly. They start to starve after only two or three hours without food. They need to consume their own body weight each 4 hours. Their heart beats up to 800 times per minute.

Microtines—Voles and lemmings. They are rodents in the subfamily: Microtinae.

Migration—A movement from one place to another. Usually in birds and mammals it is for the purpose of following annual seasons for food supplies or reproduction.

Molt—A molt or molting is the replacement of feathers. It happens at least once a year in all birds, twice in many species, three times in some and rarely, four times in a few species. Changes in the length of daylight is the principle trigger for molts. Feathers wear out and need replacement. There is a need for a change of colorations for the purpose of camouflage in some birds and for sexual activity and courtship in others. Most birds molt in a pattern, such as pairs of feathers in each wing, leaving them balanced and still able to fly. However, many waterfowls lose their flight feathers at the same time, and are unable to fly until new feather have grown in to replace them.

Morph—Form. Used in this book to describe color forms of birds and animals, color morphs.

Musk—A substance produced by the glands of many mammals. It is a long lasting scent that has been used by humans in the production of expensive perfumes.

Muskeg—Common in the northern regions and is a bog, usually a wet place of built-up mosses and other vegetation.

Mutation—A change in a gene that causes a new characteristic in following generations.

Natal Den—The lair or den of an animal used for birth and nurturing of their young.

Offal—The internal organs and intestines, also called viscera.

Ovulation—When mature eggs are produced from the ovary. The time when eggs are ready for conception.

Palm, Palmate—In respects to antlers it is a palm-shaped portion of the antler, a wide section. An antler that has a palm-shaped section is palmate.

Placenta—This is the organ that connects the fetus to the mother's uterus. The placenta and fetal membranes are expelled by the mother after giving birth and is commonly called after-birth.

Predator—Any organism, but usually meaning mammals or birds that prey on other live animals.

Quill—A sharp spine, hollow, and, in porcupines, having barbs.

Range, Home Range—The area in which an animal lives. The range of moose is the northern latitudes, circumpolar (around the North Pole). The range can also mean the home range of an individual animal. One particular moose may live within a certain number of square miles.

Regurgitate—To vomit or throw-up. Some birds and mammals use this in feeding their young.

Resident—In the context of nature, a bird or mammal that claims a certain area as his territory is called the resident of that territory.

Rhizome—A horizontal root below the ground and has nodes where it sends down roots and sends up new shoots above the ground, forming a new plant.

Rodent—A member of the order: Rodentia. This order consists of many families and include squirrels, beavers, mice, rats, marmots, and microtines (lemmings and voles).

Rut—A time when animals become sexually excited. Usually used in connection with the male while the terms estrus or "in heat" is used with the female. The rut is the mating season.

Scent—Smell or odor.

Shovel—As per caribou, the shovel is that portion of the antler extending downward over the muzzle. Usually only one antler has a shovel, however occasionally they have one on each antler and that bull caribou is then said to have a double shovel. This is a desirable condition for hunters seeking a record-book trophy.

Sibling—A brother or sister.

Solitary—Some animals lead a life alone. They do not associate with others of their species, other than in mating. These animals are designated as solitary. Bears and wolverines are solitary animals. Caribou and wolves are not, they live in groups.

Species—A group of animals that are so closely related they can breed and have fertile offspring.

Taiga—The taiga occurs only in the far north and is that area where trees are small, sparse, and there is boggy areas among and between them. It is where the tundra ends and trees begin.

Territory—See range, home range.

Tundra—Treeless terrain of the far north. Vegetation is mosses, lichens and low shrubs.

Umbilical—The navel.

Underfur—The fine, dense fur next to the skin.

Ungulate—A mammal that has hooves.

Velvet—When an antler is still growing and is covered with a velvety skin, it is in velvet.

Vent—The anus or rectum.

Vixen—The female fox.

Vulva—The external part of the female mammal genital organ.

Fauna

Although Alaska has a lot of wildlife, there is not nearly so much as nonresidents believe. Many are disappointed when they see only a couple moose on a two weeks visit. The road system will seldom produce more than that. Some well known mammals stay so far from humans that to see them one would be extremely fortunate.

Stony River is home to one of the largest land carnivores on earth, the brown bear (Ursus arctos). They can get up to one thousand two hundred pounds. Only the polar bear (Ursus maritimus) is heavier, one thousand five hundred pounds and over. The smallest mammal on earth also resides here, the pygmy shrew (Microsorex hoyi). It takes a dozen of them to weigh an ounce, and one can easily sit on a quarter.

The following is only a few of the interesting inhabitants of the Stony River area:

Arctic Ground Squirrel
Spermophilus parryii

This prolific rodent is an important prey species for several predators. They have up to 8 young per litter and weigh 2 pounds and over at maturity. Its coat is speckled gray with rusty brown about the shoulders and head. Principally a vegetarian, they are not averse to eating young birds or small mammals. They are social, living in small colonies in dens dug in the earth. The den entrance (usually only one) is plugged just before the animals go into true hibernation. In appearance, it is much like a tree squirrel, but lives entirely on the ground in tundra areas.

Beaver
Castor canadensis

Weighing 60 pounds and over, the beaver is the largest rodent in North America. It is a water animal, living in family units, using both earth dens and the familiar beaver house. It builds dams of mud and sticks to create their own water habitat. The hind feet are webbed and the tail is thick and flattened. Its large incisor teeth are used to cut down trees, sometimes several inches in diameter. These teeth grow throughout the animal's life and have to be constantly used to keep them worn down. Clumsy on land but quite agile in its water environment.

Black Bear
Ursus americanus

Stony River black bears run smaller than average and are uniformly glossy black. Three hundred pounds is very large here. Classified as a carnivore, it is omnivorous. It will kill and eat any flesh. No other predator kills more moose calves. They breed about June, but delayed implantation delays birth until one to three cubs are born in the winter den. Cubs weigh only 8 to 10 ounces. They stay with mother at least eighteen months. Black bears attack humans less frequently (percentage) than do brown bears, but are more likely to feed on the human.

177

Brown Bear
Ursus arctos

Large males can reach 1,200 pounds, females about half that. Interior browns are usually labeled grizzlies, but all are Ursus arctos despite color, size, or location. Most attacks on humans are a result of man getting too close to cubs or a bear's kill. Cubs are born less than a pound in weight and stay with the mother at least 30 months. They are not true hibernators, but go into a deep sleep from October to May (variable with weather and area). They feed heavily in the fall, putting on a thick layer of fat to sustain them and still have a lot of it left come spring.

Caribou
Rangifer tarandus

Caribou are members of the deer family as is moose. Summer coats are brown, blue-gray in winter. Males have white hanging manes about the neck during rut. Hair is hollow and stiff with excellent insulating properties. Mature males have antlers that are exceptionally large in proportion to the body. Cows are the only females in the deer family to have antlers. Caribou are herd animals, particularly during migration. A tundra resident, it spends little time in forested areas. Single fauns (no spots) in early spring are able to run within an hour.

Collard Lemming
Dicrostonyx torquatus

This is a rodent, very mouse appearing, 4 to 5 inches long and 2 ounces or better. Fur is long and dense, brownish gray in summer with a faint light collar about the neck. It is the only rodent turning white in winter. During winter, they grow extra long claws on two toes of each front foot that are used in digging their burrows under the snow. Claws are shed in spring. Vegetarian and does not hibernate, active all winter in burrows under the snow. Voles and lemmings have litters as large as eight and several litters a year. Some even have litters during the winter.

Collard Pika
Ochotona collaris

The pika is a distant relative to rabbits. Pikas, rabbits, and hares are in the same order. They are not rodents! About 6 ounces and 7 or 8 inches long with warm gray-brown fur. A light collar about the neck gives it its name. Up to 5 in a litter and may have a second litter in late summer. Does not hibernate. Actually cuts, dries, and stores hay for food during winter. Hay is stored in rocky crevasses about their dens. They are territorial and only one or a mated pair will reside in it. Their range is small and several pikas can be seen in one suitable rocky outcrop.

Dusky Shrew
Sorex obscurus

This is only one of 30 species of shrews in North America and 250 world wide. They are insectivores, not related to rodents. Most shrews in Alaska are small, no more than 2 inches long. Eyes are tiny, nearly hidden by hair. They have a long nose and short, tight gray-brown fur. Sense of smell is acute as they are constantly foraging for food needed in abundance due to a high metabolism. Feeding both day and night, they will starve if they go more than a few hours without food. They prefer insects and flesh, but will eat seeds and other high energy plant foods.

Goshawk
Accipitea gentilis

One of two true hawks in Alaska. They have short, round wings, a long tail, and a hooked beak and sharp, curved talons, well adapted to catching, holding, and tearing apart food. The goshawk is strikingly marked; the back is a soft, blue-gray with very light gray underparts. The white line above the red-orange eye makes for easy identification. The back of the head frequently has the semblance of a crest. Two feet long with a 4 foot wingspan. Very fast and agile, hunts in forested areas, and is capable of dodging in and around trees and shrubs.

Gray Jay
Perisoreus canadensis

This robin sized jay has many common names such as whiskey jack, camp robber, Canada jay, Alaska jay, etc.. It is not shy of man and will approach closely. It is omnivorous, feeding on insects, berries, small rodents, and just about anything edible. Any excess food is cached in hollows or limb crotches. This is the first visitor to the site of the hunter's kill and is usually there looking for food while the hunter is butchering. Lays three or four eggs in a nest that is usually near the trunk of trees, frequently not much more than head high.

Gray Wolf
Canis lupus

There are many wolves in Alaska, but are rarely seen. Males can reach 175 pounds. Wolves live in packs from a very few to nearly 20. Wolves hunt together and their main food is caribou and moose, which a pack has little trouble pulling down. Calves and ill or injured receive special attention, but full grown, healthy moose are regular prey. On the Kenai Peninsula alone, there are an estimated 200 wolves in 20 packs. Each pack, on the average, downs a moose every week to 10 days. This is a minimum of 750 moose annually...in a very small portion of Alaska.

Gyrfalcon
Falco rusticolus

This is the world's largest falcon, two feet long with a four foot wingspan. They live on ptarmigan, other birds, and hares at times. They are arctic tundra birds, some migrating into Southern Alaska in the fall. Three color phases, white, gray, and nearly black. Alaska has all, but the gray is predominant. Like other falcons, they are very fast, having long, pointed wings and moderately long, slender tails. The light phases have dark spots on wings and back, similar to the snowy owl. Nests on cliffs.

Marmot
Marmota caligata

The hoary marmot is one of two species in Alaska, Marmota broweri resides in the Brooks Range, Marmota caligata in the southern parts of Alaska. Habitat is alpine tundra, preferring rocky slopes of mountains. Strictly herbivore. Lives in burrows, usually under rocks, and in colonies. Plugs den entrance to hibernate, as does the ground squirrel. It is a true hibernator. This rodent is large, weighing up to ten pounds. Brown with a grizzled appearance and a short, bushy tail. Close relative of the woodchuck.

Moose
Alces alces

The world's largest deer, mature bulls frequently over fifteen hundred pounds and six feet at the shoulders. Twins are the norm, and the unspotted fauns are able to follow mother within minutes. Usually stay with mother through the following winter. Dark brown above with light tan legs. Head is unmistakable, long and drooping. Has a "bell" under the chin, varying from short to very long. The bell is nothing but skin and there has never been a logical explanation for it. Prefers forest and taiga habitat, but has been moving into tundra regions. Moose are browsers, but will feed on grass at times. Favorite food is willow and birch leaves and twigs. In winter will eat limbs up to half an inch in diameter, but gets little nourishment from them. Males have quite large antlers, sixty inches wide is not rare and they can weigh up to fifty pounds. Antlers, shed in winter, start regrowing in spring, and are fully grown by late August. Flesh is excellent for food.

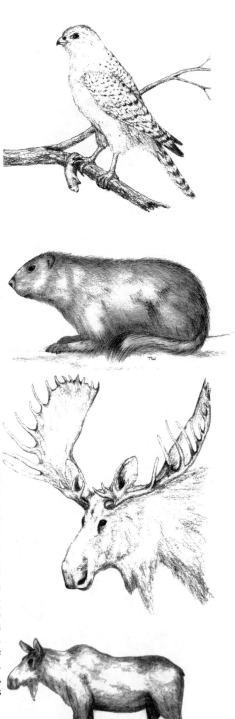

Northern Bog Lemming
Synaptomys borealis
Very much like the collard lemming, previously described, but does not turn white in winter. Voles and lemmings are microtines, herbivores, and prolific breeders. They quickly overpopulate, then the population crashes. This is in a cyclic manner, about every three to four years. At the height of population booms, they frequently migrate to find unoccupied areas, but this is seldom successful as the population boom occurs everywhere at once.

Northern Shrike
Lanius excubitor
Of the Lanidæ family, the only shrike in Alaska, closely related to the loggerhead shrike of the Lower-48, which it resembles in most respects. Robin sized, has a hooked beak, and small curved talons. Identified by black mask over eye, black wings, and tail, otherwise gray. It is a predator and feeds on birds and small mammals that are killed by biting into the spine behind the head. Too small to kill using talons as do hawks or owls. Actions are much like a goshawk, fast and agile, catching other birds in flight. Does not use feet to hold food, but places kills in crotches of limbs or similar places to tear food apart. Mimics the calls of other birds.

Porcupine
Erethizon dorsatum
A rodent, weighing up to 40 pounds. Herbivore, feeds on ground plants, roots, and berries in summer and mostly bark in winter. Good climber, dens in tree hollows or logs. Does not hibernate. Quills begin on cheeks, very short, and progressively longer toward the tail. Does not throw quills. Quills can be four inches long and are barbed on the end. Only two predators, the fisher and the wolverine, have been known to regularly kill and eat porkies without getting full of quills. Many animals are severely injured by these quills, some fatally.

Ptarmigan
Lagopus lagopus
Willow ptarmigan, Alaska's state bird. Mottled browns with white splotches in summer, molts to white in the winter except a black tail that is mostly covered by white tail coverts. White-tailed ptarmigan are entirely white in winter, mottled brown, black, and gray in summer, tail always white. Rock ptarmigan are difficult to distinguish from willow ptarmigan. Mottled in summer, white in winter, except the black tail. It has a black eye mask in winter, which others do not have. Ptarmigan are related to spruce grouse and hybrids of it and willow ptarmigan have been reported.

Snowshoe Hare
Lepus americanus

Family Leporidæ. Three to four pounds in size, it is brown in summer, white in winter (except tips of ears). Hind feet are very wide, hence its common name, enabling it to run over soft snow. Prolific, two or three litters a year, up to six leverets per litter. Young are precocial as are all hares. They are born furred, with eyes open and able to leave the nest in a few days and start eating a vegetarian diet at ten days. (Rabbits differ from hares, the young are blind, hairless and helpless at birth.) Hares are an important prey species for many predators, especially lynx, which feeds almost exclusively on them. They have a ten year population cycle.

Snowy Owl
Nyctea scandiaca

Family Strigidæ. Two pounds, five foot wingspan. Young are heavily marked with brown spots which become more scattered until an adult of several years is nearly pure white. Head is round without ear tufts, eyes yellow. Principal food is lemmings, but will take hares and birds as large as ducks. Ground nests, clutch size varies with the abundance of lemmings. Habitat is arctic tundra, but migrates south in winter or when lemmings are in short supply. I once saw one in Kansas.

Wolverine
Gulo gulo

In the weasel family, Mustelidæ. Females 25 pounds, males 35 and over. Dark brown with tan stripes down both sides, meeting at shoulder and tail. One to three kits per litter, born in late winter in snow dens. Able to fend for themselves at six months. Pound for pound, without doubt, the most vicious animal in North America. Can kill single wolves quite easily. Neck is larger than head, supporting tremendous jaw muscles that can crush leg bones of moose. Claws semi-retractable and uses them like a cat. Heavily muscled legs and oversized paws. Relentless and tireless when in pursuit of prey.

S oil in Alaska is poor, having been covered by glaciers until recently, it has not had the chance to grow plants that decompose and create a rich, thick layer of earth. Consequently, much of the area has only thin soil covering gravel and sand. Few nutrients, a short growing season, and extreme cold only supports the hardiest of plants.

Alaska has only eighty-nine plant families and some of them have only two or three represented species. In tropical climates there can be hundreds of families, each with hundreds of species. Studying botany here is therefore much simpler, but still a challenge.

To thrive, a plant must be able to reproduce. To reproduce in Alaska, the plant must do it with all haste. Most do very well in summer, growing fast and large using the long days of sunlight. Alaska's plants are individuals that have adapted to harsh conditions and are most interesting to study. The following is only a very few:

Alaska Poppy
Papaver alaskanum
Papaveraceæ (Poppy Family). A mountain plant, likes sand and gravel. Grows close to the ground. Old, brown leaf bases are dense on the caudex (stem). Flower is yellow.

Mountain Alder
Alnus crispa
Betulaceæ (Birch Family). Shrub, eight to ten feet tall. Habitat is more mountainous (subalpine) than Sitka alder. Grows to treeline where it becomes a dwarf shrub. Alders have many limbs growing from the ground, forming a bowl-like shrub. They grow near each other, their limbs intertwine, and form a nearly impassable thicket.

Sitka Alder
Alnus crispus sinuata
Betulaceæ (Birch Family). Very similar to Alnus crispa except the leaves are more lobed and somewhat larger; However, this is difficult to determine. They cross readily as Alnus sinuata, which occupies the lower elevations and coastal areas, gradually appears to change to Alnus crispa further inland and as the elevation rises. Alders are hated by hunters—wounded bears seem to always go in them. The difficulty going through alders has to be experienced to really understand. I tried one on my first Alaska hunt...and swore I would never try it again, even if it took miles to get around. That oath has been kept with one exception, when a partner wounded a bear. Luckily the bear kept going, apparently not badly hurt. I was sweating the entire time, although it was cold.

Baneberry
Actaea rubra

Ranunculaceæ (Crowfoot Family). Many plants in this family are poisonous and this one is no exception. The berries and root contain pro-tanemonin and can cause death by paralyzing the respiratory system. The strong, bitter taste is most unpalatable and poisoning is rare. The berries are a glassy red (sometimes white). Two feet tall, the baneberry dies back to the ground each fall.

Bearberry
Arctostaphylos alpina

Ericaceæ (Heath Family). Ground hugging plant forming large mats in the tundra and mountain sides. Leaves turn scarlet in fall and are showy. White flowers and edible black berries in the center. Arctostaphylos rubra is very similar, but has red berries.

Dwarf Birch
Betula nana

Betulaceæ (Birch Family). Small shrub that grows in muskeg and wet tundra. Easily identified by the small, round, dentate leaves that turn orange and red in fall. Leaf illustration is as large as the leaf gets, most are much smaller.

Kenai Birch
Betula kenaica

Betulaceæ (Birch Family). Tree up to thirty feet tall with dark bark. Habitat is open forests and lower mountain sides. Common in Southcentral Alaska. It is eaten extensively by moose. Paper birch has light, peeling bark, and its leaves have a long point. The two cross readily, and properties of both can be found on a single tree.

Paper Birch
Betula papyrifera humilis
Betulaceæ (Birch Family). This birch lives in the lowlands, much the same as Betula kenaica, but easily identified by its bark, which is white and peels easily. The leaves are more pointed. This and other birches readily cross and at times it can show characteristics not typical of the paper birch.

Shrub Birch
Betula glandulosa
Betulaceæ (Birch Family). Similar to Betula nana (dwarf birch) but is taller, up to 6 feet. Not confined to wet environment, it also likes open woods. Leaves larger than Betula nana but still turn red and orange in fall. All birches cross and this can be seen as the plant gets progressively larger as it progresses from wet (Betula nana) to semi-wet (Betula glandulosa) to dry, the tree species (Betula kenaica and Betula papyrifera).

Blueberry
Vaccinium uliginosum
Ericaceæ (Heath Family). Alpine blueberry is a one to two foot shrub, has urn shaped flowers, usually pink. Dark blue berries ripen in August, getting sweeter until frost. A favorite of both humans and wildlife. There are several local species using different habitats from wet to dry to shaded. The huckleberry is a close relative as is the lingonberry (low bush cranberry) (Vaccinium vitis-idaea). Low bush cranberry is a ground hugging dwarf shrub with red berries that look and taste like cranberries. It is not a true cranberry, nor even related to it.

Coral Root Orchid
Corallorrhiza trifida
Orchidaceæ (Orchis Family). Six inches tall, without leaves, but has tan leaf sheaths visible on light green stalk. Flowers small, upright, greenish, with white, notched lip and some dark spots. Fruit droops when mature. The root is a rhizome resembling an ocean coral, nearly white and breaks easily. Likes shade, lives in damp woods. Impossible to misidentify.

Cottonwood
Populus trichocarpa
Salicacæ (Willow Family). Every outdoor person is familiar with this large tree. Up to one hundred feet tall, it grows mostly along water courses, but can be found near treeline. There are two species, Populus balsamifera and Populus balsamifera trichocarpa, but they are so similar it is possible they are the same. The sap is very sticky and smells strongly of turpentine. Bark is deeply ridged, especially when growing near water.

Fireweed
Epilobium angustifolium
Onagraceæ (Evening Primrose Family). One of fifteen species of Epilobium, angustifolium is widespread and common. It flourishes along roads and can be found, one species or another in about every type of habitat. Angustifolium blooms in racemes, usually red to pink. Many roadsides have huge, beautiful patches of fireweed in August.

Ladies' Tresses Orchid
Spiranthes Romanzoffiana
Orchidaceæ (Orchis Family). Grows six to ten inches tall in bogs or other open wet areas. The white flowers have a sweet scent and grow in three spiral rows up the top of the stem. Flower has the typical orchid, hood-like, upper petal.

Pasque Flower
Pulsatilla patens
Ranunculaceæ (Crowfoot Family). This is its southern range, plant is small, and lives in dry, sandy conditions. Its has purple flowers in early spring and are very hairy. Leaves appear as the flower matures. Seeds ripen, forming a silky ball.

Quaking Aspen
Populus tremuloides

Salicacæ (Willow Family). Closely related to cottonwood and has been known to cross with it. Smaller, up to thirty feet and has smooth bark that is white, tinted green. White powder will rub off on dark clothing from the bark. Leaves have flattened stems, allowing them to twist and turn in the slightest breeze. They can also photosynthesize on either side. Does well in open forests and mountain sides.

Roseroot
Sedum rosea

Crassulaceæ (Stonecrop Family). Leaves are thick and fleshy, more crowded as they get near the top of the stem. Deep wine colored flowers clustered at the top. Habitat is wet tundra and rocky mountain sides, frequently along streams.

Spider Plant
Saxifraga flagellaris

Saxifragaceæ (Saxifrage Family). Lives in rocky habitat in high mountains. Does not depend on seed to propagate, stolons (runners) form buds from which new plants grow. (The strawberry also does this.) Leaves are clumped at the base, the flower stalk has up to five yellow flowers. Saxifrage means "rock breaker" and those in this family are the first plants to appear when glaciers retreat, leaving nothing but rock and gravel behind. Their humus form the first soils.

Sundew
Drosera rotundifolia

Droseraceæ (Sundew Family). Has round leaves as the name indicates. The Long Leafed Sundew (Drosera angelica) has long leaves that stand up where Drosera rotundifolia leaves lay on the ground. Otherwise, the plants are very similar. They live in bogs and other open, wet areas. Small, five inches tall, has white flowers. Leaves are clustered about the base and are sparsely covered with hairlike structures that have a tiny drop of sticky fluid on them. This is used to catch insects which the plant absorbs. It thrives without this nutrient, however.

Western Red Columbine
Aquilegia formosa

Ranunculaceæ (Crowfoot Family). This plant is well known from the cultivated species. The red and blue (Aquilegia brevistyla) both inhabit this area, in woods and along waterways. Difficult to distinguish the two when not in bloom. The red form has red petals with yellow bases, the blue has white bases, or nearly so, with shorter flower spurs.

Wild Calla
Calla palustris

Araceæ (Arum Family). Also known as marsh calla. Grows in water, ponds and marshes, the leaves upright above water, from a creeping rhizome that roots from nodes. Its flower is a spathe, which looks like another leaf; however, the front side is white and the fruit, small red berries, stand upright in front of it. The plant is poisonous when raw.

Alaska Willow
Salix alaxensis

Salicacæ (Willow Family). From sea level to treeline throughout Alaska and Northern Canada. One of over fifty species in Alaska and crosses with most of them. Many species cannot be positively identified due to this. It is a shrub in poor ground and a tree up to twenty feet tall in favorable conditions. Willows are a favorite food of moose. Bark contains aspirin and makes a tea good for pain.

Netted Willow
Salix reticulata

Salicacæ (Willow Family). This willow is easy to identify. It is a prostrate (ground hugging) shrub with round to oblong leaves, heavily veined, giving it the common name. It trails on the ground, sometimes with only one or two leaves appearing out of the moss. It is found in tundra, both wet and dry places, and crosses with several other similar species.

Index